J.R. HARBER

The
Future
Was
Now

BOOK 1 OF THE *BEYOND HORIZON* SERIES

RIVER GROVE
BOOKS

Published by River Grove Books
Austin, TX
www.rivergrovebooks.com

Distributed by River Grove Books

Design and composition by Greenleaf Book Group
Cover design by Greenleaf Book Group
Cover images used under license from ©Shutterstock.com/Valery Brozhinksy, ©Shutterstock.com/pixelparticle, ©Shutterstock.com/Benguhan

Publisher's Cataloging-in-Publication data is available.

Print ISBN: 978-1-63299-276-5

eBook ISBN: 978-1-63299-277-2

First Edition

This book is dedicated to all life on earth. May we learn to better protect our planet before it's too late.

PROLOGUE

The end of the old world surprised few.

It announced itself violently, year after year, as massive storms ravaged everything that stood, and the oceans rose, swallowing low-lying land that once held the great cities of the earth—one devastation after another.

The inhabitable zones grew fewer and farther apart, famine bred war, and war bred only more war and destruction. What the world faces now could once have been solved. A pandemic, a wave of human migration, a hurricane, an earthquake–in the past, these were merely logistical problems, tragedies nonetheless, but the whole of civilization could have absorbed them. Now they happen all at once, compounding one another. The world itself has turned on humanity.

The population knew it would happen—most people

understood what was coming. The common people of the earth pleaded for help, demanded the powerful few reckon with them—that those with wealth and influence wield their precious resources to bring about necessary, wholesale change. The world begged them to stand up and fight alongside the people, against the imminent destruction of our species and the world in which they lived.

It should have been such a logical choice: Do you wish to save the world? Or do you not? But man's greed is relentless and devoid of logic. They could have made changes to protect us all. Instead the powerful chose to do nothing, to let the world burn.

Now that is in the past, decisions left out of the hands of those who followed. Humanity must turn to the future—not for itself, but for all who are left to follow when the chaos ends.

The new plan for humanity must work. The survivors see that now, and yet the plan itself chills many souls to the core. "Everything has a price," wise confederates say, and some bite their tongues so as not to remind them that the civilization that created this phrase unwittingly choked to death on it. Yet they are not wrong: there is much more than conscience at stake.

This is the world's last chance. Ultimately, humanity must choose to save humanity. To save the world . . . no matter what the price.

CHAPTER ONE

"THERE HE IS," NAOMI SAID IN A LOW VOICE.

Gabriel nodded. "I see him."

"Of course you do." She smiled, sipping her tea.

Gabriel took a small device from his pocket and turned it on, holding it under the table as the screen lit up. Quickly, he took control of the cloaked drone already tracking their subject and brought the picture up on his screen. The man they were tracking was a block away from where they sat in the cool shade of an outdoor café. He was walking slowly down the bustling city sidewalk. He seemed to be staring straight ahead, but even from this distance Gabriel could tell he was darting his eyes back and forth, his shoulders hunched forward as if danger might come from any direction.

Naomi sighed.

"What went wrong?" she asked softly.

Gabriel didn't answer; he knew she wasn't really expecting him to. John Philip Horizon was a normal man, as far as anyone knew. He had a wife and a three-year-old daughter, and plenty of friends. Yet a few months ago, the drone feeds had been registering anomalous behavior from him: outbursts of temper, retreat from his usual friends, and this quiet paranoia Naomi and Gabriel now observed. Three days before, he had shouted at his wife, Katherine, with such ferocity that the drone outside their home had sent an emergency alert, flagging him as potentially violent. Naomi and Gabriel, Authority Figures of the State—specifically Contract Enforcers for District 7C of the city of Horizon—had been assigned to him, and now they watched as he turned onto a residential street and stopped in front of his home.

He stayed on the sidewalk, pacing back and forth. Gabriel directed the drone to zoom in, focusing on the man's face.

"What is it?" Naomi asked.

"He's muttering something," he whispered.

Gabriel squinted, trying to make out the words, but it was impossible; John wasn't talking, just moving his lips along to something in his head, as if he were reading something he'd seen a hundred times. He nodded his head decisively, and Gabriel stiffened.

"It's happening," he said, standing.

"He's shown no sign of escalation," Naomi protested, but she set down her tea.

"We have to go now," Gabriel said.

He took off running toward the townhouse before she could respond.

By the time they got there, John was no longer on the sidewalk, and the front door to the house was ajar. Naomi pointed to Gabriel, then to the side of the house, and he nodded. He crept toward the back entrance, glancing back to see Naomi climbing the steps to the front door, her hand hovering close to her stunner.

Gabriel stepped in front of the facial scanner at the back door.

"Gabriel Ward, Contract Enforcement," he said tightly, waiting impatiently as the blue light flickered across his face. When it was done, the door popped open, and he slipped inside.

"John, please talk to me," he heard Naomi say as he crept through the kitchen toward the front of the house.

"I don't have to talk to you, stalker!" John cried, an edge of hysteria in his voice.

"Of course not," Naomi said calmly. "But I can't help if I don't understand what's happening."

Gabriel peered around the corner. John had Katherine pinned up against a wall, one hand pressed against her neck. In his other hand was a kitchen knife, and he was holding the point up to her throat, just below her jawline. Gabriel didn't move, assessing: John could not see him from where he stood. Katherine was still breathing heavily. He was terrifying her, but not choking her—not yet. Naomi stood a few feet from John and was addressing him calmly, her hands behind her back in an unthreatening posture.

"I want to help, John, but I need you to step away from Katherine," Naomi said, her voice never wavering. She sounded as if they were talking about something mundane. *Please pass the salt. Come now, John, please don't kill your wife.*

"She's *my* wife!" John exclaimed, but he stepped back with a flourish, taking his hand off her windpipe. He kept the knife at her throat, his arm stretched out across the distance between them. Katherine darted her eyes around the room and stopped in surprise when she saw Gabriel. Gabriel raised his index finger to his lips, gesturing for her to be silent, and she gave a tiny nod of her head. The knife scraped against her skin, and she gasped.

"Yes, John, she is your wife," Naomi agreed. She stepped closer, and he stiffened but did not move. "You're her husband, and when you married, you decided that you would care for one another. That you would be partners in all things, isn't that right?"

John didn't answer, but his hand wavered, and the knife moved minutely away from Katherine's neck. "That's right," he said.

"Then please, care for Katherine now. Treat her as your partner. Give me the knife."

John's shoulders hunched forward. Gabriel couldn't see his face, but he heard the man beginning to weep as he lowered the knife; he clutched it in both hands like a talisman.

"I'm sorry, Katherine," John said, voice halting.

Naomi smiled. "Thank you, John," she said. She took a step forward.

"I'm so sorry," he repeated.

Gabriel froze, hit by a shock of adrenaline.

John raised the knife again and swung it around, lunging at his wife as Gabriel leapt toward him in a blur. Katherine screamed as the blade grazed her throat, and then Gabriel seized the man, grabbing him in a chokehold and yanking him down and away. He flipped John onto his face and twisted his right arm up straight, planting his knee in the man's back, then glanced back at the two women. Katherine was slumped back against the wall, her mouth hanging open and her eyes wide. A single bead of blood ran down her neck, a small cut her only wound. Naomi took her arm and gave Gabriel a nod, then started to guide Katherine to the sofa.

John's face was red with rage, pressed flat against the carpet. Gabriel looked down at him gravely, reviewing the facts of the incident once more in his mind. He took a deep breath, centering himself, then spoke.

"John Philip Horizon, by authority of the State, you will be questioned, judged, and sentenced." He waited a moment, but the subject did not attempt to move or speak. "I, Gabriel Ward, judge you guilty of violence, of violating your Social Contract with the State and all your fellow citizens. I sentence you to be terminated."

"No!" Katherine exclaimed, her hands clenched together. "Please, you can't!"

John struggled, trying to twist out of Gabriel's grasp. Gabriel sighed, set his stunner, and hit the man with a moderate voltage. John shuddered, then went limp, unconscious.

"*No!*" Katherine screamed.

"It is done—he has been sentenced," Naomi said, putting a hand on her arm. Katherine began to cry—gasping, wrenching sobs that wracked her whole body.

"Please, please, you can't. It was my fault too. We were fighting . . ." she managed to say. "I made him angry . . . you can't terminate him, please . . ."

Naomi took a seat on the couch, her hand still on Katherine's arm, and Katherine sat down heavily beside her.

"You can't," she repeated, voice softer.

Naomi took Katherine's hand between her own. "It is done," she said gently. "It is not your fault. John's actions are his responsibility and no one else's. No one can be judged for the crime of another."

"I know," Katherine whispered.

"Someone who commits such a violation of law and morality must be removed from the population. It is not cruelty, Katherine. He is too dangerous. This is the only way to be sure he will never harm anyone else ever again."

Katherine looked down at her hands in her lap. She had

knitted her fingers together so tightly her knuckles were white. "He's a good man," she said, voice thin. "He just can't help it."

"I know," Naomi said.

Katherine looked up at her in surprise. "You do?"

"Everyone has good in them," Naomi said. "But we can't make our judgements based on who people are deep down inside. We have to judge what they actually do. Not their character, but their actions."

Katherine bowed her head, looking unconvinced. Naomi looked back at Gabriel, and he slapped John lightly on the cheek. The man stirred; he was still only semiconscious, but Gabriel dragged him to his feet. His head fell to one side as he stood.

"We've got to get him processed," Gabriel said. Naomi pressed Katherine's hand and stood to help Gabriel maneuver the subject.

"Can't you . . . can't he just be transported to Work?" Katherine asked in a last, half-hearted plea. Gabriel shook his head.

"No," he said, voice like stone. "No one gets a second attempt at murder."

With that, he prodded the man, who groaned, and shoved him stumbling through the door, Naomi following close behind.

✦

"I didn't see it coming." Naomi shook her head as they walked away from Municipal Building 4, where they had left John to be processed for termination. "I thought it was over, that he was putting the knife down. I was right there in front of him, and if I'd been there alone, that poor woman would be dead."

"You weren't there alone."

"I should have seen it coming," she repeated.

"Naomi, I've been stalking for fifteen years, and that's only the second time I've seen something like that. A weapon? A man trying to *murder* his wife? The person he ought to love above anyone else? When something unthinkable happens, you just have to do your best."

They walked on in silence for a moment, then Naomi looked up questioningly at him. "What was the first?"

"What?"

"You said it was the second time you saw something like that."

"Right." Gabriel cleared his throat. "It was almost exactly like what happened today, except I didn't see it coming. He killed her, and himself, before I could stop him."

Naomi nodded, her expression unchanging. She stopped walking and looked up at the sky for a moment, and Gabriel looped back to her.

"Let's walk through the park," she said suddenly. Gabriel's heart lifted. They were off duty now. She could do anything she liked, go anywhere, with anyone, and here she was, spending her time with him.

"Anywhere you want," he said and glanced backward. Municipal 4 was still in sight, but the street was crowded around them. "Maybe we should check in though."

Naomi laughed, the clear sound ringing out in the night air like a bell. "It's not forbidden, Gabriel," she said and took his arm. "You're such a stickler," she added, pulling him close.

"I'm dedicated," he retorted, and she laughed again.

"I'm teasing. You're the best stalker I've ever known."

The path into the park branched off, and they took it. Naomi let go of his arm and strode ahead toward the high bridge. Gabriel hurried to catch up. Naomi stopped at the crest of the bridge, where you could look out over half the city or look up and see the stars—the city and the park had been planned so that there would be places like this, where the light pollution was dim enough that the sky was thick with constellations.

Naomi leaned back against the concrete bridge support, looking up, and Gabriel's breath caught in his throat. Her hair hung back in dark curls, and her expression was pensive, as if she saw something among the distant stars that he did not understand. She had changed into a loose red dress after their shift ended, and the way she stood now, it clung to her body; she might as well have been wearing nothing at all. Naomi looked at him, and he cast his eyes away hastily, feeling his cheeks flush.

"Gabriel," she whispered and held out her hand. He grasped it, letting her pull him close, until the line of her body was almost brushing his.

"Naomi," he began, not knowing what he would say next, and she reached up and ran her fingers through his hair.

"You still look at me like you're afraid to touch me," she murmured, and he put his hands on her waist, marveling at her warmth.

"I'm not afraid," he said hoarsely. "I just . . ." He searched for words, and she tugged at his hair, then let it go, tracing her hand down the back of his neck. He shivered.

"Just what?" She kissed his throat, just above his collarbone, pressing herself close against him, and he swallowed hard.

"I still can't believe it's real," he admitted as she leaned her forehead against his shoulder.

"Neither can I." She pushed away a little and looked up to see his face. "I love you, Gabriel," she whispered, and his heart stopped. He felt as if his body had forgotten how to make it beat.

He kissed her until he was desperate for air, then cupped her face in his hands, at a loss.

"Gabriel?" she said, gently prying his hands off her cheeks.

"I love you," he said, astonished to hear himself say it out loud, at last. She smiled and swayed against him, making him gasp audibly, then she took his hand.

"So then come home with me," she said and led him off the bridge.

CHAPTER TWO

ASA LEANED BACK AGAINST THE ANCIENT oak, gazing up through the green canopy of trees. *I can't wait to get out of this place.* A shallow stream rippled slowly past a few feet away. As kids this had been the usual meeting spot, where Asa and his best friend Eli took turns crossing the water on a fallen log that served as a perilous bridge. Here they both were, again.

"Asa?" Eli prompted. "What's with you today? I just asked what you're going to do next."

Asa had a sudden impulse to tell him. *Tomorrow, I am leaving this place to go and live in the city. I'm done with this tiny, repetitious world of yours. From now on, every day will be new: new people, new places—new things I haven't even imagined yet.* Eli was the only one Asa would really miss when he was gone.

Like Asa, Eli was clever but restless. They were both athletic; their talents lay not in brute strength but in agility, speed, and daring. Asa was notorious by the time Eli came along, the blond daredevil with eyes blue as the Chancellor's. When he befriended the new doctor's son, his parents—everyone's parents—had hoped the small, bookish boy would prove a good influence on Asa.

They had been wrong.

"What am I gonna do? I'm gonna move to Horizon and never come back to Rosewood!" Asa said with the dry wit he had cultivated over the years. "Come on, I've got to go to my party."

"I thought you said it was your parents' party," Eli teased.

"Yeah, well, it's their party, but it's my birthday!"

He took off at a run through the woods, down the hill toward the town, not caring if his friend was keeping up. As he reached the town square, he skidded to a stop, nearly colliding with his nineteen-year-old sister, Hannah.

"Asa!" she cried, cheeks flushed with excitement. Her light brown hair had slipped free of its braid.

Asa put on a mock-exasperated face. "What is it now?"

"Happy birthday!" she exclaimed, throwing her arms around him. Asa laughed and hugged her back.

"You said that this morning! Has the party started without me?"

Hannah shrugged. "It's all Mom and Dad's friends so far." She grinned. "Did Mom and Dad give it to you yet?"

"Give me what?" Asa pretended ignorance. Hannah rolled her eyes.

"You *know* what! Oh, come on, Asa, you're twenty-one! Aren't you even a little excited? Your life is about to officially start!"

Asa shook his head, blond hair falling across his forehead. He brushed it back. "I like to think my life started twenty-one years ago," he said dryly. "Come on, everybody's over there."

11

They started toward the party. Asa's parents, Sarah and Isaac, had gathered a few of their friends around the set of tables in a corner of Rosewood's picturesque town square, and everyone had brought food. Asa's friends Seth, Noah, Marc, and Zeke were off to one side, near the group but not part of it. His mother spotted him and waved, and he felt a sudden clench of regret.

She's going to be heartbroken.

Asa ran ahead of Hannah and swooped his mother into a hug, lifting her off the ground and swinging her around. She was wearing a long green skirt, and it swirled prettily around her ankles, the shiny, hand-sewn details catching the light and sparkling.

"Put me down!" she protested, laughing as he obeyed.

"Me next!" his father joked, putting an arm around his wife's shoulders.

"I'll do it," Asa warned.

"Isaac, don't tempt fate," Asa's mother said, and it was as good as a dare.

Asa kissed his mother on the cheek, grabbed his substantial father around the waist, and lifted him off the pavement. He set him down again almost immediately, panting. His mother was laughing so hard she had tears in her eyes.

"Are you laughing at my son, Sarah?" Isaac said with a grin.

"No, I'm laughing at my husband," she managed to say, still giggling, and Isaac kissed her forehead. Asa smiled, feeling he was on the edge of something new.

Something inside him seemed to be whispering, *This is the last day. Treasure all of it.*

He turned in a small circle, taking in the square: the pristine white monolith at the center that seemed to reflect the sunlight, brightening a day that was already bright; the trees, still young by the standard of trees, thick and green with the first leaves of the season; and the lush verdant fields beyond the square. Even the drones seemed lively, swooping around the square or hovering in place, always watching.

I can't be nostalgic for a place I haven't left yet! Asa chided himself. Yet nostalgia was not the right word—it was something like the opposite. He was twenty-one, and despite his denial, Hannah had captured his feeling precisely. *My life is about to start.*

Everything he had ever resented about Rosewood had ceased to matter; the insularity, the sheer *smallness* of the place would never bind or constrict him again.

Asa looked across the square at the little crowd gathered around the vegetable stand, picking up tomatoes and squashes, comparing and discussing them.

Most of them have their own gardens. They go to the vegetable stand for the gossip as much as for the food.

It was the kind of thought that once would have made him despair, to imagine a lifetime spent inventing little tasks and little chatter, spinning whole years out in measured circles. What would there be to look back on when it came time to leave for Sanctuary? Not a lifetime but a single day, repeated over and over until you scarcely noticed the rising and setting of the sun. But now he was free of it.

"Asa!" Hannah called.

He rolled his eyes before turning around. *I don't think I've ever heard my own name called so many times in one day.*

"Come on, there's something for you!" she called.

He trotted back to the group. Eli stood next to Asa's mother. His own parents were sitting at one of the tables. Sarah held out a small box. It was a slim white rectangle with the State seal stamped on it. In the lower corner a small label read "Asa Isaac Rosewood, 21 Yrs."

He grinned.

"Asa," his mother said, "twenty-one years ago, you came into our community, and for twenty-one years you have been cherished and educated, taught to live by the Social Contract that binds us all. Now you are fully a member of adult society."

"Thanks, Mom!" Asa said and made a grab for the package. Sarah snatched it away before he could grasp it.

"I'm not done. Now you have the means to live your life however you wish, within the bounds of the Social Contract."

"I know, Mom, you don't have to make a speech." Asa looked down at his sneakers.

"Let your mother say what she wants to say," Isaac cut in. "We're both so proud of you, Asa."

"I didn't do anything."

His parents exchanged a glance. "You'll understand when you have children," his mother said and handed him the box.

"Thanks," Asa muttered, gauging its weight in his hand.

His parents' cloying affection, for him and for each other, was stifling. He turned away and opened the box. Inside was what he knew he would find: a phone with a lightweight silver-colored casing and his name inscribed on the back.

He touched the button at the top. The screen lit up. He had seen at least a dozen others go through the process, so he quickly obeyed the instructions as they appeared onscreen, holding the device up so it could scan his face and confirm his identity. When he had provided enough confirmation that he was, in fact, Asa Isaac Rosewood, the screen went black for a moment, then lit up with a familiar face.

"Happy birthday, Asa," said the Chancellor. He smiled

warmly, little wrinkles appearing at the corners of his striking blue eyes.

Asa smiled back in spite of himself. *It's just a recording*, he reminded himself. *He can't see you.*

"I am so pleased to welcome you into adult society," the Chancellor continued. "May you find contentment and be fulfilled. And remember to be careful of bridges, Asa!" He winked, and then he vanished, the screen abruptly black again.

Asa started. It might have been only a recording, but it had been recorded specially for him. The Chancellor knew each citizen—perhaps not well, but he knew a little about them all, enough to record a personal twenty-first birthday message for every single one.

"What did he say? I didn't hear," Hannah said, pushing up against Asa's shoulder.

Asa put the phone carefully in the pocket of his jeans. "He said, 'Be careful of bridges.'"

Hannah laughed. "He really does know you!"

"I guess so." Asa smiled to himself.

Bridges were the obvious thing. When he was ten, he had attempted to climb the one spanning the South River, and he had failed. He fell into twenty feet of water and was completely submerged, even his head going under. He had managed to struggle out, somehow, as a few friends watched in horror from above. One ran for a grown-up as Asa lay gasping for breath on the bank; no one dared to go near him. The old doctor, Levi, sped up in one of the town's cars, leaping out almost before he had come to a stop. As he bent over Asa, there was no spark of hope in his brown eyes.

"Did you go all the way under, son?" he asked gently, and Asa nodded, pushing himself up to a sitting position.

He coughed and spat out water, then looked up at the doctor's grim face. "Am I going to die?"

Levi didn't answer. The doctor had Asa take off all his clothes and sealed them in a case. He sprayed Asa down with a substance that burned his skin, and another that made it numb, then gave him a worn blue robe to put on. Levi drove him home in silence.

When Asa's mother came to the door, Levi said, "Asa, go to your room."

Sarah's eyes widened. "Where are his clothes? What's wrong with his skin?"

"Is Isaac here?" was the last thing Asa heard clearly before closing his bedroom door.

He could have held it open a crack and listened, but he didn't need to. Kids knew as well as grown-ups what happened when you fell in the water.

It was an amoeba, but people called it the Bug. It got in through your mouth or your nose and crawled up in your brain, and you were dead from fever and madness within ten days. Some people didn't even make it to three. There was no vaccine against it and no cure. And while there were always stories of someone who had survived, somebody who had fallen into a lake that had killed dozens yet managed to come out unscathed, those were only rumors of rumors. Someone knew someone two communities over who had heard it from someone else. Those stories were just legends.

Asa sat on his bed and looked out the window, pressing his forehead against the glass. The back garden was outside, lush and blooming with vegetables and fruit, but all he could see was the dirt.

I don't want to die. He couldn't even cry.

Asa didn't leave his room after that. He heard people coming and going, heard sobs and whispered conversations in the living room, but he just leaned out the open window, breathing the air because it was his last chance.

Two days passed, then three, then four, and he had not yet run a fever. Levi came every day. He was the only person Asa saw besides his mother and father. Levi took vital signs and asked him questions, simple math problems and simpler questions still: How old was he? What was his sister's name?

He's trying to see if the Bug's got my brain yet, Asa thought, but he just answered the doctor's questions, then went back to the window. He memorized all the trees and their branches, all the plants in the garden. He noticed when new flowers appeared in the field or when rabbits had been eating the tops of the carrots. Six more days passed, and the whispers turned heated.

"No one . . . ten days . . ."

"Possible? . . ." His mother's voice rose above the rest.

"Stories . . . legends . . ." said the doctor.

Twenty-five more days passed; the tomatoes grew overripe. His mother was neglecting the garden. Then one morning, his father came into his bedroom.

"Get dressed, Asa," he said with uncharacteristic gruffness. "You're going back to school."

And that was how Asa became a legend.

"Asa!" called his Aunt Ruth, just arriving with some freshly baked bread, and he sighed, turned, and smiled, bracing himself for the rest of the party.

People came and went. Asa lost track of who had or hadn't stopped by. His father's two brothers showed up as the sun was setting, brandishing a fiddle and concertina, and began to play without prompting. Zeke produced a harmonica from his pocket and joined in as Seth grabbed his beloved Julia's hand. Two of her friends pounced on Noah and Eli, dragging them out to dance.

It grew dark and the lamps came on, lighting up the square with a gentle glow. Asa looked up at the sky; the stars were dulled a little by the artificial light, but they were still strewn thick across the sky, ancient and enormous. Asa shivered. For an instant, the fiddle sounded thin, the square was tiny, the people fragile.

Suddenly, the drones scattered around the square all began to hum. Conversation halted, and the music stopped, the fiddle cutting off a second late with a high-pitched squeak. The drones swarmed toward the white wall at the center of the square and circled above it. Most of the people followed, gathering around as two drones dropped and positioned themselves on either side of the blank wall. Asa lagged behind a little.

The drones' humming stopped abruptly. Both sides of the wall lit up with the same projected image of the Chancellor. Eli caught up to Asa and elbowed him.

"Hey, turn on your phone," he whispered. "Let's watch on it!"

"It's bigger on the wall," Asa objected, but he turned the phone on and held it out to Eli as the Chancellor began to speak.

"Good evening, everyone," he said with a smile, spreading his arms in a gesture of welcome. He was in his office tonight, as he often was, but he was standing, leaning back casually against his desk.

Asa glanced at Eli, who was grinning, his eyes fixed on the little phone screen.

"I can't *wait* till I have one of these," he whispered, and Asa rolled his eyes good-naturedly.

"What an exceptional week it's been," the Chancellor

continued. "Our clean water reservoir is at its highest level in years, thanks to the gifted engineers of the State and to every one of you. I know that each of us helps ensure the safety of our supply. There is truly no higher purpose than the protection of our society, and we can only achieve it together."

His deep voice reverberated with the last words, and Asa felt a sudden sense of pride. *I'm part of adult society.*

"Today," the Chancellor went on, "I'm going to take a few minutes to highlight one of the people who exemplifies the values of our society. Some of you will know this person, but all of you will know people who are very similar. You know, the reason I like to do this every week is to remind all of us just how important each of our individual contributions are and to remind us what it is we're contributing to.

"In the years of chaos before the Founding," he said, "people in communities like ours might have said things like, 'Why should I worry what happens to Fairfield?'—sorry, Fairfield, you're just an example," he said with a wink, and a laugh rippled through the crowd, then vanished as the Chancellor's face grew serious. "They might have said things like, 'Why should I worry about Fairfield? I don't live in Fairfield! In fact, if Fairfield wasn't around, maybe my community would have more!' and that ...'" The Chancellor sighed and shook his head, looking down for a moment, then he faced the camera again with steel in his eyes. "That was the tragedy of the old society, and it was the ugliness, the rot at its core. It was an insatiable greed that our ancestors lived with, and it wasn't just bad for Fairfield! It was bad for everyone. Because thinking like that will corrode you from within. It will consume a person, and it will destroy a society."

He looked grimly at them for a moment. Then his face relaxed, and Asa let out a breath he hadn't realized he was holding; all around him he heard people doing the same.

"So, we don't think like that," the Chancellor went on assuredly. "And not just because it's dangerous, but because it's a lot easier to help each other out, right? So, I like to do these little highlights to remind us all that even though we might live in communities that are far apart—even though most of us will never meet!—we are all in this together.

"The person I want to talk to you about tonight is a wonderful woman named Abigail who lives in—and you may have already guessed—Fairfield!"

A still photograph of a woman, holding a toddler, appeared on the projection. They both had dark hair and light brown skin, and both were laughing wildly. The projection switched to a drone feed video of Abigail and the child sitting on the grass outdoors. They were playing with a bright blue wooden puzzle. It had pieces cut out into common shapes, and the child was attempting to put them into place.

"Abigail is thirty years old. That is her with her young daughter, Rebecca. Rebecca is learning shapes, as you can see! Abigail is known in Fairfield as a wonderfully intuitive person. Everyone who knows her says she is a good person to help talk through a difficult problem."

The feed switched to a gathering in a community square; it could easily have been Rosewood, Asa thought, except for the unfamiliar people. Abigail was amid the crowd, talking and laughing.

"Abigail and her husband, Joshua, have been married for nine years," the Chancellor continued. "They waited to have children because they wanted to spend some time together first, just the two of them, which I think sounds just lovely." The feed switched back to the Chancellor's office. "I think Abigail is just an amazing woman, and we are very lucky to have her in the Fairfield community."

He smiled widely.

"Next week we'll all get to meet someone else, and I am so glad that we will. Although we may live in our own communities and be spread far apart from each other, we are all part of our greater community. We are, truly, all in this together. I'll see each of you again next week."

The feed switched off; the wall went blank again, and Asa stretched. The sounds of the village square rose again as people chatted, and some began to walk away toward home.

"Are you gonna watch *The Challenge*?" Eli asked, and Asa shook his head.

"Nah," he said. "I'm kind of tired."

Eli shrugged and handed back Asa's phone. "Suit yourself. See you tomorrow!"

"See you tomorrow," Asa echoed with a pang of guilt. He started off toward home; as he crossed the square, the wall lit up again as familiar theme music played.

"I wanna watch," a little boy complained as his mother tugged his hand.

"It's not appropriate for someone your age," she said tightly, glancing back at the crowd that had remained to watch. Asa passed them, looking down at the cobblestones and picking up his pace.

He didn't want to see anyone else, didn't want to repeat the lie, "*I'll see you tomorrow.*"

"Asa!" Someone called to him from a few yards away, but Asa pretended not to hear. He hurried out of the square and up the road toward home for the last time.

21

✦

In the morning, Asa told his mother and father he was leaving.

"I don't understand," Sarah said, gripping the handle of the coffee pot so tightly her knuckles were white.

"I said I'm leaving," Asa repeated patiently. He had been rehearsing this all night; he was braced for an outburst, ready to counter any of their objections.

"I understand what you said." Sarah's words were clipped as she began to move again, pouring her coffee and setting the pot back down, spooning in sugar with a crisp, angry deftness.

Isaac watched warily from the doorway; he had not yet responded to his son's declaration, and Asa could not read his heavy-featured face. Finally, Sarah sat at the table, her back straight as a post, and gave Asa a withering stare. He met her eyes, not giving ground. Sarah sipped her coffee, not breaking eye contact, then set the cup down.

"What I don't understand, Asa, is why you would choose to leave us. What have we done to hurt you?"

"What?"

"There must be some reason you're saying this, son," Isaac said, coming in to stand behind his wife's chair. He rested his hand on her shoulder, and her face lost a fraction of its tension. "Your mother just wants to know what it is. So do I. We've always tried to do the best for you."

Asa looked from his father to his mother and back again. This was the only contingency he had not planned for. He was ready for arguing, even shouting, tears and dire warnings of what happens to young men in the city. It had not occurred to him that his parents might be hurt.

"Mom, Dad, you didn't do anything wrong," he said quickly.

"I just want more out of life. I want to see what the world really is, not be stuck here in this tiny, suffocating place—" He broke off too late.

"Tiny, suffocating place? Asa, this is your home, your *community*," Isaac said, the shock visible on his face.

"I didn't mean it that way!" Asa sighed with frustration. "It was a great place to grow up. It's a great place now. I just want to try something new, now that I can."

"It's not about the place, Asa," Sarah murmured. "It's about the people."

"I know that, Mom. I just want to see a little more of the world, that's all."

His parents were silent. Isaac pulled out a wooden chair and sat beside his wife. "I suppose we can't stop you," he said doubtfully, as if realizing this new state of affairs for the first time.

"No, you can't," Asa said quietly. His mother and father exchanged a glance. His mother shook her head and took another sip of coffee.

"I don't like it," she said in an even tone. She didn't look at Asa, staring at the middle of the table as if something very interesting were happening there.

"I know, Mom."

"Asa, can you really imagine starting a new life, surrounded by people you've never met? The people of Rosewood have known you all your life. They know the whole of you—who you were the day you were born, who you've become, and everything in between. How would it be if everyone around you were a stranger? How could they truly love you without knowing the whole of you, the way the people here do?"

Her voice grew strident, and Isaac put his hand on hers. "Your sister Ruth met Matthew outside of Rosewood. She went all the way to Deerfield, remember? And they're happy as can be."

"They have no children, Isaac," Sarah said, lowering her voice.

"That's their choice," he said calmly. "All I'm saying is, I don't think it would be such a bad thing if Asa went to Pine Valley or Pleasantdale for a little while. Some young people need to breathe a different air before they can settle down."

Sarah sighed and shook her head. "I don't like it," she said again. "But maybe your father is right. Do you know where you want to go?"

Asa swallowed. He had meant to get everything out all at once, but the conversation had gotten away from him almost immediately.

So much for having an answer for everything, he thought.

"I'm going to Horizon," he said with as much confidence as he could muster. "Today."

His mother gasped, and his father's face darkened. "Asa," Isaac said, his voice taking on a firmer edge. "Horizon is quite a different thing."

"People live there, don't they?"

"People who live there have reasons," Isaac corrected. "Authority Figures, people training at the medical and engineering schools, anyone who has chosen to become a vessel of the State. People who need to be in Horizon to learn or to serve the greater good."

"Other people live there too."

"People who live dangerous lives," Sarah said. "Asa, you're a risk-taker. I know that, and it has terrified me ever since you ... I have feared for you. I've always hoped that when you reached maturity—or perhaps when you married—you would settle down, and I would stop having nightmares about what you might do next."

"Mom ..." Asa half-heartedly tried to interrupt, but his father glared him into silence.

"And now," Sarah continued, "you tell me you are about to take the greatest risk of your life—and worse, I won't even know what is happening to you, because you'll be hundreds of miles away!"

"Mom, it's only a few hours away on the rail!"

"Did you know there was a young man who moved to Horizon from here?" Sarah said slowly. "He was our age, Isaac, remember? He went when he was twenty-three."

"Adam," Isaac said.

"Adam," Sarah repeated, nodding. "He was only in Horizon for three months before he broke his Social Contract. Then he was sent to Work." She looked plaintively at her son. "Twenty-three years old, and he never saw his family again. Why must you willingly enter the same trap that he did?"

"What? I'm not Adam—I never even met this guy! I'm bound by my Social Contract just as much as you are. You raised me to know right from wrong. Do you think I'm going to become a different person just because I move to the city?"

His father opened his mouth to speak, but Asa rushed on.

"It's not like I can break my Social Contract by accident, Mom! I would never hurt anyone or anything deliberately. I would never damage the world around me. And you raised me from the day I was born to act with respect for myself, for my community, and for the State that keeps us all safe and provides everything we need." He heard himself falling into a singsong rhythm as he finished, going back to his childhood, when they first learned how to remember the words. Sarah and Isaac still looked at him sadly.

"It's not always up to you, son," Isaac said finally. "Whether or not you become a different person. People do change, and you can't know how something will change you until it happens."

"You should know me better than that," Asa said. "I don't want to become a different person. I just want to see what it's like to live differently."

"And once you experience this? Will you come back?" Isaac asked. His mother waited anxiously for his answer.

Never, Asa thought, the word on the tip of his tongue, but he swallowed it.

"Maybe," he said instead. The answer ended the argument, but it didn't seem to have reassured anyone.

His mother stood abruptly and went back to the coffee pot. She refilled her cup slowly and stood looking out the kitchen window as if she might never turn around. She was done with the argument, apparently. Isaac came up behind her and whispered something in her ear, and she leaned back against him. Suddenly uncomfortable, Asa retreated to his room.

His things were already packed—he had been packing and unpacking for weeks, carefully choosing which of his possessions he would give precious space to in his hiking backpack, then having to undo the whole thing when he inevitably needed socks. Last night, though, had been the final round. He had stripped it down to the bare essentials: nothing sentimental, nothing that could not be used every day.

He hefted the pack onto his back, testing the weight, and nearly dropped it as he turned at the sound of a knock on the door. Hannah was hanging onto the frame, half in the hallway, her eyes wide and anxious.

"You're really leaving?" she asked.

Asa set the backpack down. "Yes," he said. "It'll be okay though—we'll see each other soon. It's only a few hours away on the rail."

Hannah frowned. She hesitated in the door for another moment, then darted across the room and sat down on the bed, twisting her braided hair in her fingers. "What's wrong with Rosewood?" she asked. "Susanna would marry you, Asa, or Leah, or even some of the girls in my class, if you wanted to wait." She wrinkled her nose at the thought, and Asa laughed.

"Hannah, it's not about that. I just want to explore a little, see something new."

"What will you do there?"

"I don't know yet." Asa sat beside his sister. "I just want to try something new. You can come visit me, as soon as I have a place to live. I'll send you a rail pass, okay?"

"Okay," Hannah said, but she looked unconvinced.

Asa picked up the backpack again. *If I'm going, it had better be now*, he thought.

He leaned down and kissed Hannah on the cheek, passed through the kitchen and hugged his parents quickly, not giving them time to respond, and hurried out the door, heading for the road.

CHAPTER THREE

IT WAS NOT UNTIL THE PIERCING WHISTLE OF the tea kettle had reached its highest pitch that Gabriel heard it. He glared at it for a moment, letting the sound go on; maybe the noise could drown out his thoughts. *Get it together,* he told himself and turned off the stove, letting the sound fade away. He started to pour the water into his cup, stopping when he realized he had forgotten the tea bag. Gabriel closed his eyes and took a deep breath, then set the kettle aside and sat down at the table. He knotted his hands together, dread swelling in the pit of his stomach.

I can't do this.

He clenched his jaw, staring down at the pale, worn tablecloth. He had never liked it; now, he could not bear to move it. His phone beeped on the counter behind him, and he ignored it.

Joan. Bright, shiny, newly minted stalker with her wide-eyed excitement. Of all the partners to replace—

He shoved his chair back from the table and went to get his phone. *Nobody's replacing anyone.*

"You just have to adjust, get reacclimated to your role as an Authority Figure," the doctor had told him. Gabriel had nodded and said thank you, thinking, *Reacclimate? I was raised to this since I was three years old. A month's leave can't make me less a stalker. You'd as well make me less a human being.*

He looked at the phone. Joan had called twice. He sighed. *Have to start sometime.* Gabriel turned on the water in the kitchen sink as cold as it would go and splashed some on his face, shocking himself back to a kind of calmness.

He dried his hands and face on a dish towel. As he was replacing it, the phone rang again. He glared at it for a moment, then sighed and answered.

"Gabriel."

"Gabriel?" a young, female voice repeated.

"Yes."

"It's Joan. Your new partner? We met last week?"

"I know who you are," he said shortly, irritated at her questioning tone. Going into the field, she should have more confidence. "What do you want?"

"It's almost three. You're late. You're supposed to be meeting me at Municipal 7 right now."

"I know," he said, then, belatedly, "Sorry. I'll be there in a minute."

He looked around the kitchen. There was nothing else left to do, but it seemed strange to leave like this, just walk out of the house without a word to anyone about it. He hesitated at the door; by now it had become a habit, almost, to pause before he touched the knob, to look down before opening the door, not wanting to disturb the now undetectable spot on the floor where she had lain.

Gabriel set his jaw, opened the door, and went out into the too-bright sun.

✦

Joan was waiting for him outside Municipal 7. He saw her across the plaza as he got off the train, standing perfectly still as people streamed in and out of the building. Despite himself, Gabriel smiled.

Her expression was almost completely neutral, neither hard nor inviting. Her posture was straight without being stiff. Her eyes flickered over each person who walked by her, and he knew she was sifting, filing away details or letting the information pass through her mind, making split-second judgement calls about every piece of data. She was dressed in dark, close-fitting pants and a matching shirt. Authority Figures didn't have uniforms, but there were guidelines for every division, and for stalkers— Contract Enforcers, to use the official term—it was simple: wear anything you like, as long as you can run, jump, hide, and take down hostile threats.

"You look like you stepped out of a textbook," Gabriel said, voice dry, as he reached her.

She nodded. "See everything, notice everything, forget everything except what matters," Joan said with a faint smile. "You can't remember everything you see. Your job is to notice patterns—to notice breaks in the patterns. Raw data collection is for drones."

"So, you did step out of a textbook."

"I'm not *that* new," Joan said lightly, but there was something steely in her brown eyes.

Gabriel looked her over quickly. They'd met a week before,

at Municipal 5, where he had undergone testing for his reentry approval, but he'd scarcely been paying attention. She was not as young as he had thought, he realized now, in the bright light of afternoon. She was just small, and pretty in a delicate way that probably made people like him misjudge her all the time.

She looked Panasian—the word didn't mean much; at this point no one was quite sure whether any of Panasia was still above water, but people kept descriptions like that—and she had long, thick, dark hair. The last time he saw her, it was loose around her face, but now it was pulled back tightly, adding to her more sophisticated impression.

"What are you looking at?" Joan asked without a challenge in her tone.

Gabriel shrugged and told the truth. "You seemed younger last time."

"Gee, thanks," Joan said sarcastically, then grinned. "They told me you were coming back after—I wanted to make it easier for you," she finished disjointedly.

Gabriel laughed. "You wanted to appear nonthreatening, so you wore your hair down?"

"It's a basic technique." She lifted her chin.

"You're right out of training."

"Did you even read my file?"

"Yes. You're right out of training."

"Everyone starts that way," Joan said.

She was looking at him thoughtfully, probably trying to read his face—whatever nonsense might be scribbled there. Gabriel headed for the front door without another word. He heard her hurrying behind him but didn't slow his pace.

So now I'm stuck with her for how long? he thought, and then, *Naomi would have liked her.*

They entered the building, a large concrete structure saved from ugliness by the enormous windows on every wall. Gabriel signed himself in, which meant stepping into a small box of a room while a robotic voice gave him instructions. Because of his long absence, it was a multistep process, examinations and questions both to confirm his identity and determine his fitness for duty. Thankfully, it was all automated—all he had to do was say "Yes" and "No" to the computer-generated voice while his body was scanned, mapped, and approved for duty.

When he emerged, Joan was waiting again.

"You're starting to feel like my guardian," he remarked, and she laughed, though he had not meant it as a joke.

"They were everywhere, weren't they? Sometimes I thought there were more guardians than kids! I grew up in Sumac Ward Home. How about you?"

"Acacia," Gabriel said. "We should go. If we catch the train down the block, it's faster."

"Oh—it's a new sector, actually. We can walk," Joan said awkwardly, and Gabriel shook his head.

"I forgot. Come on."

He strode out in front of her, feeling the need to prove that he remembered where they were going. He had expected other people to wonder about his fitness for duty, but he had not expected to question himself. They were five city blocks from the municipal building when Joan called his name.

"Gabriel! Turn here. And slow down, would you? You're too tall."

"Maybe you're too short."

He looped back to meet her, but the attempt at friendly banter fell flat. Joan gave him a smile that didn't quite reach her eyes, and his stomach tensed. He knew what that look meant. Joan glanced around; they were beside an alley on a side street, as close to alone as they were likely to get.

"I just want you to know, Gabriel, I know what happened and I am so sorry," she said in a low voice. Gabriel felt his face hardening, his eyes taking on a flat glare. "If you ever want to talk . . . I just know these things are hard," she finished in a rush.

"You don't know anything." Gabriel had turned to lead. Joan drew back slightly, then straightened.

"So, tell me," she said.

Something inside him broke open. Gabriel grabbed Joan's upper arm and pulled her into the alley, and she gasped but didn't pull away. He let go and turned away, talking to a blank wall.

"Naomi was my partner for six years," he said.

"I met her one time," Joan started, and he ignored her.

"I fell in love with her. You're not supposed to, technically, but it's one of those rules that no one worries too much about. And it didn't matter. She had a boyfriend, a guy named Timothy. She was happy. I was just her partner. Sometimes it was great—we'd make an arrest or prevent a crime and she'd smile at me, and it was like we'd just saved the world together.

"It made me a better stalker, and not just because I wanted to impress her. When she was there, I was just *better*. The best version of myself that had always seemed just out of reach." He forced a hollow laugh. "Sometimes, of course, it was a little like going around all day with a pulled muscle, where no matter what you do, it just hurts more. But eventually I got lucky—she loved me too. Happy ending."

"Okay," Joan said cautiously.

"She left her boyfriend and moved in with me. For almost three months it was . . . perfect. I know that sounds like I'm remembering it with some kind of nostalgia, but it was—it was perfect. No one had ever loved me before. That sounds maudlin, but I don't mean it to be. I hadn't really expected love or wanted it. I didn't know what I was missing."

Gabriel broke off, suddenly aware of Joan's wide eyes, intent on his face.

Naomi was more than I was, he had been about to say. *Not better, although she was that, but* more. *She was exacting in her work, no less than I, but she was so compassionate to everyone we caught and sentenced. I was scrupulous about right and wrong, thinking through scenarios every night, as if I were still in training, just to be sure I would never make a mistake. But to her it was like breathing. She didn't have to think about it. She just knew.*

"Gabriel?" Joan said softly, interrupting his thoughts, and he looked at her.

"Right." He cleared his throat.

She was looking at him with a softness in her eyes, and suddenly he was tense with anger. *How dare you pity me.*

"So, one morning the doorbell rang," he said, his tone sharper. "I was upstairs. We both started for the door, but she got there first. I was still at the top of the stairs when she opened the door—it was Timothy. He just stood there for a second. He had the strangest smile on his face, and I saw the kitchen knife in his hand. I ran down the stairs. I almost fell over my own feet. Naomi tried to turn and run, but he grabbed her by the hair and yanked her back. He stabbed her over and over as I tried to get to them—it was like a dream where you're in slow motion. She was screaming. I saw her blood spray in an arc across his face, covering it. He stabbed her again and again, and then she stopped screaming."

Joan's eyes were wide, and she clapped one hand over her mouth. Gabriel couldn't tell if it was from shock or nausea, but he pressed on with a sick satisfaction at her distress.

"I reached the bottom of the stairs, and he dropped her and ran—I caught her before she hit the floor. I didn't even think of chasing him. I pressed my hands over the cut in her throat, the deepest one, but it was too late—he had sliced her carotid artery open. She was already unconscious, and she would be dead in seconds."

He paused, getting his voice under control.

"I called Emergency Services, and while I waited for them to arrive, I held her head in my lap, still covering the wound in her throat even though there was no blood pumping out into my hands. I studied her face, memorizing it because it was the last time I would see her. Her eyes were brown, and there was a little dark fleck near the pupil. I looked into her eyes, fixing on that point like I had a thousand times before, and I realized I wasn't looking *into* her eyes, I was looking *at* them. She was dead, just a thing. There was nothing left of her. I kept looking though. I didn't want to forget. By the time Emergency Services arrived, my clothes were soaked through with her blood. They took her away and said someone would come to clean the blood up so I wouldn't have to do it myself.

"I searched for Timothy. I didn't go to the hospital. What would be the point? Naomi was already gone. But it was useless. I hadn't even seen which direction he ran. Still, I swore I wouldn't rest until I brought him to justice. I would dedicate my life to it."

"And?" Joan said softly.

Gabriel gave her a sideways glance. "And nothing. Someone else found him a few hours later, just a mile or so up the road. He'd cut his own throat with the same knife he'd used to stab Naomi. So, I went home and I cleaned the front hall. I wiped up her blood and washed the tile until it was clean—I couldn't bear to have someone else be the one to strip the last traces of her from my life. I guess that makes me a romantic," he added sarcastically.

"Not really," Joan said. She looked pale and slightly off-balance.

"Breathe or you'll faint," Gabriel said shortly.

She took a deep breath and let it out slowly, then looked at him, some of the color returning to her cheeks.

"They told us she died in an accident," she said at last.

Gabriel laughed abruptly. "Time to get back to work." He strode ahead, not looking back to see if Joan was behind him.

CHAPTER FOUR

"WELCOME TO HORIZON. PLEASE MAKE SURE
you have collected all of your belongings before disembarking."

Asa lifted his head fuzzily, awakened by the pleasant automated voice of the rail announcement. He had managed to fall
asleep with his arm and face pressed up against the window, and
as he sat up, he rolled his shoulder, trying to work out the kinks.
His backpack was still between his feet, and he grabbed it and
scanned the floor in case something had fallen out.

"Welcome to Horizon. If you see someone having trouble,
please lend a helping hand," the voice intoned. People were moving past him toward the exit; Asa wasn't sure when he had fallen
asleep, but the compartment was a lot fuller than he recalled.
He watched them go by, men and women with sure steps and
compact luggage.

Does everyone but me do this all the time? he wondered.

The compartment emptied quickly, and Asa got to his feet hurriedly, falling in line behind a middle-aged man with clipped gray hair and square shoulders.

"Welcome to Horizon," the voice began again as Asa emerged into the station. "Enjoy your time here, and always report any suspicious activity. Remember, we are all in this together."

". . . in this together," Asa said under his breath along with the recording, saying the words like touching a talisman.

The rail station was bright and open. The high ceiling was made of irregularly shaped glass panels, and the sun streamed in unobstructed. Asa stared upward until someone bumped into him, almost knocking him off his feet. Asa stumbled, then recovered his footing to find himself facing a thin, dark-haired man a little older than him.

"Are you all right?" the other man said. "Sorry, I should have noticed you."

"I guess I shouldn't have been standing in the middle of a crowd, staring up at the sky," Asa said sheepishly.

The young man grinned. "Don't worry, everyone does it the first time they pass through this place. Look." He pointed discreetly across the station, where an elegant-looking woman was gazing upward, exactly the way Asa had been. As they watched, a man hurrying for the door pulled up short, barely avoiding a collision.

Asa laughed. "I guess it's not just me."

"Not at all. By the way, welcome to Horizon!"

"Thanks, I'm—" Before Asa could finish introducing himself, the man was gone, vanishing into the crowd with a final wave. "I'm Asa," Asa said quietly.

He tightened his grip on his bag and followed the largest section of the crowd out the main door and onto a sprawling plaza.

It was reminiscent of the town square in Rosewood, writ large, but it was so much more.

To begin with, it was thronged with people—more people than Asa had ever seen in one place. Some were crossing the flat, pale stones purposefully, on their way to something important, and others were sitting in the sun or playing games that Asa could not recognize from a distance. There were stone benches and clusters of tables, but what made Asa stare were the spots, scattered across the plaza, where lush plants grew boldly as if in the wild.

He went to inspect one. In a circle about ten feet in diameter, meadow grass and wildflowers rippled in the wind. Asa glanced around; the air in the plaza was still. He walked around the circle until he came to a plaque, which read "Microclimate: Meadow." Asa reached forward, about to pick a blade of grass, and his hand went suddenly numb, a buzzing sensation striking all the way up to the elbow. Asa grabbed his wrist, glancing around to see if anyone had noticed, but no one was looking at him.

He looked at the plaque again. In the bottom corner, small script read "Do not touch: microclimate protected by electrified air barrier."

"Probably should have read that," Asa mumbled to himself, flexing his hand as the feeling slowly returned to it.

Despite the shock, he went to another one. It was the same size, a large circular space, and this one was mostly sand and rock, with strange flowers scattered thinly on the ground.

"Microclimate: Desert," Asa read aloud.

He looked on for a moment, then was startled as a small animal darted from behind a rock, vanishing under another too fast for Asa to see what it was.

Leaving the desert, Asa made his way to another one of

the spots, labeled "Microclimate: Forest." This one looked as if it could have come straight from Rosewood, with shady trees, maybe fifteen feet high, with heavy leaves. Asa sat down on a nearby bench, feeling a little more at ease with trees standing beside him. He took off his backpack and sighed.

Now what?

He had considered everything up to this moment, directed all his thoughts and plans toward getting to Horizon. Now that he was here, the future was a vast open space. He didn't know what to do; he didn't even know what he *could* do.

Asa squinted up at the sky. The sun was falling; it was late afternoon. *I should probably find a place to stay,* he thought.

He got up and started out of the plaza, picking a direction at random. The first large building he saw had a sign that read "Bank" above a row of doors, each leading into an individual booth. He picked one and went inside.

"Good afternoon, Asa Isaac Rosewood," said an automated voice as he entered.

"Um, hello. How did you know my name?"

"Your name is Asa Isaac Rosewood," the voice replied pleasantly.

"Right . . ."

"How can I help you, Asa Isaac—"

"Please, just call me Asa."

There was a brief pause.

"How can I help you, Asa?"

"Yeah." Asa took out his phone and held it up. "Can I check my account, I guess?"

"You have 199,988 credits available." As the autom spoke, the number appeared on his phone's screen. Below the total, in smaller print, a deduction was listed: twelve creds for his train ticket.

"Oh. I can just use them, right?" he asked awkwardly.

"You have 199,988 credits available. They are valid for all transactions except those in violation of your Social Contract."

"Right." Asa hesitated.

The bank autom wasn't really equipped to answer his real questions. *I can really go where I want, do what I want? I don't have to ask anyone because I'm not a kid anymore?*

"Would you like to view the bank's official financial planning advice video, covering such topics as budgeting, spending priorities, and saving for a secure future?"

"Not now," Asa said.

"Is there anything else I can do for you, Asa?" The autom's voice didn't change, but Asa felt a little like he was being asked to move along.

"Not now, thank you," he said.

Asa looked down at the phone in his hand. *Financial planning.* Two hundred thousand credits, deposited every year on his birthday, seemed like more than he could ever need, but he had heard stories about people who lost everything, getting sent to Work for their foolishness.

I don't know how much it costs to live in an apartment, he thought. *I don't know how much food costs in Horizon.* He wavered at the door, feeling briefly guilty for skipping the bank's video. *I can watch it another time. It's not like the bank's going anywhere,* he decided.

The sun was close to setting when Asa emerged from the bank. He looked up and down the street with rising excitement. Even though the bank autom was just an autom, the interaction had lifted him up; now he wanted to talk to someone else. But no one magically stopped to chat, so once again, Asa picked a random direction and started walking.

He tried not to gawk, but the city was everything he had hoped for: it was nothing like Rosewood. The main streets were straight and wide, crossing regularly in a slightly off-kilter grid, and the buildings varied widely: some were simple—square and concrete, and a little ugly—while others looked like pieces of art, daring structures with jutting curves and colorful patterns. He paced back and forth beneath a strange tower whose height seemed to shift depending on which angle he saw it from.

Asa kept walking, gazing up at the strange buildings until his neck began to cramp. As it grew dark, he began to notice lights coming from the narrow alleys. They were not dead ends, as he had assumed. He hesitated a moment, then quickly slipped between a square concrete block of one building and another that appeared to be an enormous fountain, water running continuously down its walls and into an invisible gutter.

Careful not to get wet, Asa went into the alley. It was long and narrow and opened out into another narrower alley. He followed that, then turned the next corner and found himself back on the main road, about a block from where he had started. Asa smiled and set off down another alley, which took a sharp left turn down another alley before opening onto a new road, not as wide as the main streets and lined with smaller, much less impressive buildings than the ones on the outside. All around them, the backs of the enormous buildings loomed, hiding the main street from view.

It was like a whole hidden section of the city—he would never have known it was there if he hadn't followed the lights on a whim. Asa stared for a moment, feeling as if he had stumbled on a secret treasure. This was, he thought, the thing he had always wanted but never knew existed.

Some of the buildings were marked with brightly lit signs,

and one across the road caught his eye. "Zipporah's Nightbar." Asa's pulse rose.

He had heard whispers about places like this, but he doubted most of the adults in Rosewood had ever seen one. People always said strange things could happen in Horizon's nightbars. Maybe even dangerous things. No one had ever specified what those things might be, and the vague warnings had given these places an alluring edge to Asa and his friends.

He crossed the street and went inside.

Asa looked around. It was dark and a little grimy, with patrons seated at a long bar counter or at little tables along the facing wall, and when he walked in, half the people there raised their heads simultaneously, looking him up and down as if taking his measure.

This is just like Tom's place back home, Asa thought with a pang of disappointment. *Right down to the stares if you don't belong.* Nevertheless, he went up to the bar and waited while the stone-faced redheaded barwoman gazed off into the distance, apparently unaware of his presence. He moved three feet to the left, placing himself directly in her line of sight. Her eyes narrowed.

"I haven't seen you before," she said.

"It's a big city," Asa offered warily, wondering if this would be some strange dominance test.

But she just asked, "What do you drink?"

"Moonshine," Asa answered honestly, and she laughed. He felt himself flush and looked down at the bar.

"New in town?" the bartender asked with a kinder tone, and he nodded. Her lips twitched into a smile. "Welcome," she said, looking him up and down deliberately. Asa smiled slowly. This he was used to.

"Leave him alone, Zip. He's too young for you!" a man called good-naturedly from down the bar.

Asa winked at the barwoman. "Don't listen to that guy. He's drunk," he quipped, and Zip—presumably the Zipporah the place was named for—laughed and pulled a glass out from under the bar. She poured something into it from an unmarked bottle and set it in front of Asa.

"Here you go, blue eyes. Moonshine, from my personal distillery. Welcome to Horizon."

Asa sipped the drink and grimaced; it was nothing if not authentic. And possibly corrosive. More at ease after chatting with the overly friendly Zip, he looked around again, hoping for another conversation. The patrons were dressed in a variety of fashions, old and new, only a few of which were familiar to Asa. He took another sip of his drink and nearly choked as he saw *her* across the bar.

The sight of her hit him like an actual blow to the chest: a young woman, perhaps a little older than he was, with long, straight black hair almost down to her waist and smooth, light brown skin that seemed to glow under the dim light of the nightbar. She was wearing white, which shone in bright contrast to the darkness of the place. She was looking down into her drink, and her large dark eyes and full lips were almost expressionless. She didn't look bored, exactly. She actually looked restless.

Asa tried to catch her eye, but she didn't look up. He hesitated and brushed his hair back carefully to appear more mature. He was not usually nervous around women—most reacted to him much the way that Zip had—but she was different. She seemed like something new.

Asa finished his drink quickly, and the rush of alcohol steadied him as he made his way down the bar to where she sat. There was an empty stool beside her, and he grabbed it. She glanced at him from the corner of her eye, the movement scarcely visible, and Asa grinned.

"Hi. I'm Asa," he said. She turned her head, then laughed suddenly.

"Did I say something funny?" he asked.

She shook her head. "No. About five minutes before you got here, a guy asked me if I wanted a wild ride, and fifteen minutes before *that* someone else asked if I wanted to 'plant my melons in his community garden' in a very inappropriate manner. I know it was a sexual euphemism, but I still can't for the life of me figure out what it's a euphemism *for*."

"Well, 'Hi. I'm Asa,' only has one meaning, as far as I know."

"Glad to hear it . . . Eve."

"What?"

"My name is Eve. In case you were curious."

"Eve—yes, I was curious. Thanks," he added with a giddy, off-balance feeling. She—Eve—kept catching him off guard, switching the conversation before he was ready for it, but it didn't make him feel silly. It was exhilarating.

"I'm from Rosewood," he said. "Asa Isaac Rosewood."

"Asa Isaac Rosewood," Eve repeated slowly, holding the tones in her mouth as if she were tasting each of them. Asa felt his face getting hot, and he slid off the stool, stepping in a little closer to her in the process. She didn't move away.

"Where are you from?" Asa asked. A stricken look came over her face. "I'm sorry!" he said quickly. "Is that a bad question—"

He was cut off as someone seized his arm and yanked him backward, almost pulling him over.

"What the hell do you think you're doing with my girl?" a man growled into his ear.

"Daniel, stop it!" Eve cried, leaping off the stool.

"Stay out of this, Eve!"

"I didn't mean anything," Asa stammered, and the man holding him back let go and shoved him forward. The barstool caught him in the stomach, and he gasped for air, struggling against his own lungs.

"Hey!" Zip shouted. "Not in here, Daniel!"

"Fine," the man snapped. He grabbed Asa by the collar and yanked him toward the exit. Asa struggled away from him, facing his attacker for the first time.

"I didn't do anything!" he shouted.

Daniel snorted. "Yeah, they never *do* anything." He was a lot older than Eve, maybe close to forty, and while he looked as though he was in good shape, his eyes had dark circles under them, and his face looked haggard.

"Come on, man, we were just talking."

"We were just talking, Daniel!" Eve called out.

"Stay out of it!" he snarled and grabbed Asa again by his shirt collar.

Asa fought to push him away, then kicked him, his foot landing hard on Daniel's kneecap. Immediately Daniel launched himself at Asa, punching his solar plexus, then the side of his face. Asa doubled over, gasping for breath again. Daniel hit him from the other side, his fist landing right over Asa's eye. Asa reeled momentarily, then hurtled himself forward, slamming Daniel's head backward into the wall.

"Hey!"

A whistle sounded, and the next thing Asa knew he was on the floor, his whole body vibrating with a bizarre, intense pain that seemed to go on for hours. When it stopped, he lay with his eyes closed for a moment, afraid it would happen again. When it didn't, he opened his eyes to see Daniel lying on the floor beside him, writhing in pain.

"That's enough," a crisp female voice said, and Daniel's convulsions stopped. Asa pushed himself up to a sitting position, the room still spinning around him.

"What happened?" he managed to say. A man crouched to his level quickly and gave Asa a scrutinizing look, his dark eyes seeming to read far beneath the surface.

"By authority of the State, you will be questioned, judged, and sentenced, Asa Isaac Rosewood."

CHAPTER FIVE

"GABRIEL." JOAN PUT HER HAND ON HIS ARM, then pulled it away sharply. Gabriel didn't look at her.

"Are you okay?" she asked softly, and he turned to her with a grin.

She flinched but recovered quickly, and he held the smile a second longer. Gabriel was no longer bothered by the reaction his appearance provoked. Only Naomi had ever told him he had a nice smile with a straight face, and she had been lying.

Descriptions he'd overheard ranged from "unsettling" to "death's head." Frowning, neutral, or even with a faint smile he was handsome, but with a wide, cheerful grin he looked monstrous. He'd tried practicing in the mirror as a child, but he couldn't help the way the muscles bulged under his thin, pale skin, the way his dark, hooded eyes began to resemble the hollows of a skull when he bared his teeth.

Later, when Gabriel understood that he would become a stalker, he stopped trying to fix it. A face like his would come in handy.

"I'm fine," Gabriel said. "This is the best thing that could have happened to me today. This man has been on my list—on everyone's list—for years."

"That kid looks like he just stepped out of *Innocent Farmers' Weekly* magazine," Joan said dryly. "And the other one is just a drunk. I asked around. People in the nightbar say he's seen stumbling home in that sector at least once a week. Which one are you making that ghastly face about?"

"The drunk. Leave him alone in there for a while. I want to talk to *Farmers' Weekly* first."

✦

Asa was losing track of time.

They had taken his phone when they brought him in, and it felt as if he had spent hours already in this little featureless room, tense with anxiety. His eye was swollen half-shut, mercifully blotting out a little of the bright white light that contributed to his splitting headache. He could feel other bruises on his face.

His abdomen, where the man had landed two heavy blows, was sore all over. There was no way to sit that didn't make it worse. He stood for a while, but the ceiling was too low for him to stand up all the way, and eventually he gave in and sat, shifting positions every few minutes to distribute the discomfort.

The room was strange, not really a room: the off-white plastic walls were rounded and cramped, and they seemed to be all one surface with the low ceiling and the floor, which was covered in a thin carpet of the same color. There were two facing benches, both of them built seamlessly into the walls. Asa couldn't tell where the door was or even whether there was one. Maybe the little pod had been built up around him.

Probably not, he thought. He lay down on one of the benches and closed his eyes, then immediately felt himself begin to slide off it.

He opened his eyes and sat up hurriedly. Inspecting the benches, he saw they were tilted almost imperceptibly toward the center of the pod. If he didn't stay awake, he would fall to the floor.

I wonder if people sleep on the floor, he thought. He wasn't actually tired, but he could only sit tied in an anxious knot for so long, and curiosity was getting the better of him.

Asa bent down to feel the carpet, then yelped and snatched his hand back. His palm was covered in tiny red dots, as if it had been stung in dozens of places at once. Asa blew on it, then crouched to see what he had touched. It took him a minute to spot it: what he had thought was a carpet was tiny, thickly concentrated spines protruding from the floor of the pod. He looked at his palm, which began to burn steadily. It was red all over now, the skin puffed up slightly.

He flexed his fingers; he could move them, and there was no pain beyond the surface of his skin.

It's not spreading, then. Asa turned his attention back to the spines. With his undamaged hand, he touched a finger to one carefully, yanking it back at the sting again.

"I wouldn't do that," said a woman behind him. "They are poisonous. Not *very* poisonous—you'd have to roll your whole body in them before you got really sick. But it's still not very nice."

Asa turned carefully, easing himself onto the bench. It was one of the stalkers who had brought him in. She was looking at him expressionlessly, and he had the sense that she didn't really care whether he poisoned himself or not. He held up his hand, showing her the palm. The corner of her mouth twitched.

"So, you burned one hand and figured you'd make the other match?" She seemed to be suppressing a smile, but Asa wasn't sure why.

"I was wondering what it was."

"Synthetic nettle," a man said, stepping into the room, and Asa shrunk back unintentionally.

It was the man who had detained him. Now he swept his eyes up and down Asa's body as if he was summing him up. "I'm Gabriel Ward, Contract Enforcer. That's Joan." Joan gave Gabriel a look of annoyance.

"Joan Ward, Contract Enforcer. We need to ask you about what happened last night."

"I don't know what happened!" Asa said, the words tumbling out all at once. "It's my first day in Horizon. I started talking to that girl, then that man attacked me. I don't know why."

Now they know, he thought, relieved. *Now that they know what happened, it will all be okay.*

Joan Ward sat down on the bench opposite him. Gabriel Ward remained standing, his posture straight.

"Why were you in that nightbar?" Joan Ward asked.

"I . . . I'd never been in one. At home we don't have them. Actually, now that I've been to one, I think we do. They just don't call it that."

"What do they call it?"

"Just . . . Tom's."

Joan gave him an encouraging smile, then Gabriel sat abruptly next to her, almost pushing her out of the way. She made room, not looking at her partner.

"How do you know Daniel James Horizon?" he demanded.

"What?" Asa asked, startled. "I don't know anyone. Here, I mean. I don't know anyone here."

"In my years of experience, I've found that most acts of physical violence take place between people who know each other well," Gabriel said in an ironclad voice. Joan glanced at him nervously but said nothing.

"Is he the man who attacked me?" Asa asked.

"Yes, he's the man who attacked you," Joan said quickly. "Do you know why?"

"I mean—the girl was shouting something . . ." Asa put his hands to his temples. "I don't know—I think he didn't want me talking to her."

"Why wouldn't he want you talking to her?" Joan asked. Gabriel was watching with a narrow gaze, and Asa sensed that he was memorizing everything as it happened.

"Asa?" Joan prompted, and he sighed.

"I don't know. Sometimes people get jealous, I guess, but we really were just talking."

"Did he say anything to you during the encounter?" Gabriel asked.

"He said, 'Stay away from my girl,'" Asa said. "I forgot about that," he added, embarrassed. "I guess he didn't want me talking to her."

"Did he say anything else? Anything that wasn't about the girl?"

"Like what?"

"Did he give you anything?" Gabriel persisted.

Asa gestured to his swollen eye.

"That's not what I meant," Gabriel snapped. "Did he give you any object?"

"What? When, while he was punching me?"

"Did he hand you something?"

"No, he didn't. You searched me. If he had you would have found it." Asa's voice rose as he spoke. He took a deep breath, composing himself. "I'm sorry. I don't understand anything you're talking about."

Gabriel looked blankly at Asa, as if considering his fate. "Come on, Joan," he said finally.

The two stalkers—Contract Enforcers—stood, and without any visible signal, a door appeared and slid open at the front of the pod.

"How long will I be here?" Asa called, suddenly panicking. Joan stopped on the threshold.

"Stop touching the nettles," she said, then followed Gabriel out. The door slid shut, then vanished into the wall as if it had never been there.

✦

"I think he's telling the truth," Joan said once the pod door had closed behind them.

Gabriel sighed. "I know. Leave him there overnight." He strode ahead along the long hallway lined on either side with pods identical to the one they had just left.

"Can we talk about strategy for the other one?" Joan asked.

Gabriel shook his head. "No. I'm going in alone."

Joan stopped walking. Gabriel took a few more steps before stopping and turning around.

"I'm sorry about Naomi," Joan said firmly, setting her jaw. "I really am. I wish you'd never had to go through that. But I am your partner now, and you have to treat me like one. I don't care if you don't like it—it's your duty, and mine."

Gabriel could see the tension in her posture, but she didn't waver. He took a deep breath and walked back to her. "You're right," he said.

"So, tell me what our strategy is."

"I am going in alone," Gabriel said.

"Gabriel!"

"I need to go in alone," he said hastily. "Daniel isn't a normal detainee. We can't question him like we did that kid—we need to catch him off guard."

"So why can't I go in?"

Gabriel sighed. "Okay, partner," he forced himself to say. "It's because Daniel knows who I am. He'll know about Naomi and why I was on leave."

"How would he know that?"

"He knows a lot of things. The point is, if I go alone, he'll wonder."

"He'll wonder if you're stable."

"Ideally." Gabriel flashed her a grin, and she smiled back.

"I'll watch from outside," she conceded.

"Good."

Gabriel stopped in front of a pod identical to all the others and stood in front of the door, waiting for the facial scan to complete. Once he'd entered the pod, the door closed behind him with a hiss, leaving him alone with the man inside.

"Hello, Gabriel," Daniel James Horizon said politely.

Gabriel smiled widely. Daniel was not an imposing figure: his close-cropped brown hair only emphasized his oversized ears, nose, and mouth, giving him an affable, almost goofy appearance. He was unshaven and unkempt, his clothes wrinkled, and he smelled like three-day-old whiskey.

"What a pleasure to welcome the uncatchable Daniel James Horizon," Gabriel said lightly.

"Is that what they call me?" Daniel asked nonchalantly. His eyes were intent on Gabriel's face, despite his pleasant expression. It was a little like being scrutinized by another stalker, Gabriel realized.

"It's your name," he said.

"I meant 'uncatchable,'" Daniel said.

"Well, not anymore," Gabriel said, giving him another ghoulish grin. "And to be caught in a drunken brawl, that's just embarrassing for someone like you."

"It should probably be embarrassing for anyone. But I've been a drunk long enough—it was bound to happen."

"I meant being caught brawling instead of one of your more impressive activities."

Daniel laughed abruptly. "What impressive activities? I'd like to know so I can brag."

"You know what I mean."

Daniel lifted an eyebrow. "But do you? Sit down, Gabriel. I keep thinking you're about to hit your head on the ceiling."

"I'll stand."

"Please sit. I feel like a bad host." He gave a rueful smile.

Gabriel stared at him. *Do I hate you or like you? I can usually tell.* Daniel met his gaze mildly and did not look away.

"I'll sit," Gabriel said dryly, "but I wouldn't worry much about hosting. You're not the one who can open the door."

"Are you sure about that?" Daniel didn't break eye contact.

"Yes." Gabriel sat on the facing bench, planting his feet on the ground so he would not slide down the sloped surface. "Talk."

Daniel stretched his arms over his head, then slid down in his seat and extended his long legs to the opposite bench, resting his feet inches from where Gabriel sat. Gabriel didn't move, but his eyes flicked to the door. Daniel was, technically, blocking his exit, even though Gabriel could easily push him aside.

"My mother always said I was a disappointment," Daniel said idly. "And my father said my ears were too big, but I prefer to think it's my head that's too small. What do you think?"

"Tell me about mayflies."

"Old-world insect, I think. Lived and died in three days, always near the water. Of course, the water was different back then. These days, three days would be a lot."

"Yes, thank you. Tell me about mayflies in the context of unsanctioned technology."

"I can't imagine extinct bugs have much use for unsanctioned technology," Daniel said, making a puzzled face.

Gabriel exhaled slowly. "Tell me about your income sources."

"I get a two-hundred-thousand-credit stipend from the State every year on my birthday. It's a very good system. Makes for a nice birthday party."

"Have you ever obtained, used, or sold technology not issued by the State?"

Daniel tilted his head to the side. "I'm sorry, stalker, but I'm missing something. What do insects and innovative technology have to do with this little spat I was in last night?" He smiled pleasantly, meeting Gabriel's eyes again and holding them.

I have to stop, Gabriel thought. Daniel's eyes were hazel, he noticed idly, with a little fleck of black in one iris. *He's right. I'm straying too far from the incident. I'm at the edge of jurisdiction.*

"Just trying to get a clear picture," Gabriel said and cleared his throat. "Did you know the other party?"

"Never met him before. Little blond boy, almost as young and pretty as my Eve."

"Eve was the woman involved in the dispute?"

Daniel's head jerked up. "Involved in the dispute? Wait, you didn't arrest her, did you?"

"No," Gabriel said. "She did nothing wrong."

Daniel nodded, a shaken look on his face. Even the thought that she might be in custody had disturbed him deeply.

"Daniel," Gabriel said more gently. "Why did you assault that boy?"

Daniel cast his eyes down, looking almost ashamed. "Everyone heard me shouting it, didn't they? I may as well admit it. I didn't want him talking to my Eve. I know it was wrong, but you know how it is. Love can make a man crazy."

Gabriel froze, holding himself perfectly still. *Love can make a man crazy* . . . "I guess that's true," he said, each word as cold as ice.

He stood abruptly and started for the door, knocking Daniel's feet off the bench as he did. Daniel let out a shout, and Gabriel turned rapidly to see him land hard on the floor, the side of his face touching the carpet.

Gabriel rushed to help him up, but Daniel waved him off.

"It's fine, I've been burned before," he said.

"I'll send in a medical autom," Gabriel said. The right half of Daniel's face was already bright red and beginning to swell.

"Ask it to bring a beer," Daniel joked, his speech slurred by the carpet's poison.

"I didn't intend to do that," Gabriel said, and Daniel nodded.

"I know. Sorry for what I said—it wasn't a dig at you. And I'm sorry about Naomi. No one deserves that, not you, and not her." There was genuine pain in his voice, though it could have been the nettles.

Gabriel blinked and looked away. "Yes." He cleared his throat. "I'll send a medical autom," he repeated.

When he was back in the hallway, Daniel sealed behind him in a pod, Gabriel took a shaky breath. "Medical autom to pod 3575892," he said loudly. "Authorization voice print Gabriel Ward."

"Acknowledge voice print, Gabriel Ward," said an automated voice.

Gabriel started quickly down the hall, back the way he'd come. After a moment, he heard footsteps behind him. He didn't slow his pace as Joan caught up.

"What was that?" she asked breathlessly.

"It was an accident."

"I know, I was watching. That's why you shouldn't leave me out of these things."

"Thanks for the tip."

"I didn't mean that. I meant the questions. What's a mayfly? Why were you asking him about it?"

"What he said was true. It's an old-world insect."

"Right. Because you have a reputation for asking irrelevant entomology questions of detainees. Seriously, Gabriel, who is he, and what were you talking about?"

Gabriel hesitated, then relented. He scanned the wall of pods until he spotted an unoccupied one. "Come on, partner." He grabbed Joan's arm lightly and escorted her to the empty pod.

"Are you detaining me?" she joked, but there was an edge of fear in her voice.

"No. I want to talk privately." He positioned himself in front of the facial scanner.

"Everything in the pods is recorded," Joan pointed out as he guided her inside and let the door close behind them.

"Yes," Gabriel said. "And so is everything out there. But the records from in here are more highly classified."

"So, anyone eavesdropping will be qualified to do it?"

It was the third time in a row she'd framed something as a joke, he noted; he couldn't tell yet if it was a habit of hers or something about him.

"Yes," he said in response. "Mayflies, in addition to being extinct insects, are untraceable credits."

She frowned. "I don't understand."

"I haven't explained. A mayfly is an encrypted line of code, essentially, that transfers credits into or out of an account. Most transfers are direct, right? I buy tea at the supermarket, the cred goes from my account to the supermarket account, and anyone looking at either account can see what happened."

"I understand how banking works," Joan said dryly.

"Good," he said, ignoring her tone. "Say I wanted to buy something I didn't want anyone to know about. I'd buy a mayfly from a dealer, at a markup. Money transfers unaccountably out of my account. I pay for whatever it is with the mayfly, and money goes unaccountably into the other account."

"So, you're just covering where money goes and comes from."

"Yes, if I use my State account, which of course would flag it as suspicious. But most people doing any kind of major trade in the underground markets aren't using the State bank. There is an illicit, untraceable banking system, and it runs on mayflies. It's what feeds the trade in unsanctioned technologies and a number of other enterprises that undermine our communities and the State."

Joan was looking at him wide-eyed. "You think Daniel is involved in that?"

"I know he is. We all know he is. But we don't know how, and we can't prove it."

"Then how are you so sure?"

"Did you hear him in there? He was playing with me." Gabriel ground his teeth. In the moment he had been holding steadily on the surface, playing the game as Daniel set it out. Now fury rose in his chest. "Talking about bugs. 'Innovative technology'—that's not what we call it up here. It's a trade term." Gabriel sighed and leaned back, pressing his hands to his temples. "Joan, we—stalkers, I mean—have known about him for almost twenty years, and this is the first time anyone has had a reason to bring him in and question him."

He sat up straight, meeting her eyes. "And I have to let him go."

✦

"I said stop touching the nettles."

Asa lurched out of a restless doze at the sound of Joan Ward's voice. He quickly got to his feet. He had fallen asleep on his knees on the floor, resting his head in his arms on the bench. His pants had a few pinpoint holes, but they were sturdy canvas, and he hadn't felt the sting of the nettles.

He looked Joan straight in the eye. "What nettles?"

She shook her head, seeming to suppress a smile. "Most people can't sleep there. It's designed that way."

Asa shrugged, deliberately casual, and gestured at his pant legs. "Most people don't wear quality fabric."

"Well, you can go now. Your record has been updated." She walked out of the pod, leaving the door open behind her.

"Wait, what?" Asa rushed after her, his legs stiff from the cramped position he had slept in.

She didn't slow down, and when at last he caught up with her, they were walking down a hallway filled with squarish pods, all presumably identical to his own.

"Do all of these have people in them?" he asked.

"No," she said.

"Hey, wait!" Asa stopped walking, and after a moment Joan did as well.

"Yes?"

"I don't understand what's happening. You're saying I can just go?"

"Through that hallway. Your personal items will be returned to you before you leave." She pointed to a gap between two of the pods, which opened into a small hallway Asa had not noticed before.

"Okay. Thank you," he said automatically.

Joan gave him an odd look. He nodded and started down the hall, feeling her eyes on his back.

He passed into the hall, and behind him a sliding door closed swiftly. Asa spun around; where the door had been was only a blank wall. He looked around. There was no door at the front. What Joan had referred to as a hall was actually a closed room, similar to the pods but without the benches—the complete featurelessness was disorienting. He bent over and touched the floor. It was smooth and did not sting, at least.

"Asa Isaac Rosewood?" said an automated voice.

Asa straightened. "Yes," he said loudly. *I've heard my own full name more times in the last two days than in my whole life*, he thought.

"Please confirm that all your personal items have been returned to you."

A drawer appeared in the wall and slid out. Asa went to it.

Inside was his backpack, and he opened it and went through his possessions swiftly, trying to remember what he had packed in the first place. In the front pocket of the bag was his phone.

"I guess that's the most important thing," he said.

"Please confirm that all your personal items have been returned to you."

"Um, confirm. All my personal items have been returned to me."

"Asa Isaac Rosewood, you are now free to go. Your record has been updated to reflect this incident."

The front wall of the room slid open, revealing an unfamiliar street.

"Thanks," Asa said, grabbing his bag and hefting it onto his back. He was at the door when the autom's words registered. "Hold on. What did you say about my record?"

"Your record has been updated to reflect this incident," the autom said pleasantly.

"What does that mean?" Asa felt the blood drain from his face. "Do I have a mark?"

"Asa Isaac Rosewood, you are now free to go."

Asa waited, but nothing more was forthcoming from the autom. He stepped out into the street and turned back to watch as the door closed and vanished. From the outside, the wall was ugly gray concrete.

"Now what?" he muttered and was slightly relieved not to be answered by a calm automated voice. He looked up and down the street. Nothing was familiar, so he turned left and started walking.

Asa had gone less than a dozen steps when he heard the door hiss again. He turned to look, stepping into an alcove between two buildings, as a man emerged from the door, shielding his eyes with one hand. Asa drew back farther into the corner. It was the man from the night before—Daniel James Horizon, the stalkers had called him.

He was tall, and his clothes hung loosely on him. He looked exhausted. Asa watched as he leaned back against the wall, closing his eyes for a moment, then felt around in his breast pocket for something. After a moment he took out a flask and took a quick sip from it, then sighed heavily. He straightened, looking a little less drained, and started walking in Asa's direction. Asa stopped breathing, trying to make himself smaller, but Daniel walked on past without breaking stride, not even looking in his direction. Asa remained motionless for a long moment, then peered out cautiously. Daniel was gone. Asa tugged on his backpack strap nervously, then set off in the opposite direction.

◆

Asa walked for what felt like hours without paying attention to where he was going, turning corners at random and scarcely looking up from the pavement.

"Your record has been updated to reflect this incident." Updated how? I didn't DO anything.

The thought filled him with a useless rage. Asa had never considered the possibility that it was possible to break his Social Contract without intending to—without even realizing he was doing it.

He *attacked* me. *How can I be responsible? I didn't even hit back, did I?* He stopped walking and closed his eyes, trying to picture the scene. *I was talking to the girl, Eve, then he grabbed me—he hit me—*Asa touched his eye lightly and winced, wondering briefly what his face must look like. *He hit me again, then I slammed him into the wall. Okay, I did hit back. But he started it!*

Asa opened his eyes just in time to leap out of the way of a fast-moving family of four talking animatedly among themselves, apparently as unaware of the rest of the world as he was.

Asa sighed and looked up at his surroundings for the first time. He had reached a break in the closely packed buildings and was standing on what he now realized was a bridge arcing over an enormous park, or maybe a garden.

Leaning over the low wall of the bridge, he could see the whole park from where he stood. It was a rough oval, with clearly marked paths where people were walking. The perimeter was planted with a kind of tree Asa had never seen before, the leaves small and pale pink. In the far corner he could see some kind of animal moving, maybe a deer, and he felt a pang of homesickness.

Maybe this was a mistake. Less than a day in the city, and he'd been hauled off by stalkers. *All I did was talk to a girl. Maybe I should go home.* Asa turned away from the park beneath him and leaned back against the bridge wall. *I'd have to find my way back to the rail station.*

He pictured it, climbing back onto the train, the journey back, arriving home to the relief and mild scolding of his parents. The very thought of it was comforting, and the tension in his chest eased a little.

But then what? Find a girl, get married, live just like my parents? I'd rather get sent to Work. I'd rather go to the Waste.

"Are you all right?" a woman asked, and he pulled himself out of his ruminations.

"What?"

"I said, are you all right?" She was a little younger than his mother maybe, a short-haired woman in a bright red dress. "Your eye."

"Oh," Asa said. "Yeah, fine." He turned away, back to the garden below.

"Sorry to bother you," he heard her say, and he couldn't tell whether she meant to be sarcastic. He hung his head.

A pretty woman asks a question, and you're rude to her? But after last night, who knew what might happen—he didn't know the rules of this city. He didn't know his own Social Contract as well as he thought he did. He glanced up. The woman who had stopped had reached the end of the bridge.

"I'm sorry!" he said, knowing she was too far away to hear him.

A high-pitched tone sounded, and Asa jumped. It sounded again, and he realized it was coming from his own backpack. He fumbled open the front pocket and took out his phone. The screen was lit up, displaying the name *Eve Layla Ashland.*

His heart skipped, and he answered the call.

"This is Asa?" he said and heard a laugh from the other end of the line.

"Are you not sure?" Eve asked.

"I'm sure. I . . . just got this phone," he admitted, just stopping himself from saying, *It's my first call.* "How did you call me?"

"You told me your full name, remember? *Asa Isaac Rosewood.*"

"Right. I guess some parts of last night slipped my mind," he said ruefully.

"Yeah. I'm really sorry about that."

Asa searched for words. "It wasn't your fault," he finally said.

"I know. I'm still sorry it happened. Listen, I'm calling because I want to see you again. Can you meet me at my apartment tonight?"

"What?" Asa stared at the phone, startled. *That guy attacked me for talking to you. Won't he kill me if he catches me at your apartment?*

"Asa? Will you come over?" Eve repeated.

"Yeah, yes, of course."

"Oh, good." She sounded relieved. She gave him the address. "Will you be able to find it?"

"Yeah, no problem," Asa said. "I'll figure it out."

"Great. See you later tonight, around eight." Eve hung up, and Asa stared down at the phone in his hands.

What just happened?

CHAPTER SIX

"YOU HAD TO LET HIM GO. YOU DIDN'T HAVE A choice," Joan pressed, managing to keep up with him stride for stride, though he was half a head taller.

"There's always a choice," Gabriel retorted.

"In this case, your other choice would have been to detain him without merit," Joan said harshly, and he glanced at her.

"Fair enough. But there should have been something I could do."

"You couldn't have asked him anything else. You can't stray beyond the bounds of the incident investigation."

"But we *know* there's more."

"Then you have to find more," Joan said placidly. He glared at her, then sighed. "What?" she asked, looking nervous again.

"Nothing. You just keep being right. It's annoying." He smiled at her, and after a second she smiled back, still looking uneasy.

"Come on," Gabriel said, picking up his pace as they rounded the corner and Municipal 7 came into view.

"Why?" she asked warily. "We have to file."

"You're going to file."

"What are you going to do?"

"I'm going to find more on Daniel James Horizon," Gabriel said grimly. "I'll be in the Crypt when you're done."

Joan nodded. "Okay. I'll come find you."

Without waiting for a response, she veered off toward the main entrance. Gabriel stopped for a second, watching her walk briskly inside, before he headed for the sunken side entrance to the Crypt.

Officially, it was the Archive, but it was dark and cool for the preservation of all kinds of historical and contemporary materials, and it was underground. People had started calling it the Crypt almost as soon as the building was finished. Gabriel waited impatiently as the door scanned his face, then slid open to admit him. He breathed in deeply. He had always liked the smell of the place—some combination of chemicals for preservation and the cool air, probably. The Crypt underlay the whole of Municipal 7—all the municipal buildings had Archives, but this was the largest—and it was laid out like a maze.

New Bureaucrats and fresh Authority Figures sometimes wandered lost for hours, too stubborn to ask the autoims for help. Gabriel had memorized the schematics before he ever had to set foot in the Crypt, and by now it was like navigating his own home. He made his way through a series of hallways to a wall lined with soundproof viewing booths and let himself in to the one at the farthest end.

"Welcome to the Archive's viewing facilities. Please let me know what I can show you," the booth said pleasantly once he'd shut the plastic door behind him.

The booths were shaped a little like the detainment pods, though they were painted in various pastel colors and lacked the poisoned carpets and uncomfortable seating. This one, which Gabriel preferred, was light green. The front wall was taken up entirely by a video screen, and a movable control desk was pressed up against one wall, a variety of green chairs lined up on the other. He selected a straight-backed, armless one and pulled the desk out to face the screen.

"I need drone feeds for habitation 47BQ9J," he said.

"Authorization voice print required for that request," the booth said.

"Authorization voice print Gabriel Ward."

"Acknowledge voice print, Gabriel Ward." The screen flickered on. It was divided into quarters, three of them lit up with video. The fourth was blank.

"I want to see *all* the drone feeds for habitation 47BQ9J," Gabriel said, irritated. "I'll select from there."

"Drones Gamma-631, Sigma-487, and Mu-248 are pictured. Those are the three drones allocated to the surveillance of habitation 47BQ9J," the booth replied.

"A building that size should . . ." Gabriel broke off. *Of course he's somehow managed to limit the drone activity around his home.* "Never mind. Leave these up."

"Acknowledge, Gabriel Ward."

Gabriel turned to the controls and flipped through the feeds. They all showed the same thing: the reflective exterior of the building where Daniel James Horizon lived. *I wonder . . .* Gabriel took control of the drone whose feed was on the screen and pulled it out from the building, trying to orient himself. As he moved, the sun glinted off the wall, blinding the camera.

The building's covered entirely in plasmonic solar panels. Very civic-minded, whoever sculpted that one. Probably generates power for that whole sector of the city. Coincidentally very good at preventing surveillance. Still, it can't prevent everything.

Gabriel pulled out farther, flying the drone down to ground level and making it circle the building until he came around to the door. He angled it to show the sidewalk in front of the building as well and set it to hover. "You stay right there," he murmured, then more loudly. "Leave that feed up, please," he squinted at the letters in the bottom left of the screen. "Leave the live feed up for this one, Sigma-487, and show me archival footage of all three drones."

"Archival footage for what date?"

Good question.

"One week ago," he said at random. "I just want to confirm something."

"Acknowledge."

The screen split into quarters again, the sidewalk feed remaining in the top right corner. The rest of the screens filled with the mirrorlike solar panels. The cameras circled the building slowly, blinded now and then by the reflection of the sun. It was impossible to see what levels they were at, and nothing but the glare ever crossed the screen.

Gabriel's phone sounded, and he picked it up without looking at the screen. "Gabriel Ward."

"Gabriel? Where are you?" Joan asked.

"Viewing booths," he said and ended the call, his eyes still on the screens. A few minutes later she knocked on the door.

"Open door," Gabriel said, and the screen went blank. Then the door opened and Joan stepped in. "Put the drone feeds back up, please," Gabriel said wearily.

"New authorization voice print required, Gabriel Ward."

"Authorization voice print Joan Ward," Joan said quickly, and the screen came back on. "What are we looking at?" she asked Gabriel.

"You got here fast," he remarked, and she held up a folded piece of paper.

"I copied the schematic," she said, and he chuckled. "What?" she demanded.

"Nothing. I did something similar when I was new. Get a chair. Come look at this."

"What is it?" she asked, pulling over a high stool. When she sat down, she was a little taller than he was.

"It's all the drone feeds from Daniel Horizon's building. The top right is a live feed. I moved the drone to show the entrance, but look at the rest. This is the usual view."

"There's only three? And the reflection . . . was he the one who had the building sculpted that way?"

"Let's find out." Gabriel glanced at her. "Go get a portable viewer. I want to leave the drones up. We'll take a look at the layout of his apartment too—it's the penthouse."

Joan rolled her eyes. "Of course it is. I'll be right back," she said. "Open door." As the door slid open, she unfolded her home-made map again.

"Switch all drones to the live feed, please," Gabriel said. "The one I just moved, Sigma-487."

The front door and sidewalk of the building filled the screen, and he sat back to watch. No one had come or gone when Joan returned with two portable viewers. They were smaller versions of the main screen, with thin cords that plugged them into the booth's database.

"Two?" Gabriel asked, and she shrugged.

"You look at the pictures. I'll read up on known associates."

"I know all that backward and forward," Gabriel said absently.

"Then I should too," Joan said in the pleasant, unbending tone he was growing familiar with.

"Pay attention to the girl," Gabriel said. "I haven't given her much thought, but she's the first thing Daniel's been willing to get locked up for. She's got to matter to him. And see if the farmer has any connection to either of them."

Joan looked surprised but hid it quickly.

"I'm not sidelining you, Joan," he said. "Naomi once said I had the welcoming spirit of a steamroller, but that doesn't mean I'm unaware of your contributions. You might see something I've missed."

"That's practically a compliment. Could you write it down? I'd like to frame it," Joan said wryly. But her face was flushed.

"Find the farmer and look closer at the girl," Gabriel said, turning his attention back to the drones.

✦

Several hours later, Gabriel had repositioned the other two drones and was using them the best he could. He had first tried to requisition more drones for the area, but Daniel's interference, whatever he had done, blocked Gabriel's request. All he could do was move around the ones that were already there. What Daniel had not been able to do was block the drones' life-sign capture: as long as Gabriel brought them close enough to the walls, he could tell how many people were in the apartment and roughly where they were.

It made it impossible to capture pure images at the same time—everything in the drone's eyeline showed up as a flat, monochrome blue, with living beings appearing in blurry red

72

silhouette. But Daniel had already rendered the image-capture useless with the mirrorlike façade of the building, so Gabriel made the switch and began scanning the walls of the penthouse. After a painstaking search, he had managed to discern one person in what the schematics claimed was the bedroom and another on the far side of the house, close to the wall. The one in the bedroom hadn't moved at all; the other one kept pacing, then stopping in the same place.

"Do you have anything?" Gabriel asked, and Joan looked up from her screen, rubbing her neck. "You can adjust the screen height," he added as she stretched.

"I know," she said. "I meant to—I got distracted. I don't know if I have anything. I can't find Asa anywhere he shouldn't be. Born in Rosewood, turned twenty-one two days ago, bought a rail pass to Horizon the next day, got detained—by you and me."

"That's it?"

"There's one thing," Joan said. "But I don't know if it's relevant."

"Everything's relevant." Gabriel looked back at the drones. Nothing had changed.

"There's a medical report from eleven years ago. He fell off a bridge."

"When he was ten?"

"A bridge over a river."

"What?" Gabriel turned, giving her his full attention. "Don't play for suspense. Tell me what happened."

"He was playing with some friends, showing off, and he fell off the bridge into about twenty feet of water. He was completely submerged. The doctor followed protocol, disinfected him, burned his clothes, but . . ."

"You can't burn the Bug out of someone's brain once it's in there. They're sure he was submerged?"

"Three witnesses, four if you count him. Anyway, he just . . . survived. Nothing happened. No signs of brain damage, ever. No fever, no dementia—no physical or mental symptoms at all. After a month or so they ended the isolation. He's been perfectly healthy ever since."

Gabriel sat back, looking thoughtfully at her. "You're right, I don't know if that's relevant. There have always been rumors of people who survive. It's remarkable, but it's got nothing to do with what we're looking for. Okay, forget Asa for the moment."

"Gabriel, he's right there!"

Joan pointed at the wall screen, and Gabriel flipped the sidewalk feed to fill the screen. He maneuvered the drone, circling above the young man who stood at the door, apparently struck by the building's appearance. Asa peered closely at the wall, then moved back to take it in from a distance. He looked up at the shining sculpture, exposing his face unmistakably to the drone.

Asa Isaac Rosewood had come to visit Daniel Horizon.

✦

Asa double-checked the address—47BQ9J—then took a few steps back from the building and stared. There was no door beneath the address, but that barely registered as he gazed upward. The whole neighborhood was packed with the fantastical "sculpture" buildings, but this one towered over all the others.

It seemed to be made from enormous slabs of glass, raggedly cut and stacked so thickly that the walls they made were iridescent but opaque. The top was a rough, unsettling peak; it was hard to tell how the slabs of glass came together. Asa walked down the street, then back up again, trying to take it all in. The sun was setting, and the west-facing wall appeared almost to be on fire, the light shimmering, glinting shades of orange and pink off the jagged surface. From a distance it would be alarming.

The high-pitched noise of his phone emanated from his pocket, and he reached for it, his eyes still on the mesmerizing play of light. He answered without looking at the name on the screen.

"This is Asa," he said.

"Are you going to come upstairs or stand there gawking like you've never seen plasmonic solar panels before?" Eve's voice came cheerfully from the device.

"I've . . . never seen them look like this," Asa said. "It's beautiful."

"Yeah. It is." Eve sounded thoughtful. "Anyway, go to the door so I can let you in," she ended the call.

"Okay," Asa said.

He hurried to the front of the building. Just as he arrived back at 47BQ9J, a panel slid open, revealing a wide lobby. He hurried through the opening.

"You Horizon people really like hidden doors," he muttered.

"Invisible doors prevent the functions of the building from interfering with the aesthetic lines of the sculpture," an autom replied, and he jumped.

"Um, thanks. I'm supposed to go upstairs, I think? I'm meeting Eve . . . Layla Ashland," he said.

"Your name?"

Asa sighed. "Asa Isaac Rosewood," he said, already sick of the ritual of repeating his full name every time he wanted to do anything.

"You are expected," the autom said.

"Great."

He looked around; the space was empty. The floors were pale

blue, and the glass was transparent from inside. At the back of the lobby, it billowed out from the rest of the building, creating a low roof, and he walked over to the area. Through the ceiling, he had an unobstructed view of the sky.

"Though light pollution prevents true stargazing, our residents enjoy . . ." the autom said.

"Yeah, nice," he interrupted. "You said I'm expected. Can you tell me how to get where I'm going?"

"The elevators are along the west-facing wall."

The wall was blank. Asa opened his mouth to object, then stopped. "Right. Invisible doors, aesthetic lines. Can you open it?"

A panel slid open, revealing an elevator, and Asa hurried to it, almost running. As soon as he was inside, the door slid shut, and the elevator car shot upward so fast his stomach lurched. It stopped smoothly and the door opened. Asa didn't move right away, still a little stunned from the ride.

"Are you all right?" Eve asked, appearing in the doorway like a vision.

She wore a short sleeveless dress of rich, bright green that made her dark eyes seem to glow. Or maybe that was just the way her eyes always looked. Asa swallowed.

"Yeah. Yes. Fast elevator."

She laughed. "The first time I rode it I almost got sick," she said and held out her arm. "Come on, let me show you around."

Asa took her arm and followed as she showed him into the living room, a wide, open space with two couches facing back to back, one into the room and one looking out at the transparent wall. From here he could probably see the whole city. Asa took it in, trying to pay attention to something other than her skin beneath his fingers; he could feel her pulse as if it were his own.

"Eve," he said, his voice coming out hoarse. She turned to him with a radiant smile, and words failed on the tip of his tongue. "I ..."

"Asa, I'm so glad you could come." A man strode into the room with a hearty greeting, and Asa drew back, dropping his hand from Eve's arm. It was the man who had assaulted him the night before.

"You're Daniel," he said. He looked quickly back and forth between them. "What's happening?" Asa eyed the exit. Daniel stood between him and the elevator; he was stuck.

"Asa, wait," Eve said. "We want to apologize for what happened last night."

Daniel shook his head. "Eve is too kind to me. *I* want to apologize for what *I* did last night." He looked at Eve fondly. "Things don't just happen by themselves, love. We've all got to take responsibility where we find it."

"You should stay for dinner," Eve said.

There was something pleading in her voice. Asa looked at her, not understanding, but he nodded.

"Yeah, okay," he said warily, half-regretting the words as he said them.

"Good!" Daniel clapped his hands together, and Eve jumped, startled. Daniel chuckled. "Sorry, darling." He turned to Asa. "Want anything to drink? Here, I'll get us all something."

He bounded over to a cabinet across the room and took out three glasses and a bottle. He was a tall, thin man, and he moved in sudden, graceful fits of speed as he poured the drinks. It was disconcerting. Asa glanced at Eve, who gave him a faint amused smile. Daniel pressed a glass of dark blue liquid into Asa's hand.

"Thanks," he said awkwardly.

Daniel held a glass out to Eve and she reached for it, but he lifted it away with a teasing smile, holding it above her head for a second. He bent down to kiss her, and Asa cast his eyes away, embarrassed. When they broke apart, Daniel handed Eve her drink, and she sipped it without expression.

"Asa! Let's have a toast!" Daniel exclaimed, and Asa raised his glass, waiting as Daniel mused, seemingly to himself. "To good friends? You haven't had enough time to decide that yet. To health? I can't swear that . . . Asa! Asa, where are you from?"

"Rosewood," Asa said.

"To Rosewood!" Daniel cried, raising his glass with such enthusiasm that his drink sloshed over the side.

"To Rosewood," Asa echoed. Eve said nothing. Asa sipped his drink, and his eyes widened. "What is this?" he asked. Daniel grinned.

"It was a gift. Ancient recipe. Do you like it?"

Asa nodded. His head felt light but clear. The liquor tasted like nothing he'd ever had before.

"It's sweet without the sweetness," he said at last.

Daniel laughed, delighted. "Sweet without the sweetness," he repeated, shaking his head. "What do you think, love? Does he mean the liquor or you?"

"Daniel," Eve said. She sounded sad, and again Asa looked away.

"Let's eat," Daniel declared and ushered them into a dining room.

The space was beautiful but odd; the furniture seemed to be made of the same material as the building itself. In addition to the dining table and chairs, there was a long couch facing the transparent wall.

Every room must have those, Asa thought, walking toward them.

He peered out cautiously, feeling as if he might fall through the clear barrier. It was dark now, and lights were on all over the city. It looked a little like the night sky, seen from the other side.

"Asa?" He turned at the sound of Eve's voice. "Table's over here," she said, pointing.

The table was set for three with white-and-silver place settings, and Asa noted another bottle of what appeared to be the same dark blue liquor.

"Your home is really nice," Asa said, remembering his manners.

"Thanks," Eve said. "It's Daniel's, really."

"What's mine could be yours," Daniel said lightly. "But I can't take credit. The artists designed this one inside and out, right down to the glass in your hand."

Asa looked down at the glass in his hand. On closer examination, he could see that it was a little concave at the sides, not quite an ordinary glass.

"It's nice," Asa said.

"Well. Glasses, people, it's all the same. It's what's inside that counts!"

Daniel grabbed the bottle on the table and refilled his own glass, then glanced at Asa and Eve, who both shook their heads. Eve set her glass on the table and crossed the room to a bare wall.

"Is dinner ready?" she asked.

"Yes, Eve," an autom replied, and a panel in the wall slid open, revealing a number of covered dishes on a narrow counter.

"Thank you," Eve said.

She went back to the table and sat down. Daniel went to the counter, grabbed two dishes, and set them on the table. Asa stepped over to help, but by the time he got there, Daniel had transferred everything himself.

"Sit!" Daniel said, gesturing expansively.

He sat down across from Eve, leaving Asa the chair next to

hers. Asa sat, feeling for the sixteenth time as if he were walking into a trap.

"Everyone, take what you like," Daniel instructed, removing the covers from the dishes, and Asa was glad to see that they contained food he mostly recognized. He took a spoonful of each and sat down, watching his hosts for cues. "Asa, tell me what brings you to Horizon," Daniel said, and Asa swallowed a bite of what he was fairly sure was chicken.

"I just wanted to get away from Rosewood," he said, then hesitated. "Sorry, that sounds like there was something wrong with Rosewood. There wasn't. It's a great place—I just wanted to see something new. Something bigger."

"Me too," Eve said.

"Right," Asa said, relieved that she was finally joining the conversation. "I was surprised to see your name was Ashland—I guess I expected Horizon. You seem so . . . sophisticated." He glanced nervously at Daniel, who winked.

"Don't worry, Asa. Eve would be a polished gem if she'd been raised in mud. I can't blame you for seeing that."

"Daniel, what does that even mean?" Eve protested, but her cheeks were flushed, and her tone was light. It was the first sign of affection she'd shown for him, and Asa felt a stab of jealousy, then regret.

It's not as if I would want her to be unhappy, he reproached himself.

"Ashland is practically Horizon," Eve said, turning her attention to Asa.

"Everyone from Ashland says that," Daniel interjected. "Everyone from Horizon disagrees."

Eve gave him a dirty look. "It's just barely outside the city. I moved to Horizon proper when I was seventeen, me and my brother."

"Just the two of you?"

"Our parents died in an accident," Eve said. Her voice was detached, placid. "Saul was twenty-four, so he was my guardian until I turned twenty-one. You know how the communities are. So small—everyone knows you from the day you're born."

Asa nodded vigorously.

"We couldn't take it," she went on. "Every moment of every day, every person we saw was trying to offer us help, sympathy, comfort—if we'd stayed, I'd have been stuck with sixty replacement mothers, and Saul would have been married to everyone's favorite daughter. It was all out of kindness—but it was too much."

"So, you came here," Asa said.

"Yes. I've been here ever since."

"And is Saul still in Horizon, or did he go back to Ashland to marry one of those daughters?"

Eve's face turned to stone. "No," she said.

"I'm sorry," Asa said quickly. He realized he'd been indelicate somehow.

"It's fine. Saul isn't in Horizon anymore. I met Daniel through him."

Asa looked at Daniel, expecting a response, but Daniel only raised his eyebrows and reached for the bottle to pour himself another. He raised it toward Asa, offering, and Asa shook his head, showing his still half-full glass. He flicked his eyes toward Eve, but she didn't seem to notice.

"Asa," Daniel said heavily. "I asked you here because I want to apologize. I want to make things right between us."

"You did apologize," Asa said. "As far as I'm concerned, it's behind us."

"That's not what I mean. How's your eye, by the way?"

Asa shrugged. "I've had worse jumping out of trees. It'll heal.

How's the back of your head?" he asked with an edge. *That fight wasn't all one-sided.*

Daniel looked at him, puzzled, then put a hand on the back of his head and winced.

"I thought that was just the hangover," he said. "What did you do to me?"

"I . . . um, I shoved you into a wall. Your head made a pretty good cracking sound."

Daniel laughed. "I can't say I didn't deserve that." He grimaced. "Worst headache I've had in years. Congratulations."

"Thanks."

Daniel leaned in, crossing his arms on the table. "Listen, forget my head and your face. Those stalkers hauled you in because of me, and I am sorry. That should never have happened."

"I shouldn't have hit back, I guess." Asa sighed. "I never knew I could break my Social Contract without meaning to."

Eve laughed, a sudden, agitated sound, and they both looked at her.

"Nothing," she said. "Make nice with each other. It's warming my heart."

"You weren't taken in because of your Social Contract," Daniel said grimly. "What did they ask you about?"

Asa studied his weather-worn face for a moment. "They asked me about you," he said finally.

Daniel finished his drink and poured the rest of the bottle out into his glass. So far, he didn't seem drunk.

Asa took a long sip of his own drink. "They said my record had been updated to reflect the incident," he said, coming to the thought that had been gnawing at him all day. "What does that mean? Do I have a mark?"

"Don't worry about it," Daniel said.

"It seemed worth worrying about." Asa sounded harsher than he'd intended. Daniel didn't seem to notice.

"I mean, I'll take care of it. Don't worry about it."

"What?"

"I'll take care of it. Have another drink." Daniel leapt up from the table, almost knocking his chair over, and went to the panel where the food had come from. He knocked on the wall. "Another bottle, darling," he said.

The panel slid open, revealing another bottle filled with the blue liquor.

"Please return the previous bottle for sterilization and reuse," the autom said.

Daniel held out a hand, and Asa snatched the empty bottle off the table and gave it to him. Daniel swapped them, cracked the new one open, and poured a measure into Asa's glass, filling it almost to the top.

"Thanks," Asa said and took a sip.

"Stop!" Daniel said, and Asa jumped, almost spilling his drink, then set the glass down carefully.

"We have to toast!" Daniel bellowed. "Come here, love, give me your glass. We'll raise a toast."

Asa looked at Eve. She shrugged, finished her glass, and let Daniel pour her another.

"What will we toast to now?" Daniel asked, looking around the room. His eyes landed on Eve, and he walked to her, brushing past Asa as if he weren't there. Daniel cupped Eve's face with one hand and kissed her lightly on her forehead. "May I toast to you, my love?" he asked softly, his lips brushing against her hair.

"Don't," she whispered.

He closed his eyes and kissed her temple, and for a moment Asa froze, suddenly aware that he was intruding on something painful: Daniel looked as if he was holding on to Eve for dear life. Then he let her go and turned to Asa with a wide grin. "We'll toast to our guest! To Asa!"

"To Asa," Eve echoed. She sipped her drink, then smiled at him. "I really am glad you came," she said.

"Me too. Daniel—what did you mean, you'll take care of it?"

"It's only fair. I got you into trouble, I should get you out! I'll fix it. Don't worry."

This was clearly the tipping point: Daniel had gone from apparently sober to extremely drunk in less than a minute. He was red-faced and merry and making less sense than before.

Asa pressed the point. "I don't understand *how* you're going to take care of it."

"Never you mind," Daniel said. "You shall be expunged! I mean your record. It will be clear. No marks." He held up his hand and connected his thumb and fingers in a ring to make a zero.

"He can do it," Eve said. "I don't know exactly how, but he can."

"If you don't know how, how do you know?" Eve gave him a strange look, and Asa shook his head. "How do you know he can do it?" he asked more coherently.

"Like all magic, it must be seen to be believed. She has seen!" Daniel exclaimed.

Asa looked at Eve, who sighed. "He saved my brother's life."

"I did," Daniel agreed. "I did, my love. I did that for you."

"I hope you did it for Saul," Eve said sharply, and Daniel's face fell.

He nodded somberly. "I did. I did it for Saul. I loved Saul like a brother. Brother-in-law."

"Don't," Eve said.

Daniel shook his head. "I won't," he whispered. "I won't."

"Saul was part of Daniel's organization," Eve said.

"Organization?"

"Yes. He was going to be sent to . . . Work, and then we found out he was slated for termination. Daniel saved his life." She said it all at once without inflection, as though she had practiced in the mirror until she could speak the words without breaking.

"I'm sorry," Asa said, slightly perplexed. "That sounds awful. But Daniel did save his life?"

Eve smiled, but it didn't touch her eyes. "For a little while. Saul couldn't stay here. He'd have been caught again and terminated immediately. Daniel rescued him, but he had to go into the Waste. That was five years ago."

"Oh," Asa said. Eve looked utterly heartbroken, and he was at a loss. "I mean, there's all sorts of stories of wasters . . . of people surviving out there," he tried. "He could still be alive."

Eve looked at him. The glow of her eyes had become a void. "He isn't," she said.

"Enough of this," Daniel broke in. "Enough of the past. There's been so much of it. Tomorrow is my birthday."

"Happy birthday," Asa offered, still a little rattled.

"It's not his birthday," Eve said.

"It is!" Daniel argued.

"It's next month," Eve said. It sounded as if they'd had this conversation before.

"Next day, next week, next month—time goes so fast as you get older, love. It speeds up until it makes you sick and dying. I'm dying, and she doesn't even take me seriously," he told Asa, who drew back, wide-eyed.

Eve sighed. "He means we all die, and he is getting older. *Just as we all are,*" she said pointedly, but Daniel didn't seem to hear her.

"She is the moon and the sun and all the stars," he said, addressing the room at large. "But she will not shine on me."

"I should probably go . . ." Asa began, but Daniel grabbed his arm, pinning him in place.

"My father died when he was forty," he said. "He was forty, and he dropped dead like a stone. Next month or tomorrow, I'll be dead."

"Just because your father died at forty doesn't mean you will," Asa said, trying to remove his arm. Daniel's grip was iron.

"You think I'll die sooner?" he said, his eyes locked on Asa's. There was a black fleck in one of them, and for a second Asa had the disorienting feeling he was being stared at through a third pupil.

"No!" he answered quickly.

Daniel released his arm and roared with laughter, his face red. "Don't worry, my friend. Don't worry about your record, and don't worry about my dying."

"Okay." Asa got to his feet. "I should go."

"No, stay!" Daniel waved his arms in protest. His speech had begun to slur. "Stay. Eve likes you. I can tell. Come on, let's go look down at the city beneath our feet."

He stood, not waiting for an answer, and went to the couch, taking the half-empty bottle with him.

Asa glanced at Eve. "Okay. Do you mind?"

"I don't," she said. "Come on."

Asa followed her to the couch and sat at one end, facing Daniel; it was curved in a half circle, so they could all see one another. Eve didn't join them. Instead, she went to the glass and gazed out. Daniel watched her as if he was waiting for something.

Asa raised his glass and cleared his throat. "To you, Daniel.

I don't know how you're going to clear my record, but I appreciate it. Really."

"Least I can do," Daniel said, one word sliding into the next. "I like you. Eve likes you. You like him, Eve? I've brought you something that you like, at last?"

Eve sighed. "Daniel . . ."

She went to the couch and put her arms around him; he rested his head against her stomach, just below her breasts. Asa looked away hastily, but he could still see them in the glass. Daniel hugged her, gripping the fabric of her dress with both hands, and Eve stroked his head, whispering something Asa could not hear. Asa sipped his drink and stared out over the city, trying not to eavesdrop.

"But you don't," Daniel said loudly, and Eve hushed him.

"I do, Daniel. I do. I'm here." She sat down beside him. "Come on, get some sleep, okay?"

Daniel mumbled something incoherent but pulled his legs up on the couch, laying his head in her lap. Eve leaned down and kissed his cheek, then stayed where she was, unmoving for a few long minutes. Finally, Daniel began to snore.

"Asa," Eve hissed, and he turned. She gestured to Daniel on her lap. "Help me," she whispered.

Asa realized she was pinned in place. He helped her lift Daniel gently so she could slip out. His snoring kept an even pace as they laid him back on the couch. Eve pointed to the door, and they went slowly, careful not to bump the table and rattle the dishes. In the living room, Eve closed the door behind them and leaned against it, pressing her forehead to the opaque glass.

"Are you okay?" Asa asked softly.

She nodded, then wiped her eyes and turned around. "I'm

sorry about that," she said. "He really will fix your record. He's a genius, even if he acts like an idiot."

"I never met a genius," Asa said. "As far as I know, he's a perfect specimen."

Eve laughed, but the sound was brittle.

"Will he be all right?" Asa asked, and she nodded.

"He always is. He's just a maudlin drunk. I guess I am too. He just always gets there first." Eve went to the couch facing the city view and sat down heavily. "He's right, though. I do like you. I don't like many people."

Asa tried to keep his face neutral, but his heart picked up its pace. "I do like most people, actually. I like you more than most, though," Asa said as he sat down beside her, leaving some distance between them.

She shook her head. "Aren't you charming," she said wryly.

"My mother always says so."

She smiled, but it faded quickly. Asa looked out over the city, then back at her.

"Hey, I'm sorry to push it, but it's my life. Do you know how he can fix this stuff? I already got in trouble. I don't need to make it worse."

Eve narrowed her eyes at him and tilted her head, and Asa shivered, feeling as if she was reading his thoughts. *Don't picture her naked,* he thought.

At last she looked away. When she looked back again, her face was unguarded. "He can do it. How? You might not want to know that."

"I do. I swear."

"Do you know anything about Intech?"

Asa shook his head.

"Intech—short for innovative technology."

"What does that mean?" Asa asked. "Isn't all technology innovative?"

"Yeah, when it's new. That phone you've got is ancient tech—it's old-world scrap-heap material. A hundred years ago or so, a ten-year-old kid wouldn't use it. State tech is incredible, but they hand us that junk."

Asa's phone was in his pocket, and he touched it self-consciously. "It works okay," he said, defensive.

Eve shrugged. "It does what it's supposed to. I'm just rambling. The point is that Daniel can fix your record because he has access to the Network—the system—that's all."

"Okay . . ." Asa frowned, suddenly grasping her meaning. "Wait. The system. Do you mean the State system of records? Social Contracts and things?"

"Social Contracts, births, deaths, arrests, transportations, terminations, farm yields, weather records and predictions, demographic statistics, road maps, blueprints for every building and rail station—and every personal record for everyone who's ever lived."

"How?" Asa stared at her, shocked. "Is he . . . what is he?"

There was only one person with that kind of access.

"He's not the Chancellor in disguise," Eve said dryly, echoing his thoughts. "Daniel's grandfather was one of the Founders. He built the framework for the system, and Daniel has access."

"But how?"

"Look, all I know is what he blurts out when he's drunk. It doesn't add up to much, and what I do know I shouldn't tell you," Eve said brusquely.

"So, what, you're mad at me for listening?" Asa eased away from her.

She drew her legs up onto the couch and reached for a

small pillow, which she wrapped her arms around as if it were a stuffed toy.

"Look," he went on, "I really hope you and Daniel are telling the truth. I really hope that he can fix my record. But that was the most uncomfortable dinner of my life. You know that, right?"

Eve laughed; it was a peculiar laugh, short and distressed. She'd done it before, and Asa wasn't certain what it meant—if it was at his expense, at her own, or at the world's.

"How long have you been with him?" Asa asked more gently.

Eve buried her face in the pillow. She stayed like that until Asa began to think she might smother herself, and he touched her shoulder. She turned her head, resting her cheek on the pillow, and looked at him for a long moment.

"Have you ever lost something—someone—who was your whole world?" she asked.

"My grandmother went to Sanctuary," Asa said slowly, and her eyes seemed to dim a little; it was the wrong answer. "I almost died once, though," he offered. "I thought I was dying. Everyone else did too. For almost a month, I stayed in my bedroom and looked out the window at the world, thinking I'd never be a part of it again, that I was just . . . waiting to disappear."

Eve's eyes softened, and she sat up straighter, putting the pillow aside. "What happened?"

"I didn't die."

"I mean, how did you almost die?"

"I fell off a bridge into twenty feet of water."

It sounded strange to say it aloud—back home, everyone just knew. Eve's eyes widened, and she leaned almost imperceptibly away from him.

"How?" she asked, almost in a whisper.

"I don't know," he said. "I was a kid. I got lucky. You hear rumors of people who survive—I'm one of those rumors."

Eve shook her head. "You went all the way under? Your head too?"

"Yeah." Asa shifted uncomfortably, suddenly uncertain why he had brought it up. "You were telling me something," he said. "About you and Daniel."

"Right. Me and Daniel." Eve sighed. "He's a genius."

"You said that."

"He's a good man." She took the pillow onto her lap again. "He saved Saul's life, he really did, and it wasn't easy—he did it at great risk to himself. He did it for both of us, Saul and me. Saul had been with his organization for three years by then, and Daniel—he had always had a kind of thing for me, although he was careful about it. I was underage. Saul was an innovator, he was brilliant." When Asa nodded along, she gripped the pillow with both hands. "Anyway, when Saul was due to be transported to Work—really, to be terminated, as we found out—I had just turned twenty. I had no creds, no income, no phone—you know, before you reach maturity, you might as well not exist. I couldn't buy myself a sandwich without Saul. I would have been assigned to a Ward for that last year, but Daniel took over as my guardian."

"How?" Asa asked, then caught himself. "Right. He has access."

Eve nodded. "He put it into the system, and there I was. Taken care of."

"So then . . ." Asa broke off, not wanting to ask the question.

"He didn't touch me before I was twenty-one," Eve said hastily. "That's a crude way to put it, but it's the truth. He loved me, and I knew it, but he kept his distance until I was of age."

"And after?" Asa asked carefully.

Her eyes looked enormous; in the brighter light of the apartment, her smooth skin glowed. Sitting less than a foot away, he was dying to hold her, to kiss her, to feel her body pressed against his. It seemed wrong, somehow, to ask her questions about Daniel while it was all he could do not to touch her.

Eve looked out the window, leaning forward so he could only see her in profile. "I went to him on my twenty-first birthday. It seemed only fair." She gave Asa a sideways glance, as if she might be worried what he thought of her, and he nodded, trying to look encouraging, and trying not to reach out and stroke her hair. "It was more than that," she went on, staring back out at the city below them. "I was utterly bereft. Saul was everything to me, and without him I felt like I was just . . . waiting to disappear." She gave Asa a smile. "Daniel kept me from vanishing. I think he still does. He loves me into existence."

"That's . . . sweet?" Asa hazarded, though it sounded grotesque. Eve shook her head and leaned back again, placing herself only a few inches from him. His breath caught in his throat; he could feel her warmth radiating.

"It's not," she whispered, sounding as if she was about to cry.

"Why don't you leave?" Asa asked. "You're not married, right?"

"No, we're not married." She turned her face toward his. She was almost close enough to kiss him.

"Then what is it?"

"I'm afraid to leave him alone."

"What do you mean?"

"I'm going to have to, though," she went on as if he had not spoken. "I'm twenty-five this year."

"Oh," Asa said. "You're—"

"Running out of time," she finished. "I love Daniel. I don't know if it sounds like that's true right now, but I do love him. But I want a family, and I've got less than a year."

Asa nodded, alarmed on her behalf. The idea that someone would want a family and not have one was awful—everyone he'd known who chose to declare as single *chose*. He searched for words, but she went on before he found any.

"Daniel says . . ." she said, lowering her voice to a near-whisper. "Daniel says he could . . . that he could give me children."

"He's almost forty. He said so," Asa said. "How could he have children?"

"He said he was never sterilized," Eve whispered. "It could be true—he said he just changed the records and never had the procedure. I know he's capable of it."

Asa shook his head. "Maybe. Even so, he's past his time. It's not right. It's not fair to the children—they won't be healthy."

"That's what I've told him," she said.

Asa looked at her, feeling helpless. "I don't know," he said finally. "I think you have to be happy."

"Oh, is that what you think?" She smiled.

Asa nodded. "Absolutely. I think it's crucial to having a great life."

Eve laughed, and this time it sounded genuine. The hours melted away like minutes as they talked, until unexpectedly, daybreak began to illuminate the sky.

"Hey, look, the sun's coming up," Asa said. The transparent walls ignited with color, the whole sky visible above the city as the dawn broke. They watched in silence, and after a moment, Eve let her shoulder touch Asa's, leaning against him ever so slightly.

"Thank you," she said. "It's been a while since I talked to someone." Asa turned his head slowly, afraid of scaring her away.

"Anytime," he whispered, his lips just brushing her silky hair. She gave a small, contented murmur. *If this could go on forever, I would be happy,* Asa thought.

Something shattered noisily in the next room. Asa and Eve startled, and the top of her head smacked against his chin.

"Sorry," she said hurriedly.

"Come on," he said.

They rushed into the dining room and halted abruptly. One of the floor-to-ceiling wall panels was open, and Daniel was standing on the edge, looking down over the precipice. The source of the crash was obvious: the liquor bottle was smashed on the floor beside him.

"Daniel!" Eve shrieked. "What are you doing?"

"Stay back, love. Last thing I want to do is take you with me."

"Daniel, you're not safe," Asa said, trying to sound calm. He crept toward the gaping window, inch by inch. Daniel didn't seem to notice. His eyes were on Eve.

"I didn't want you to see this," he said sadly.

"Then don't do it!"

"Eve Layla Ashland, I love you with all the heart I never thought I had. You've made my life bearable, but even a brilliant flame can't light an abyss."

"Daniel, no." Eve was crying. "Please, don't do this."

Asa was almost to the window. Another foot and he could grab Daniel and drag him in. *Keep your eyes on her,* he begged the other man silently.

"I'm sorry," Daniel said. "I'm done."

He gave Eve a strange, sad smile and turned his back to them. Asa held his breath, sidling closer. *There.* He lunged forward to grab Daniel, bracing himself against the wall, but it was too late:

Daniel jumped. He plunged, slipping through Asa's arms like smoke as he plummeted toward the street.

"*Daniel!*" Eve screamed, running to the window, and Asa caught her around the waist, holding her back. "Let me see! I have to see!" she cried, and he loosened his grip, still holding on to her as she stared down in shock at Daniel.

He had landed on his back. From so far up, it was hard to make out his face, but he was motionless. Dark liquid spread slowly out from his head, running down a slight incline in the pavement like a river.

CHAPTER SEVEN

GABRIEL STARED AT THE SCREEN, LIGHT-HEADED.

"Is he dead?" Joan whispered beside him.

He didn't answer. He reached for the controls automatically and tilted the drone down to show the alley below. Daniel's body was motionless.

Gabriel steeled himself, then sent the drone plunging down to ground level. He hovered it beside Daniel and switched to read for life signs. For a moment, his silhouette flickered on the screen, then it faded; the screen was a flat blue.

Gabriel switched back to image-capture, and Joan gasped. From the corner of his eye, he saw her turn away. He walked closer to the screen. Daniel's head was crushed. His face was unbroken but strangely distorted, surrounded by a halo of bone fragments, brain matter, and blood. Gabriel glanced at Joan; she had turned back to the screen, but she looked as if she was about to be sick, her jaw clamped tightly shut. He angled the drone's eye away from Daniel's body, aiming it at the end of the alley.

"Shouldn't we send a medical team?" Joan asked.

"He's dead," Gabriel said shortly. "There's no hurry. I'll send a team in a minute. Split the screen with Sigma 487."

The screen split; now they had eyes on both the entrance to the building and the alley where Daniel lay.

"There could be a back way out," Joan said, having regained most of her composure. Have Gamma 631 circle the building, please."

✦

There's no way he's still alive.

Asa stared down at Daniel. He couldn't look away; to move, even to blink, seemed impossible. He was dimly aware of Eve clutching his arm, her nails digging half-moons into his skin, but he could not look away from Daniel.

"There's no way he'll survive, will he?" he repeated aloud. He sounded hoarse, as if he hadn't spoken in days.

"No," Eve whispered.

Her voice was enough to shake him out of his petrified state. He looked at her. She was staring, but not downward. She nodded at the open window, scarcely moving, and he followed her gesture. Hovering at eye level, humming steadily, was the round silver body of a drone.

Asa drew back sharply, and Eve leapt forward and pressed a hidden button. The window closed quickly, seamlessly vanishing into the translucent wall. The drone hovered for another moment, then turned and zipped away, flying in a quick straight line toward the center of the city.

Asa watched it go, then turned to Eve—it was only as he took in her wide, frightened eyes and her stiff posture that it dawned on him: "The drone feed," he said in a hushed tone. "It's going to look like I pushed him, isn't it?"

Eve nodded. "We—" She broke off, then cleared her throat. "We have to get out of here."

"There must be another drone, another camera angle that shows the truth! They're everywhere," Asa said with sudden hope.

Eve shook her head, and his heart sank. "Not around here. Daniel limited their access. Asa, after that fight . . ."

"I know," he cut in. "As soon as a stalker lays eyes on me, I'll be questioned, judged, and sentenced. Work or termination." He sat down heavily on the couch behind them. "The drone's already on its way to wherever it reports."

"It reports instantly—it's already sent the feed."

"I'm as good as dead," Asa said, the words sounding dramatic and unreal even as he spoke them.

"Not just you," Eve said. "I was on camera too."

"But you didn't do anything!"

Eve gave him a faint smile. "I didn't have to. I was there. I didn't try to stop you—that's as good as helping. Besides, without Daniel's protection I'll be transported anyway, just for being his . . . and that's if one of his associates doesn't get to me first. With Daniel gone, I'm as good as dead!" She clapped a hand over her mouth, shaking her head. "Daniel, how could you be this selfish," she whispered. "What have you done?"

She went back to the transparent wall and knelt, gazing down at the place where he had fallen. Asa watched her without moving, determination swelling in his chest.

I'll protect you, he vowed silently.

"Eve," he said, summoning a firm tone as he stood. Eve didn't seem to hear him. She placed her hand on the glass carefully, as if it might feel her touch. "Eve!" he said more loudly, and she turned almost as if in a trance.

"What?" she whispered, the word barely audible.

"We have to get out of here. I don't know what we do next, but I am not going to let anything happen to you."

"You can't promise me that," she said. "You don't understand what's happening."

"So, tell me, but do it while we're moving. We can go to my parents. They might know what to do, and we can figure out our next move from there."

Eve didn't answer. She was looking down at the street again.

"Eve!" he said, almost snapping. She turned with a glare. "I'm going to protect you," he said more quietly. "But I can't do that if I'm dead, so we have to go, right now."

Her glare faded, and she met his gaze with a sudden intensity. "David," she said abruptly and got to her feet.

"Who's David?" Asa asked, but Eve was already moving.

He trailed behind her as she ran to the bedroom, grabbed a black backpack out from under the large bed, and started snatching things from around the room, seemingly at random.

"David?" Asa asked again.

Eve didn't stop moving; she zipped the bag shut, apparently done packing, and tossed it at him. He caught it, watching as she opened a closet and crawled inside, disappearing entirely. Asa heard a long series of high-pitched tones, then the dark closet lit up with the electric blue of a facial scanner.

A few seconds later Eve emerged, carrying a second, identical backpack. She took a thin rectangular black box off the bed. It was flat, about the size of a throw pillow—Asa, barely glancing at the room's decoration, had assumed it was one. Eve wedged it into the backpack with some difficulty.

"Give me your phone," she said and held out her hand. "We have to leave them here."

"What? Why?" Asa asked. "How are we going to get anywhere? How will we get rail passes?"

"I'll take care of that," Eve said grimly. "Asa, come on, give it to me."

Reluctantly, he handed his phone to her, and she crawled into the closet again. When she emerged, she swung the bag she'd packed onto her back and headed toward the elevator. Asa just barely remembered to snatch his own backpack before the door opened, and they stepped inside.

Asa flinched as they came out into the lobby. Daniel's lifeless body was visible through the transparent back wall.

"How come no one has seen him yet?" he whispered.

"It's early," Eve said. "Stay here." She took off her backpack and thrust it into Asa's arms, then headed for the door alone.

"Where are you . . . oh." He let the question fall short as he watched her leave the building and circle around to where Daniel lay.

Eve knelt, took Daniel's hand in hers, and lifted it to her lips, then bent over him, resting her cheek against his.

Asa averted his eyes, looking out onto the street. The sun had scarcely risen, but the city was awake; every few minutes someone walked past the building. Asa glanced nervously at the elevator wall.

How many people live in this building?

Eve was still at Daniel's side. She had her hand on his chest and looked as if she was saying something. Asa bit his lip, wavering on the verge of going after her. The hiss of the elevator doors caught his attention, and he stopped himself from turning, try-ing hard to hold a casual posture. The two women who had come down glanced at him with curiosity as they passed, and he smiled apologetically.

"Just visiting," he said.

One nodded vaguely as they continued to the front door; the other didn't respond at all. Asa watched them leave, his heart racing with the awareness that his presence alone might attract suspicion.

✦

Gabriel kept his eyes trained on the drone feeds. "You might want to look away," he warned, but Joan shook her head.

"I'm fine."

He followed Eve as she knelt beside Daniel. She lifted his hand to her lips, then her face twisted in grief, and she clutched his shoulders and pitched forward, hugging his body. She clung to him for a long moment, and Gabriel sat down heavily in his chair, his heartbeat roaring in his ears; his knees felt as if they might buckle. After a moment, Eve sat up. She wiped her eyes and took a deep breath, then bent over and slid her hand into the front pocket of Daniel's pants.

She came out with nothing, then tried the other. Gabriel and Joan watched as Eve rifled quickly and methodically through Daniel's clothing, checking each pocket, moving him from side to side to be sure she had looked everywhere. Several times she stowed something in her own pockets, but the items were all too small for them to see. At last she seemed satisfied. She opened her mouth, beginning to speak. Gabriel peered at her lips, trying to read the words, but he could not make out what she was saying.

She bent down and kissed Daniel's broken cheek. She was silent a moment, then she began to sob. Joan averted her eyes, but Gabriel watched as Eve wept and then composed herself, taking deep, shuddering breaths. Finally, she stood and left the alley, not looking back.

✦

Asa glanced over again and saw that Eve was gone; Daniel's body lay alone in the alley. *She's left me behind!* Asa thought in momentary panic, then looked down at the bags at his feet. *She wouldn't have left me with all this,* he thought, just as Eve rushed in through the front door, her face red from crying.

"Are you okay?" Asa asked, the question sounding silly as soon as it came out of his mouth. *Of course she's not okay.*

But Eve just nodded brusquely and grabbed the bag she had thrust at him. She unzipped it and shoved something in before Asa could see what it was.

"Come on," she said and headed for the door. Asa swung one backpack across his back, carrying the other on one shoulder, and hurried after her.

Outside, Eve slowed her pace. "Look normal," she said.

"Yeah, got it. Don't act like I just killed someone," Asa said with an edge of irritation.

"You didn't," Eve said fiercely, and he looked at her with surprise. "You didn't," she repeated more quietly. "He killed himself. Remember that, okay?"

"Yeah," he said, softening his tone.

They walked in silence for a while, Eve moving decisively, weaving through main roads and back alleys until Asa started to feel as if they were going in circles. He said nothing, assuming she had reasons for the circuitous route. At last they emerged into the plaza in front of the rail station, where he had stood so eagerly less than two days before.

"How are we going to get on the train?" he asked as they approached the rail pass machine.

Eve shot him a look. "I said I'll take care of it," she said.

"Okay, fine." Asa took off the second backpack and switched it to his other shoulder.

"Sorry," Eve said, her expression pained. "I'll explain as soon as we're on the train. We just have to move fast."

"Deal," he said and smiled at her.

She smiled back thinly, then turned back to the machine. Asa watched as she took a thin square of something—plastic or maybe metal—out of her pocket. She scrolled quickly through a series of screens on the machine, ordering the passes, then slipped the square under the phone scanner.

Asa held his breath as the scanner's blue light moved back and forth, but Eve just looked impatient. After a second, the machine spat out two strips of metal. Eve put the square in her pocket and handed Asa his pass. He glanced at the code strip, nervous that something might have gone wrong, then flipped it over to read the text displayed on the tiny screen: round trip to Oakville. Asa opened his mouth, then stopped himself, realizing the answer to his question—two tickets to Rosewood would raise suspicion if anyone was looking for him.

They went to the platform to wait, but the train came quickly. Eve went first, sliding her pass into the porter slot, and Asa watched as the device slurped up her pass, then his.

They walked through to the back of the train, and Eve paced the length of the compartment, back and forth, making sure they were alone. Apparently satisfied, she sat at a table in the back corner, taking the seat that faced the rest of the compartment. Asa sat hesitantly beside her. She heaved a sigh and put her head in her hands.

"Eve?"

She sat up, brushing her hair back, and looked at him, shaking her head. "This is as far as I've gotten. I don't know what happens now." Her focused energy, the force that had carried them this far, seemed to have drained away all at once.

"I do," Asa said quickly. "I mean, not everything, but once we get to Rosewood, we'll go to my parents."

She nodded, not looking reassured.

"We'll figure something out there," he pressed. "I promise." He gave her what he hoped was an encouraging smile, and she returned it weakly.

"I'm going to hold you to that," she said lightly.

"Me too." Asa met her eyes, and she looked back at him.

"You have the Chancellor's eyes," she said at last, and he grinned.

"I know, right? I just hope he doesn't want them back!"

She stared at him blankly for a moment, then burst into laughter. She covered her face with her hands, but her shoulders still shook with it. Asa put a hand on her arm, and she turned to him and pulled him to her. He put his arms around her, holding her as she laughed or cried—he couldn't tell exactly which. The corner of the table was jamming into his side, but he didn't care. For a moment, he didn't care that they were on the run, their position hopeless. All that mattered was that she was in his arms.

After a while, Eve straightened, moving away from Asa and wiping her eyes. "Thanks," she said quietly.

"Yeah, I mean, of course," he said, feeling awkward. She

turned to look out the window, and he remembered what had been tugging at the back of his mind. "Who's David?" he asked, and she turned back. She looked at him appraisingly for a moment. "You may as well tell me," Asa said gently. "I mean . . . we're in this together."

She gave him a wry smile. "I guess we are."

Eve reached under her seat for the backpack she carried and set it down on the table with a clunk but did not open it.

"David is Daniel's grandfather," she said. "He was one of the Founders." Asa's eyes widened. "I think he can help us," Eve went on.

Asa stared at her. "One of the Founders?" he repeated.

He has to be dead, Asa thought, feeling even more off-balance than before. Eve, by contrast, was beginning to seem calm.

"David can help," she repeated. She leaned forward, lowering her voice. "He was . . . well, all the tech we have—government tech, innovative tech—it all stems from the work he did. When Daniel stopped Saul's termination, it was possible only because of David."

"How?"

Eve started to unzip the backpack, then stopped. "I'll show you later," she said. "David had a way into the Network—like a secret passage or something. Daniel knew how to use it. But I don't even understand it."

"So, you can't wipe our records clean," Asa said, suddenly deflated. He had not realized how much he had fixed his hopes on her unexplained confidence until now.

"I can't, no."

"Then what are we doing?" He spoke more loudly than he meant to, then lowered his voice. "Eve, I thought you had a plan."

"I do. Kind of." She sighed. "Look, I know it's a long shot, but if we can get to Sanctuary, David will help us. I've brought Daniel's laptop."

"Laptop?"

"It's a kind of computer. Technology from the old civ."

"Oh." Asa seized again on the vital detail she seemed to be ignoring. "But, Eve, if he was one of the Founders, he can't possibly still be alive."

Eve smiled, a spark in her eyes. "Asa, you've heard the rumors about Sanctuary, right? That they've managed to slow the aging process?"

"Sure, but not that much!"

"He'd be one hundred and fifty, maybe one sixty. It's not impossible."

Asa opened his mouth to object, but Eve leaned closer to him, whispering, "You know what they say about the Chancellor." Her lips brushed against his ear.

She drew back, and Asa swallowed, then nodded.

"Yeah," he said.

"He's barely aged in decades."

"It's just the luck of good genetics."

"That's what they say. I think the State's biotech is better than anyone admits. And I think if anyone is getting the best of it, it would be one of the Founders."

Asa slowly shook his head. "I don't believe it. If that were true, it would be available to everyone."

"Maybe. I know Daniel thought it was true."

"So, you just believed everything he said?" Asa was growing irritated. Eve stared at him without hostility, and he looked down at the table. "That came out wrong," he said. "Did Daniel think his grandfather was still alive?"

"He never said so. But he got information sometimes, messages through the computer." She pulled the bag on the table closer to her. "I know only one person contacted him that way—I was the only one who even knew he had it, besides whoever that contact was."

"And you think the contact was David, the grandfather?"

"Who else could it be?" She looked at him nervously, and Asa realized she was waiting for him to answer.

"I don't know," he said at last. "It makes sense, I guess. But how does this help us? Can you contact him with that thing?"

Eve shook her head. "I can't even turn it on. We have to get to David."

"David's in Sanctuary?"

"He's definitely over sixty," she reasoned. "Where else would he be?"

Asa looked at her dubiously. "So, if we can get from here to Sanctuary, there might be someone who might be alive, who might be able to help us?"

"If he's willing to," Eve said. "I've never met him. I don't know if he'd even know who I am."

"Solid plan."

"Can you think of a better one?"

Asa sighed. "No."

Eve turned away to look out the window again. After a moment, she pulled the backpack off the table and onto her lap. She hugged it to her chest, resting her chin on top of it, and Asa looked away, not sure what to say or do.

He didn't have to endure the silence for long. Only a few minutes had passed when the screens at the front of the compartment lit up. Asa glanced at Eve. She looked lost in thought, her eyes fixed on nothing, holding the backpack as if it were a child's stuffed toy. Quietly, Asa got up and walked to the seats by the screen to watch.

This time it was not the Chancellor's face that appeared but a stark cityscape: low gray concrete buildings, unpainted and dreary. The streets were narrow and empty. The words "*The Challenge*" appeared, transposed over the image, then faded away as a piercing whistle sounded.

"The morning call to duty has just sounded for the citizens of Work," the narrator intoned in his dry, familiar voice, and Asa settled back in his seat to watch the broadcast. "This day begins like every other day, as the workers leave their quarters and go to their designated task zones." As he spoke, people began to file out of the nearly identical drab buildings, filling the streets. The camera focused in on one, then another, then pulled out to the crowd again. Asa watched with a grim fascination.

He had always liked the Work broadcasts—the repetitious banality of the transported criminals' lives was almost unfathomable. *How can they live like that?* he always thought.

But that was the point of the program, of course: both entertainment and warning. He had grown up watching it: the people—dressed in shabbier clothes than anyone at home, all in the same dull gray—getting up each morning, going to their task zones to do the labor of the State, then going home again to cramped apartments, knowing the next day would only bring more of the same.

Their constrained lives were their own fault, Asa had been taught, although no one had told him so in quite those words. These people had broken their Social Contracts; they could not be relied upon to be productive members of their communities, contributing to the greater good willingly, and so they had to be forced to do so. It was in Work that everything from solar cars to shoes to water filters were manufactured. Work was necessary; their labor was not a punishment. Work gave purpose to those few people who, thanks to inferior genetics or poor choices, could not uphold their Social Contracts. Work was their second chance at being part of the State.

Now Asa watched the broadcast with growing anxiety, searching the faces of each worker the camera focused on. *What did you do wrong?* he wanted to ask. *How do you survive each day?*

Every once in a while, glimpses of happiness appeared: workers smiling to greet each other, sometimes even laughter at a joke. Some workers cohabitated as couples, others by themselves. They had time in the evenings to socialize or relax, but this was merely surviving, not really the same thing as living.

The broadcast was leading up to a special event, something Asa might have eagerly awaited at home, but now he felt the blood drain from his face as the narrator announced it: "Caleb and John were neighbors for three years without incident when an argument over a noise complaint finally boiled over. We hear first from Caleb."

"He just wouldn't stop playing that horrible thing," Caleb told the camera. "He'd sing along. I'm an understanding man, to a point. I didn't care that he's the worst musician I've ever heard, but I'm talking about all hours of the night. I haven't had a good night's sleep since the day he got here!"

"Now we turn to John for his perspective," the narrator intoned.

"I've played the electric lute since I was three years old, and I'm not going to stop on account of him," John snarled. "He's had it out for me ever since I got assigned to these quarters—he was hoping for a transfer, but he didn't get it, did he?"

"Resolution," said the narrator, "has been attempted and has failed. Caleb and John's dispute will end in a few minutes' time, when we go live to see the final verdict."

Asa looked back at Eve, who was still gazing blankly out the window. He watched the screen as the narrator recounted more details of the dispute, tuning out the information. *I can't end up there. I can't end up there,* he thought, repeating the words in his head like a mantra.

Suddenly the screen brightened as the picture switched to the bleak town square of the zone; it was the live verdict. Asa stood to watch, adrenaline rushing through him as if he were the one standing on the concrete. Caleb and John stood back to back at the center of the square, almost touching. Around them a crowd was gathered, murmuring agitatedly to one another. Some looked excited, others angry or afraid.

A woman in a long gray dress stepped into the open space, and silence fell. She walked toward the two men, her shoes making a harsh clacking noise against the hard concrete. When she reached them, she said something quietly to them both, then pressed an object into each of their hands. She walked back to the crowd and disappeared into it, and then it began. John and Caleb spun to face each other. They circled a little, both looking for an opening, their postures crouched and tense. Caleb grinned and tossed his knife from hand to hand; John flinched, and Caleb attacked.

The fight didn't last long. They wrestled on the ground, John making a few shallow cuts to Caleb's forearm as the larger man pinned him to the ground. Caleb hesitated for a moment. He looked to the side at someone in the crowd, then he took a deep breath and slashed his knife across John's throat. John's eyes went wide; his mouth opened and shut without sound as blood gushed from his neck, pouring out so fast it seemed unreal.

Caleb didn't move away from him, keeping his hand on John's shoulder as his body convulsed. Then the flow of blood came to a stop, and his face took on the stillness of death. Caleb put a hand over John's face and closed his eyes, leaving streaks of blood on his cheeks. Then he stood. There was no cheering from the crowd; Caleb did not look triumphant, only exhausted.

"And it's a clear verdict!" the narrator announced enthusiastically as music began to play in the background.

Asa couldn't move. He'd watched dozens of these duels—they were just something that happened in Work, a part of the world the workers had created for themselves by breaking their Social Contracts—but he had never studied the faces of the workers who were fighting. Then again, he had never imagined himself as one of them.

I can't go there, he thought.

The broadcast ended; the screen went dark. Asa looked over his shoulder at Eve. She was still lost in her own little world.

CHAPTER EIGHT

AFTER LOSING SIGHT OF THEM, GABRIEL punched the button hard in aggravation, relinquishing control of the drone and sending it back to its watch station. He sat back and closed his eyes, suddenly feeling a decade older. He could feel Joan behind him wavering uncertainly. "What is it?" he asked, hearing the strain in his own voice.

"I've . . . never seen anyone die before," she said.

Her voice sounded small and unlike her. He rubbed his temples, trying to banish the image of Eve clinging, anguished, to the corpse.

Naomi. The moment when your life slipped away. Her skin had turned to wax, and it was as if his insides had been scraped out; he was so hollow it hurt to breathe. Gabriel pressed his hand against his chest, seized again by the raw, aching emptiness.

"Are you okay?" Joan asked, sounding more like herself.

Gabriel ground his teeth, forcing himself back into the present moment. "Fine. Get a passenger drone. We're going after them."

"We don't know where they're going. We can't requisition a drone."

"They'll go to Rosewood," he said.

"How do you know that?"

Gabriel stood and turned to face her. "Asa Isaac Rosewood had never left Rosewood before he came to Horizon. He just committed murder. I don't know why he did it, but I know he's going to head straight for the only safe place he knows."

"What about Eve?" Joan asked. "Why would she go with him? Everyone she knows is here."

Gabriel smiled wryly, and she looked away. "With Daniel dead, 'everyone she knows' wants to get their hands on her and shake her until she gives up all his secrets. And when she has, they'll make sure she can't tell anyone else."

"Oh." Joan looked at him wearily. "I'll go start the authorizations for a passenger drone."

"Good, call me when you have it." Gabriel sat back down and pulled his chair up to the controls.

"Door open," Joan said, then hesitated on the threshold. "What are you going to do?" she asked.

Gabriel pressed a few buttons, and the still image of Daniel on the ledge appeared on the screen, bigger than life. "I'm going to watch a murder."

Joan left without a reply, and Gabriel leaned forward, scrutinizing the picture from top to bottom.

"Replay Mu 248, beginning at 5:37 AM," he said.

Three life signs appeared in the blue rendering of Daniel's apartment, two to the far side of the apartment and the other moving around restlessly in the bedroom. They had spent hours positioned like this. Presumably the pair were Daniel and the girl, Eve, and the third was Asa, but what was he doing there?

Gabriel had gone over every word of their records, scrutinizing all three for connections. Daniel and Eve had been tied together for years, first through her brother, Saul, then through their relationship. None of it was news.

As for Asa the Indestructible, he appeared to be . . . exactly what he appeared to be.

He had never gotten into any trouble, besides the famous encounter with the river. If he had ever met Daniel or Eve before the evening of the fight, the connection was completely hidden. To hide something like that would require erasing drone feeds, scrambling phone communication, and a network of people willing to keep secrets. It would take someone like, well, Daniel. But after hours of searching, Gabriel couldn't come up with a single reason Daniel would want to do that.

Unless . . . some kind of research, maybe—into the Bug? Samples of his blood must have been taken to Medical Research when it happened . . .

Onscreen, the two people in the living room moved to the bedroom, joining the third at the far end of the room, their red life signs grouped tightly together. Gabriel had ordered the drone to zoom in, but it didn't help—the three bodies were still an overlapping red mass, and he couldn't tell what was happening.

Something was different with the wall . . . It was at this point that he thought to switch to image-capture.

The screen went blank, then snapped back with the image: a floor-to-ceiling window had opened in the wall, and Daniel was on the edge, his eyes wild. Before Gabriel could react, Daniel lurched forward and fell, disappearing from the picture. The drone stayed steady on the window, where Asa Isaac Rosewood stood, white-faced, in the gap where Daniel had been.

Eve rushed forward, screaming something, and Asa caught her around the waist, pulling her back from the edge. They were still for a moment, then the wall slid shut, and breaking dawn blazed over the surface of the building.

"Stop. Replay Mu-248, same selection." Gabriel paced back and forth as the drone feed played again. He wanted to see Daniel's final moments from every angle.

CHAPTER NINE

IT WAS ALMOST MIDDAY BY THE TIME THE train pulled into the rail station at Rosewood. When the autom announced the stop, Asa stood wearily, grabbing the two bags he had been carrying. Eve was holding hers in her lap, resting her chin on top, still staring bleakly out the window.

"Eve," Asa said gently. "We're here."

"I know," she said.

The doors opened with a hiss, and she got up slowly, as if it were a struggle. Asa held out a hand, but she didn't seem to see it. She followed him out onto the platform and hoisted her bag onto her back. "Let's go," she said shortly. Asa nodded, and they left the station.

"We should go through the forest," he said. "We'll be seen on the road. Come on."

He caught Eve's hand and hurried across the street into the

woods, pulling her with him into the cover of trees. Suddenly she stopped dead, dropping his hand.

Asa turned back in alarm. "What is it?" Eve was looking up, and he tried to follow her gaze. "Eve, tell me! What's wrong?"

"Nothing." She gave him a quick smile, then turned in a slow circle. "I've just never seen anything like this before."

Asa laughed. "Really? But those microclimates in the plaza . . ."

Eve shook her head. "These trees are so much bigger."

"The ones you've seen were saplings. Younger trees. These have been here longer. Some of them even from before the Founding."

"There are so *many*."

"That's what makes it a forest. Haven't you seen pictures?"

"Sure. This is different."

She went to the trunk of an enormous oak and put her hand on its surface. Asa felt a quiet rush of pride.

"I'm glad you like it," he said. "Come on, we should hurry." Eve nodded, and they set off toward the village.

✦

Asa's house—*I guess not my house anymore,* he thought—was not far away, and they reached the small parcel of land his parents farmed in less than an hour. When he saw the house, Asa's spirit lifted.

Everything will be all right. He pictured his mother and father sitting at the table and chatting, their heads bent together companionably. *They'll know what to do.* He strode out into the field, then turned around; Eve had stopped, hesitating at the tree line.

"You're sure we can trust them?" she asked, her eyes shrouded in worry.

Asa was aghast. "They're my *parents*," he said and held out a hand as he might to a recalcitrant dog. "Come on."

Eve stepped out of the trees and took his hand, gripping it tightly as they walked toward the back door of the house.

As Asa raised his hand to knock, Eve caught him by the wrist.

"Remember, you can't tell them anything," she whispered.

He pulled her aside, huddling against the wall so they would not be visible through the door.

"I told you, we can trust them," he said.

"I believe you. We can't tell them because they can't know—Asa, there will be stalkers after us. They'll question your family. Don't put them in that position."

He stared at her, struck dumb by the obvious. *Contract Enforcers.*

"But we covered our tracks," he argued weakly.

Her dark eyes were kind but resolute; she looked sad, as if she had somehow failed him. "It will slow them down, that's all," she said. "Asa, I'm sorry."

"It's not your fault . . ."

Asa broke off as the door swung open, and his father's cheerful face appeared.

"Asa! How long are you and your beautiful new friend going to whisper outside? Haven't you told her we won't bite?" He winked at Eve. "I'm Isaac Thomas Rosewood, Asa's father, as you probably already know. Sarah! Come see who I found!" he called back into the house.

"Dad! Dad, let us in, quick!" Asa rushed Eve through the door as his father stepped back to let them in. Asa closed the door behind them and latched it as his mother came into the kitchen.

"Asa? You're back!" She nearly ran to him, grabbing him in a quick hug and kissing both his cheeks before he could stop her.

"Mom!" he said, pulling away. "Listen, I have to . . ."

"Sarah, look, he's brought a young woman," Isaac interrupted, laying out plates on the dining table with an exuberant clatter.

Sarah turned her attention to Eve, whose face had gone stony, her posture straight. On the surface, at least, she seemed to have regained her confidence. Sarah looked appraisingly at her, then turned to Asa.

"What's wrong?" she asked sternly.

"Wrong?" Isaac stopped moving, his hands full of forks and spoons.

"Isaac, stop bouncing around and look at your son's face! Something is wrong. Tell us."

Asa glanced at Eve, who shook her head ever so slightly.

"I can't," he said.

His mother's face hardened. "And why not?" she asked, looking at Eve, who merely looked back placidly.

"I'm in trouble," he said, the calming words he had rehearsed in his head vanishing from memory. "I didn't do anything, but it looks like I did, and now we're going to fix it, but we need to look at Grandfather Herschel's maps," he finished.

"Maps?" Sarah knotted her fingers together anxiously. "Why do you need those?"

"We just . . . do," Asa answered.

The pit of his stomach had turned to lead, and he bit his lip. Isaac left the room, and Asa looked nervously at his mother; her face was twisted as if she were in physical pain.

"Mom, I'm sorry," he began, trailing off as Isaac returned with a large wooden box. He set it firmly on the table, rattling the dishes.

"Grandfather Herschel's maps," Isaac said grimly. "Not that I know what use they'll be. They're fifty years out of date."

"Thank you," Eve said quietly, and the sound of her voice roused Sarah, who turned on her.

"Who are you? What have you gotten him into?" she demanded.

"She didn't get me into anything!" Asa exclaimed, but Eve gave him a level look.

"Yes, I did." She turned back to Sarah. "I'm going to get him out of it. I know someone who can help. We just have to get to him."

Sarah shook her head. "I don't believe you. You're in so much trouble you can't even tell us about it? Asa, what have you done? I can't lose you! I can't watch you die like a beast in some televised duel!"

She began to cry in earnest, and Isaac put a hand on her shoulder. She turned to him, letting him pull her into an embrace, and she wept against his chest as Isaac stared at his son, tears shining in his own eyes. Asa looked helplessly at Eve, but she was staring fixedly into the distance, ignoring them all.

"Mom," Asa said. "Dad, listen, you won't lose me. I'm . . . we're going to fix it, I promise. We just need an hour here, maybe two, then we'll go."

"One hour. I want you out of here before sundown," Isaac said, his voice colder than Asa had ever heard it.

Sarah had composed herself, though she looked odd, as if she weren't quite present. Asa looked at his father, surprised, but Isaac was unflinching.

"I'd lay down my life for you, son," he said, "if I didn't have another child to think of."

He left the room without waiting for a reply. Asa stared down at the table, tears springing to his eyes.

"Asa," his mother whispered.

"I'm sorry," he began, and she shook her head.

"I love you more than you will ever know," she said. She hugged him, standing up on her toes to kiss his temple. "Don't say goodbye," she said. "Just go when you're done."

"What?" Asa pulled back, hurt.

"It's better if they don't know when we leave," Eve said clearly. "That way it'll be harder to estimate how far we've gone."

Sarah raised her eyebrow. "Yes," she said. She walked out briskly, not looking back.

"You didn't mention maps," Eve said when they were alone. Asa lifted the box off the table and set it on the floor.

"I didn't think of it until we got here," he said honestly. "My grandfather—my mother's father—he was old when she was born. He lived through the years of chaos before the Founding." Eve's eyes widened. "He helped build the town," Asa went on, "and he kept some records: maps, population data, things like that."

"I don't know how that will help."

"It might not." Asa opened the trunk and coughed as a cloud of dust arose. Eve stepped back, waving her hand to clear the air. "The thing is, how do we get to Sanctuary, right?" he said.

She nodded, and he handed her an unwieldy pile of papers, yellowed with age. She set them on the table, moving a plate, and sat down.

Asa took the rest and sat down beside her. "He might have maps from before the Founding," he said in a low voice.

"Oh," Eve said. "Oh!"

"Right."

"Maps that show the Waste or the future site of Sanctuary." She looked at him incredulously. "How could you not think of this before?"

Asa shrugged, slightly embarrassed. "I was too busy running for my life?"

Eve smiled, shook her head, and turned her attention to the maps.

✦

They went through the papers as fast as they could, scanning for anything that might be useful. About ten pages in, Hannah knocked on the door frame.

"Can I help?" she asked.

"No," Eve said automatically, then looked up in surprise.

"My sister, Hannah," Asa said, getting up to hug her.

She squeezed him tightly, then leaned past him, trying to see what was on the table. "What are you doing?" she asked.

"We're looking for something," Asa said.

"No," Eve said again, more gently this time.

Hannah narrowed her eyes, affronted. "Who are you and why are you giving my brother orders?" she asked, and Asa laughed suddenly.

Eve smiled, her face lighting up. "I'm not giving Asa orders. I swear," she said.

"What's your name, then?" Hannah asked.

Eve stood up, and Asa saw her as if for the first time again: her shining black hair, her smooth, light brown skin, her shimmering green dress, and her luminous eyes. He glanced at his teenage sister, who was staring openly.

"Hannah," Eve said seriously, "Asa and I have to do something very important. People might ask you questions about us, and it's best if you don't have the answers they are looking for. Does that make sense to you?"

Hannah looked as if she wanted to object, but she nodded. "Is Asa going to be okay?" she asked, and Eve nodded.

"Yes."

"How can you be sure?" Hannah pressed.

Eve wavered. Asa looked back and forth between them, feeling as if he should intervene, but Eve spoke before he could.

"I can't be sure," she admitted, sitting back down. She picked up the map she had been looking at and placed it on the reject pile, smoothing it down like cloth. "I can be sure that Asa and I will do everything in our power to make it back here safely."

Hannah shook her head in frustration. "Why do you have to go at all? I don't understand."

"I'll explain when we come back," Asa said, but Hannah glared at him, and he stepped back, uncertain why she was so intent on hearing this from Eve.

Eve folded her hands and leaned forward on the table. "Asa told me the story about the bridge," she said.

"Everyone knows that story."

"What does everyone think it means?" Eve asked. Hannah looked suspicious. "It's not a test. I'm not patronizing you. I'm really asking. What do the people here think it means about Asa?"

Hannah hid a smirk. "That he's a reckless fool," she said, giving him a sideways glance.

Eve grinned. "He is that. Anything else?"

"Yeah." Hannah paused, looking off to the side as if choosing her words. "They think it means there's something special about Asa—something tough. The little kids think of it like he fought the Bug and he won, and if he can do that, he can do anything."

"Really?" Asa was taken aback. "Little kids know about that?"

"Believe me, I'm not the one telling them," Hannah said dryly. "They ask me about it when I'm taking my turn teaching."

"What do you think?" Eve asked, ignoring the intervening conversation. Hannah turned back to her.

"I think Asa's a reckless fool," she said. She turned to Asa and gave him another fast, rough hug. "I'll see you when you get back, fool." She kissed him on the cheek and hurried from the room.

Asa watched her go. *Abandoned in my own house,* he thought morosely, looking around the familiar room. *How could I have been so eager to get away?* His sister's constant questions, his parents' incessant chatter of advice, their embarrassing affection for Asa and for each other—it all seemed like a small price for the warmth of a loving home. *I wanted to go away and never come back. I guess I'll get what I wished for.*

"Asa," Eve sounded impatient.

"What?"

"I said your name twice. Come look." She held up a paper and waved it at him.

Asa sat down beside her, and she passed him the map. It was hand-drawn in black ink, and Rosewood was a single dot on a larger landscape. It showed all the communities, and the city of Horizon, all cordoned off from the Waste with a thick dotted line.

North of the Waste, accessible only by the State railway through the mountains, was Work. The Waste took up the whole center of the map, more immense even than Asa had imagined it. It was a blank space, with no landmarks noted—why would there be? Along the far western side of the Waste was a wide river, and across the river was Sanctuary.

Asa considered it for a moment. "I never saw where everything was, all laid out like that," he said.

"Me either," Eve said. "I thought Horizon was more like

there," she added, pointing to a spot just past the boundary to the Waste.

Asa laughed. "I know people say things about the city, but I think you'd know if you were living in the Waste!"

She grinned and turned back to the map. "Asa, I don't know about this."

"This was your idea!"

"I know, but I thought there must be some way to get to Sanctuary. Look, there's literally no way to get there from here."

"Sure there is." Asa bent over the map, looking more closely.

"No, there isn't. It's cut off by the Waste and the water. I don't even know how they get people out there."

"Well, they do," Asa said. "They get people to Sanctuary, so there's a way into Sanctuary. And if there's a way in, then we can get in."

Eve traced her finger slowly along the edge of the Waste. "I guess I assumed that we could get there from *here*," she said. "Asa, we're going to have to go into the Waste."

"Yeah."

"You knew?"

"I figured."

Eve was quiet for a moment, then she folded the map briskly and slipped it into a pocket of her backpack. "Anything else you want from here?" she asked.

Asa looked around the room helplessly. *Everything. I want everything from here.*

"No," he said. "Nothing." He cleared his throat. "The cars are a pretty short walk from here. We'll have to take one and just bring it back when we can. It should get us through the Waste, and the river ... there's got to be a way across, maybe a bridge. That's an old map. It wouldn't show everything."

"Okay, then." Eve got up and slung her backpack onto her back. "Let's get a car."

✦

"This is it?" Eve asked, surveying the charging station as if another car might pop into existence.

"It's not a big community," Asa said, slightly insulted. "There are usually five. The other ones must be in use."

Eve walked in a circle around the two remaining cars, an anxious look on her face.

"What?" Asa asked. "I know they're old, but they're all in good shape. It doesn't matter which one we take."

"It's not that," Eve said. "They're plug-ins! Asa, doesn't the community have solar cars?"

"Yeah, of course . . ." He surveyed the station quickly. "But these aren't them." He joined her beside the nearest car and peered in the window. "This one's fully charged," he said. "It'll get us about five hundred miles. That should be enough, right?"

Eve leaned back against the car and put her hands over her face. She sighed, then let her arms fall to her sides. "That map didn't show distances. It might be enough. It might get us there but not back. Or it might leave us stranded in the middle of the Waste."

"We could wait for one of the solar cars to come back," Asa said doubtfully.

"How long will that take?"

"Hours. Days. Minutes. I don't know. People don't use cars when they're going somewhere nearby."

"We can't risk it."

Eve took off her backpack and got something out, a flat black device with a few wires sticking out of it. She dropped to her knees and ducked her head under the car, just behind the front wheel, then came back out and lay flat on her back.

"What are you doing?" Asa asked as her upper body disappeared under the car. He averted his eyes as her short dress rode up even higher on her thighs.

"Disabling the tracker," she said, her voice muffled.

Asa waited a moment, then went around to the back and opened the trunk, checking the emergency supplies. When he was satisfied that everything was in place, he added their bags. As he closed the trunk, Eve wriggled back out from under the car, her forehead streaked with wheel grease. Asa smiled.

"What?" she asked.

"Nothing. You've got . . ." He gestured.

"Oh. Thanks." She grabbed a rag and wiped her face clean, bending over to use the side mirror of the car.

"I checked the emergency supplies," he said as she scrubbed at the grease. "We've got five gallons of water and a portable purifier, a week of rations—but that's for four people, so we can stretch it longer—blankets, stuff like that."

Eve nodded, but he couldn't tell if she had been listening. "Come on, get in," she said, opening the driver's side door.

"Wait, you spent most of your life in Horizon. Have you ever driven a car?" Asa asked.

"I'll figure it out," she said shortly.

"Eve, I know how to drive," he said, perplexed.

She stopped moving. "Right," she said. "Of course." She kept her hand on the door handle.

Asa frowned, then understanding dawned.

"You're not alone in this," he said. "Let me help."

She looked at him fixedly, her expression blank, and then she stepped away from the car and nodded. "You drive," she said. As she passed him, she paused, grasping his shoulder for a moment. "Thanks," she whispered.

He nodded, and they got into the car. Asa let the scanner read his face, then started the car, pulled out into the road, and drove the other way out of town.

"I've never gone this way," he said.

"How come?"

"I don't know, I just never had a reason to." Now it seemed odd that there was a path so close to home that he had never even tried to follow. "There's nothing that way but the mountains, I guess," he added, justifying his lack of curiosity.

He glanced at Eve. She had unfolded the map on her lap and was scrutinizing it.

"The mountains, then the river," she said quietly.

"Then the wall, then the Waste," he finished. "I know."

They drove in silence.

The road narrowed as they approached the mountain range until it was scarcely wide enough for a single car, and the woods thickened around them. The mountains had always been part of the background of Asa's life, but they were only scenery. They were beautiful, but no one he knew went to them. Slowly, the road began to climb, and Asa could see that it would wind back and forth among the mountains, climbing only the lowest points.

"What is it?" Eve asked, and he glanced at her, embarrassed.

"I kind of thought we'd have to go up one side of the mountain and down the other," he admitted, and she laughed. "Hey!" he protested. "I've never done this before."

She shook her head. "I was thinking the same thing," she said, smiling. "You mean we're just going to go around?"

"I mean, around, over, through—it's a tricky road. But yeah, it's easier than I imagined." He grinned at her, feeling as though some of the tension had broken.

Eve settled back in her seat, looking out the window. "Do you think it's true, that they just let you out into the Waste?" she asked after a moment.

Asa hesitated.

"I don't see why not," he said at last. "The way I always heard it was, if you don't want to be part of the Founders' plan for us, no one can make you. It's only fair for people to be able to leave if they want."

"It's just getting back in they don't allow," Eve said darkly.

"Well, that makes sense too," Asa said. "You can't have people just coming and going, abandoning their communities and then wanting to be welcomed back. It would cause instability. Plus, the Waste changes people—it's dangerous out there, violent. You know what it's like."

"Do I?" Eve murmured.

Asa glanced at her nervously, but she was staring out the window. He fixed his eyes on the road again, winding through the mountains.

✦

It took less time than Asa had expected to cross the mountains. The sun had not yet set when the road began to straighten out, and they emerged into the lush forest again. Eve was curled up against the window, asleep, her hair covering most of her face. The trees thinned out as he drove on, and as he rounded a curve, the river came into view. He pulled off to the side of the road and stopped.

"Eve," he whispered.

She didn't respond, and he reached out and tapped her on the shoulder. She straightened up slowly, pushing her hair back.

"Where are we?" she asked sleepily.

Asa pointed. She looked; then without a word, she got out of the car and walked toward the water. He hurried to follow her.

Eve stopped a few feet from the riverbank. They were standing at least five feet above the water, but the river was nothing like the one outside Rosewood. Now that they were outside the car, it roared; the sound was overpowering. The water rushed so fast it looked white, cresting and splashing against rocks at a violent speed.

"Is this what you fell into?" Eve asked him, grasping his hand as he came up beside her.

"No. That one was . . . slower. Smaller."

Eve took a step closer, and he held on to her hand, not moving.

"Eve, you're making me nervous," he said. She turned away from the water and came back to him.

"Sorry," she said. "It's mesmerizing."

"Yeah."

"We have to go."

"I'm not the one who got out of the car," she laughed.

It was only a few more minutes before the bridge loomed into view, a sturdy gray metal structure twice as wide as the road itself. Asa paused on the brink of it.

"Ready?" he asked.

"Ready," she said with a quick, firm nod.

Asa sped across the bridge, looking straight ahead. Once on the other side, he let out a long breath; Eve did the same and grinned at him.

"You were holding your breath too?" she said.

He shrugged. "Superstition. Look."

He pointed ahead. Through the woods, the wall was just visible, the color of sand, rising taller than the trees themselves.

"The edge of the world," Eve said, echoing his own thoughts. He nodded curtly and drove on, his stomach fluttering nervously.

The road began to follow the wall, running alongside it close enough that they could see the large bricks of its construction. Eve had pulled her backpack up onto her lap again, and she was fiddling with something in her right hand, too small for Asa to see what it was. He looked back at the road, staring straight at the pavement ahead.

"There!" Eve said, and he jerked his eyes up, racing to a stop just in time.

The road forked, one path continuing straight ahead, the other turning sharply to the right. Asa started the car again, guiding it to the right. Ahead of them, the wall broke; there was a gap as wide as the narrow road, which appeared to simply continue through to the other side.

Asa slowed to a crawl. "I thought it was a checkpoint. Shouldn't there be someone . . . checking?"

"I don't know," she said. "There's probably a drone or two hanging around, concealed. Maybe that's all they need."

"Maybe." They looked at each other. Eve's face was tight; Asa was sure his own expression mirrored hers. "Are you ready?" he asked.

She shook her head, then took a deep breath and held out her hand. "Are you?"

"I'm ready," he said and clasped her hand.

"Me too," she said.

"Okay, then." Asa forced himself to smile.

He tightened his grip on Eve's hand, and they drove toward the gap.

CHAPTER TEN

THE SCREENS WENT BLANK AS JOAN ENTERED the viewing booth. This time Gabriel didn't reactivate the clip.

"Are we ready to go?" he asked, standing.

"I wasn't able to requisition the passenger drone," Joan said, her voice a little too loud for the space.

He turned. "Why not?"

"We have to go before the Bureaucrats," she said. She sounded challenging, as if she thought he was going to argue with her.

"Why?"

She shook her head, her posture relaxing a little. "I don't know. The autom told me I didn't have authorization. Then I got a message for us both to report to Hiram."

"Hiram?" Gabriel raised his eyebrows. "What did you input? They've already got a head start. If we don't leave now we could lose them altogether."

Joan spread her hands in a helpless gesture. "I input the facts," she said. "I don't know why Hiram's getting involved."

"Well, he'd better make it quick," Gabriel said darkly. "Come on."

The Bureaucratic Authority was spread through all of the municipal buildings, but they had to walk a few blocks to get to Municipal 3, where the office of the Penultimate Authority for Contract Enforcement, Hiram Ward, was located. As they approached the building, Joan glanced nervously at Gabriel.

"I hate talking to the burrs," she said in a low voice.

He laughed curtly. "Well, not calling them that will help."

She blushed faintly—she had probably not intended to use the common slang for the Bureaucrats in front of him.

"It probably has to do with Daniel," Gabriel said. "There are bound to be other threads tangled up with his death. We'll need to be briefed."

They went the rest of the way in silence. As they approached Hiram Ward's office, the door was already open, waiting for them ominously. Gabriel squared his shoulders and knocked on the frame.

"Come in," Hiram said.

They entered. Hiram Ward was a small, wiry Panafrican man with dark skin and extremely short hair who always looked like his clothes had just been ironed. He always seemed calm.

Gabriel had never met anyone who could remember him so much as raising his voice. Rather, he wielded his power as Penultimate with a quiet yet inflexible certainty; anyone who tried to argue with him, once he had made up his mind, would exhaust themselves. He would patiently listen, his eyes kind and unyielding, then repeat his decision in precisely the same words. Most people gave up after a few rounds of it.

Hiram stood. "Gabriel. I haven't seen you since you returned. It's good to have you back."

"Thank you," Gabriel said, obviously uncomfortable.

"Naomi's passing was a great loss for the State." He shook his head, voice accented with regret.

"Yes." Gabriel waited.

Hiram sat down, motioning them to do the same, and Gabriel and Joan sat in the straight-backed chairs facing his desk. They were hard and uncomfortable. Gabriel knew the one Hiram sat in was identical. He thought it promoted good posture, which, at least in his case, it seemed to.

The rest of the office was severe as well: there were no decorations on the gray walls, only Hiram's large standard white desk in the middle of the room. A small personal monitor, a square about six inches across, faced his chair, and three distinct keypads were built into the desk's surface in front of it. Gabriel had seen the same desk in every Bureaucrat's office he'd ever been to: neat, visually pleasing, and yet somehow slightly inadequate.

"Do you remember Omar Ward?" Hiram said, gesturing to the wall on their left, where a video screen was located.

Gabriel nodded and addressed the man on the screen. "Sir."

"Sir," Joan echoed, startled.

Omar Ward was the Ultimate Authority for Contract Enforcement, the only person, save the Chancellor, above Hiram in the hierarchy. Gabriel had met him only a few times before. He was a hefty man who had to be nearing sixty, though it would have been outrageous to speculate. He was completely bald, and his skin seemed to be perpetually sunburned, brightening his stern features.

"Gabriel," Omar said. "Please consider Hiram's words a reflection of my own sentiments."

135

"Thank you, sir."

"Continue, Hiram," Omar said, settling in to watch.

Gabriel glanced at Joan, who looked anxious. She was probably right to be. It wasn't often that Omar felt it necessary to sit in on routine meetings.

"Gabriel, why do you want to requisition a drone?" Hiram asked with what sounded like genuine interest.

"As you know, Daniel James Horizon has been murdered," Gabriel began.

"No," Hiram said before he could go on.

"You didn't know? I'm sorry, I thought Joan . . . I mean, I thought we'd completed the filing."

"Yes, Joan did complete the filing, and I'm well aware of the death. But I'm concerned that you're so certain he was murdered."

Gabriel was astonished. He searched for words. "I saw it happen," he said at last. "I don't know what else there is to say."

Hiram smiled. "Gabriel, we both know how unreliable witness testimony can be," he said gently.

"What?"

"You saw it happen in the moment. That makes you a witness—you were having all the reactions we know witnesses to have: you were shocked, and at that moment your brain was trying to explain something terrible. What you saw cannot be relied upon, unless additional evidence exists."

"I . . ." At a loss, Gabriel glanced at Joan, and she felt startled, as if just realizing that she, too, was allowed to speak.

"I saw it too, sir."

"It's a drone feed, sir—there's video," Gabriel hastened to add. "I've watched it a dozen times. Asa Isaac Rosewood pushed Daniel out of that window."

Hiram was nodding. "Yes, I understand that."

136

"So, you see why we need to hurry."

"I see why you feel this way."

"Sir?" Gabriel realized he was clenching a fist, and he pulled it behind his back, slowly easing his hand open.

"You have been watching and rewatching the video of an event you have already interpreted. Each viewing reinforces your original impression."

"That's textbook," Joan said under her breath. Hiram cast an amused eye at her but said nothing. Instead he turned back to Gabriel.

"I know you are accustomed to having free rein," he said, looking into Gabriel's eyes for an uncomfortably long moment. "We have always trusted you implicitly. But this is different. In this case, you are a witness to a violent death, and you must admit that even you are human. And after what you've been through, it must be said that your reaction to violent death cannot be fully—"

"Fine," Gabriel said, struggling to keep an even tone.

Hiram showed no reaction to being interrupted.

That's the problem with Hiram. He's so calm, he makes everyone else want to blow up. Gabriel clenched his fists, then relaxed them slowly, breathing out. "Why don't we all watch the video together?" he suggested when he could speak with composure, and Hiram nodded.

"I think that's an excellent idea," he said.

A slim monitor the size of his personal screen slid out of the right side of the desk and swiveled to face Joan and Gabriel.

"Can everyone see?" he asked. "Omar, can you see this on your end?" Omar nodded, and Hiram started the feed.

Gabriel waited as the drone feed started, with the fuzzy blue and red of the life-sign capture. It went blank, then flipped back on and abruptly switched to the image of Daniel, balanced for a moment in the open window, then falling forward and vanishing from view, revealing Asa and Eve behind him. Hiram stopped the feed, and the screen froze.

"Do you have image-capture footage of the moments before he fell?" he asked.

"No," Gabriel said shortly. "Daniel had all but three drones in the vicinity blocked. This was the only one present." He cursed Daniel—and himself—silently, but Hiram only nodded. "You can see it even from this feed," Gabriel said steadily. "They're right behind him. You can see his body lurch forward at the last second. He was pushed."

"I disagree," Hiram said.

Gabriel stood, throwing his hands up in frustration. "Then what do you think happened?" He took a deep breath, pulling his temper back into check. "I'm sorry. I don't understand what else you could possibly have seen."

"I saw a man fall from a window," Hiram said.

"Yes." Gabriel bit off the word delicately. The man was maddening on the best of days, and now . . . "Sir, I don't mean to speak out of turn—"

"We're having a discussion," Hiram interrupted. "You are free to say what you wish."

"Thank you, sir. It's just, every second that we stay here *discussing* this, they're getting farther and farther away. We have to act now!"

"Gabriel," Hiram said. "Please sit." Gabriel took a deep breath and obeyed. "Thank you. As tragic as all of this is, the man is already dead. Speed will not return his life."

"But . . ."

Hiram held up a hand, and Gabriel fell silent again. "I can

only guess how you must feel. It's terrible that this is the case you've returned to, and if you would like, I can assign a different team to it."

"I can handle it," Gabriel said, suddenly alert. *He could take me off the street if I screw this up, stick me behind a desk.* It was the first time the possibility had occurred to him.

"Hiram," he argued, "this is what I do, it's what I was . . . what I was *created* for."

Hiram nodded. "Yes, I know. We all were."

"Of course, sir," Gabriel said hastily, rebuked.

However out of touch with the stalkers on the street the Bureaucrats might seem, everyone in the Contract Enforcement Authority had been raised in the Wards, inculcated from childhood into their service to the State. Gabriel was exceptionally good, but he was not unique. Hiram did not appear offended, however.

"I will tell you why I'm concerned, Gabriel. I'm not making assumptions because of what happened to Naomi, although her death will no doubt affect your judgement, just as all our experiences affect our judgement. I am talking only about what you witnessed here. I told you I saw a man fall from a window. I wasn't being glib: that is what I saw. I did see the young man behind him, but he could just as easily have been reaching out to save Daniel's life."

"No," Gabriel said. "He wasn't."

"Do you have evidence of that?"

"We detained both of them the night before last," Joan jumped in, and Gabriel looked to her, surprised to be almost grateful for her presence. "They were fighting in a nightbar."

"What was the fight about?"

"We don't know for sure," Gabriel said.

"They both said it was about the woman, Eve," Joan said. "They seem to have no other connection."

Gabriel gave her a sidelong glance, then caught himself. *She's only telling them the truth. She should be telling them the truth. Our only allegiance is to the State, and the State's allegiance is to all of us. We are all in this together.*

"She's right," Gabriel admitted. "They don't seem to have any other connection."

"Joan, what did you think of the video? Did it appear that Daniel was pushed?"

Joan glanced at Gabriel, who nodded. "I ... don't know. I thought when I saw it that he was pushed, but ... now I don't see enough evidence to reach a reliable conclusion," she said, the last words coming out in a rush.

"All right," Hiram said. "What else, then, Gabriel?"

"Can you continue the video?" Gabriel asked.

Hiram started the feed again, and they waited as the drone hovered over Daniel's body until Eve appeared. Gabriel looked away, instead staring at Hiram intently as Eve sobbed over Daniel's corpse and then searched his pockets.

"Does that look like the action of an innocent woman?" he demanded when Hiram stopped the video.

"It's still circumstantial," Hiram said placidly. "I can't allow you to hound our citizens without conclusive evidence."

Gabriel stood and turned away, pressing his hands over his face.

Breathe.

"Look, I understand that all of us were created for this," he said. "But you know as well as I do that there is a *reason* I am accustomed to free rein. There is a *reason* you have always trusted me implicitly! My record is impeccable, and the fact of my partner's murder is not my fault." He stopped for a moment, so tense he was nearly shaking.

"It is precisely this lack of emotional detachment that I am concerned about. You're obviously distraught," Hiram said mildly.

Gabriel clenched his fists again, then let them go.

Breathe.

"I am emotionally detached from this case. But we aren't even talking about this case. We're talking about my fitness for my . . . my own *life*. I'm not distraught. I am *frustrated* by the fact that I am being judged not on my record as a Contract Enforcer but for the death of the woman I loved!"

Hiram opened his mouth to speak, but Gabriel pressed on.

"I mastered sifting when I was a child. When the other kids were sorting out shapes, I was sorting through the subtext of human interaction. I was given my commission as a Contract Enforcer at the age of nineteen, with an exemption granted for my youth by the Chancellor himself. No decision of mine has ever been found wanting. My actions have been scrutinized over and over again and each time found to be exemplary." He turned on Joan. "That textbook you're so cozy with was rewritten five years ago. Do you know why?"

She shook her head, wide-eyed, and he turned to Hiram.

"Do you?" he asked in a low voice.

Hiram nodded. "Yes, Gabriel," he said softly. "Of course I do. Joan, the textbook he is referring to is several books—it's the series on Practicalities: all the techniques, large and small, all the habits and practices of the ideal Contract Enforcer. It was rewritten because Gabriel so radically changed our view of what is ideal. He was—is—the model. For you and for all of us."

Joan looked from Hiram to Gabriel, then to Omar on the screen, who smiled at her.

"Gabriel, please do not think for a moment that you are any less our ideal Contract Enforcer than you ever were," Omar added. "You are exemplary, and I take personal pride in watching you."

"As do I," Hiram said.

"Thank you, sir . . . sirs," Gabriel said, his face flushed. He was wavering between righteous indignation and embarrassment, and the feeling was awkward. He sat down, oddly deflated.

"However," Hiram continued, "I cannot allow my own judgement to become clouded by my respect and affection for you, Gabriel. You do not have enough evidence to pursue this case in the manner you desire."

"But they'll get away!" Gabriel nearly leapt from his seat again but stopped himself, gripping the seat of the chair until his knuckles went white.

Hiram looked puzzled. "It's not as if we don't have jurisdiction in Rosewood," he said. "We'll go find them when you discover additional evidence that proves a crime has occurred."

Gabriel shook his head in frustration. *How can they not see this?* "The dead man is *Daniel James Horizon*," he said. "Suspected of running, or at least being deeply involved in . . ." he grasped for words. "*Everything* illicit that happens in the city and beyond. In supporting, or more likely controlling, the illegitimate black-market bank that supports the whole criminal underground."

A new alertness came over Hiram's face, and he exchanged a quick glance with Omar, who still watched silently on the monitor.

"Do you believe that Eve is involved?" Hiram asked. "I'm intimately familiar with Daniel's history and the suspicions around him. There's never been any whisper about Eve. It's actually somewhat surprising—he seems to have gone out of his way to keep her clear of his criminal activity."

"Do you really think that's plausible?" Gabriel asked.

"Even Daniel's involvement is impossible to prove," Hiram reminded him. "Everything is done through proxies, hidden beneath layers of secrecy. There is no reason he couldn't have kept her in the dark as well."

"By the same argument, he could have shared everything with her, and we wouldn't have a clue."

Hiram and Gabriel stared at each other; Gabriel was the first to break.

"Look, check their phones, see where they are now," he began.

"It's not warranted."

"It could prove their innocence! If they're—I don't know—at Municipal 2, reporting Daniel's death, I'll let this go right now."

Hiram glanced at Omar, who gave a curt nod. He typed instructions quickly, and they all waited as he looked patiently at the screen only he could see.

"They appear to be in Daniel's apartment," Hiram said.

He started typing again.

"Check the—"

"The drones? Yes, thank you, Gabriel." An edge of sarcasm had slipped into Hiram's voice. Gabriel fell silent. After a moment Hiram looked up. "No life signs in the apartment."

"If she's been in on Daniel's activities, she could be the key to dismantling the underground banking system," Gabriel said tightly. "And if I don't go now, she could vanish. Daniel's organization could hide her. If she doesn't know anything and Daniel committed suicide, why are they running? They could even go out into the Waste."

Hiram looked at him sharply. "If they do, it's no longer our problem," he said.

"No, sir, it's not."

"I mean these words, Gabriel. If they go out into the Waste, they can't return—they are no longer a threat to the State, no longer within your jurisdiction."

"I understand, sir," Gabriel said quietly.

Hiram paused for a moment, then looked back to his superior with a thoughtful gaze.

Omar cleared his throat. "Hiram. He's been our best Contract Enforcer for fifteen years. The best we've ever had. If we can't trust him, the whole damn system is broken. Give him the passenger drone."

Hiram nodded. "I agree." He met Gabriel's eyes. "Move quickly."

✦

The drone made no sound as it flew in a straight line toward Rosewood. Joan kept looking around nervously, as if she was afraid they might fall out of the sky.

"Ever flown before?" Gabriel asked finally, hoping to distract her.

She snapped to attention. "Of course. During training." She glanced outside again. "Only once, though."

"It takes getting used to," Gabriel said.

For him, though, it hadn't. As soon as he'd climbed into the round belly of a passenger drone, he'd felt an instant thrill. The drones were essentially transparent bubbles. Only the floor was opaque, covered in gray rubber. Gabriel had read they were originally clear everywhere, so you could see through the floor, but the effect of looking down from thousands of feet in the air made too many people sick.

Joan looked down again. They were flying over the community

of Fairfield, high enough to make the people on the ground look like ants.

"It's odd people can't see us," she said.

"Passenger drones are always cloaked," Gabriel said. "People are used to the small ones, but these larger models would cause unnecessary stress to the public."

"I know—hence my comment," she said. "It just seems . . . strange. That's all."

He shrugged. "So stop looking down. Start focusing on how we're going to find these runners."

It was midafternoon when they arrived.

They touched down in an open field far enough away so they wouldn't be spotted. Gabriel would have preferred to land directly in front of the house, which usually intimidated subjects. Instead, they walked for five minutes through a glade before the quaint little farm came into view. As they approached the house, Gabriel saw a curtain twitch in the front window.

"They're expecting us," he said.

Joan nodded. "Good," she said. "That means they know some-thing."

The door swung open as soon as Joan knocked on it. A woman stood in the entryway, her face flushed.

"Yes?" she said, her eyes flicking from Joan to Gabriel and back again.

"Contract Enforcement. I'm Gabriel," he said. *She's frightened. Be kind. She'll tell you more if you're nice.* "This is my partner, Joan. We're here to ask you some questions about Asa. Your son."

"Yes, I know." She cleared her throat. "Come in."

She held the door open for them to enter. Gabriel glanced around, scanning the room, but there was nothing of obvious interest. Joan was doing the same but more slowly, more carefully.

They're not here, he wanted to say. *The mother's almost calm. They've got to be gone already.*

Asa's mother led them into the kitchen, where a burly man and a teenage girl were already sitting at a plain wooden table. The girl was playing nervously with her hair, twisting it around one finger repeatedly. The man had his hands folded on the table in front of him, his elbows resting on the edge. The man gave Gabriel a hard stare as he walked in, and Gabriel met his eyes, holding his gaze until he looked away.

"How can we help you?" the man said as the wife came to sit beside him.

"You're the family of Asa Isaac Rosewood," Joan said. There was a new, hard edge to her voice. "Isaac Thomas Rosewood, father. Sarah Anna Rosewood, mother. Hannah Sarah Rosewood, the younger sister." She recited their names as impersonally as a census autom.

"Yes, that's correct," Isaac said quietly.

"Do you know why we're here?" Gabriel said.

"We do."

"So where is Asa?" Joan asked in the same, near-robotic tone. Gabriel looked at her with interest. It was not a technique she'd been taught in training, and he wasn't sure what to think of it.

"We don't know," Sarah said quickly. "He refused to tell us anything."

"And why was that?" Gabriel asked.

"So we couldn't tell you. So you'd leave us alone." The sister, Hannah, stared at him defiantly.

Gabriel suppressed a smile. "That was unwise of him," he said, letting the warmth drain from his eyes as his expression hardened. He leaned over the table until he was only a few inches from Hannah's face. From the corner of his eye, he saw Sarah begin to move toward the table. Isaac put a hand on her arm, restraining her. "It was unwise for your brother to keep information from you. I need information, and it will be better for everyone if I get it now."

Something smacked the table, rattling around under Gabriel's lean torso. He straightened.

Sarah was standing, shaking with rage, a heavy wooden spoon in her hand. "That's enough."

She rapped the spoon on the table again, and Isaac touched her arm a second time; he was still seated, his broad face impassive.

"Sarah, please remain calm," Isaac said softly.

She didn't respond, but she seemed to relax slightly at his touch. Gabriel watched the interaction with a pang of déjà vu he could not quite place. It wasn't a memory, just recognition.

When Naomi touched me, everything weighing on my shoulders lightened too.

He waited. Sarah slapped the spoon lightly into the palm of her hand, then wrapped her fingers around it tightly, holding the utensil in front of her as though she could shield herself with it.

"Asa came here late this morning," she said. "He said he was in trouble, and he couldn't tell us why. He didn't stay long."

"Was he alone?" Gabriel asked.

"Yes," she said.

"She's lying," Joan said. He glanced at her, having almost forgotten her presence.

"I know," he said mildly. *When I need your help, I'll ask for it,* he thought. "Sarah, tell me the truth, please. Who was with Asa?"

"A woman." Her lips went tight every time she stopped talking, as if she was physically trying to keep the words inside.

"Her name?"

"Neither of them said. I didn't ask."

Truth.

"What about you?" Gabriel turned to Hannah, who shrank back from his gaze. "Did she tell you her name? Did either of them say her name?" Hannah shook her head mutely. "What did she look like?"

Hannah swallowed. "She was beautiful," she managed to say.

Sarah broke in. "Please, leave my daughter alone. We will tell you everything we know."

"Actually, I need to know everything that you know and everything she knows as well."

"Then let me ask her the questions. Hannah, did Asa or his friend say anything to you about where they were going?"

"No," she whispered.

Gabriel nodded. *Truth, but not all of it.*

"What else did you talk about?" he demanded.

"Stalker!" Sarah hit the table again.

Gabriel made a point of waiting a beat before looking at her. "Are you challenging my authority to pursue these suspects?" he asked calmly.

She shook her head. "There's something else you need to know," she said. Gabriel raised an eyebrow, and she tapped the spoon against her palm, nervously this time. "Asa didn't just say that he was in trouble. He said, 'I didn't do anything, but it looks like I did.'"

"Do you believe that?"

"Yes, I do."

Truth.

Gabriel turned to Isaac. "Come with me. I need to speak with you outside," he said curtly. "Joan, the girl is hiding something. Please find out what it is."

He walked to the door, not looking back. As he opened it, he heard Isaac push his chair back from the table, murmuring something to his family. A moment later, he walked out of the house.

"What's this tactic?" Isaac demanded. "Separating us to see if our stories match?"

"No," Gabriel said. He walked toward the garden and stood at the neat break in the grass where it began. "Who does the planting?"

"We all do," Isaac answered. "Don't play games, stalker. Just ask me what you really want to know."

Gabriel smiled. "Not many people call us that name to our faces," he said, turning around with a sinister stare.

If Isaac found his face disturbing, he did not show it. "I like to call things how I see them," he said.

"Good," Gabriel said. "So, what time did your son leave?"

"I don't know."

Half-truth.

"Tell me the truth."

"That is the truth."

"Not quite."

"It's the truth," Isaac repeated, crossing his arms over his chest.

"I know it isn't everything you know."

"Do you think we're stupid out here in the country? That we believe those made-up rumors that stalkers can tell if you're lying? I'm telling you the truth."

Gabriel smiled again. "I had no idea that was a rumor. So, tell me where Asa is going."

"I don't know."

Truth? But he has some idea.

"Is he going into the Waste?" Gabriel stared intently at Isaac's face; his expression was enough to answer the question.

Gabriel nodded. "Thank you."

"I didn't say anything. I told you, I don't know where he's going!"

"You've been very helpful," Gabriel said curtly, walking back into the house with a newfound energy.

"I said I don't know anything!" Isaac yelled, rushing in behind him. Joan stood to attention quickly as Gabriel entered the kitchen.

"Time to go," he said.

She nodded, and they started toward the front door.

"Wait, what's going to happen to Asa?" Sarah shouted, scurrying behind them.

Gabriel caught Joan's eye with a quick shake of his head. When they reached the door, he turned to face the family. Hannah's eyes were red, and Sarah looked as if she might snap her wooden spoon.

Without emotion, Gabriel said, "Asa and his companion have gone into the Waste. Thank you for your time."

For a shocked moment, none of them spoke, then the family collapsed in on itself, clinging together in disbelief.

"No, he hasn't!" Hannah screamed, her voice raw, and she began to sob, the choked noise of her grief wracking the quiet countryside as her parents clutched her between them. Gabriel and Joan turned away and started walking back the way they'd come.

"Is that true?" Joan asked as soon as they were out of earshot.

"I believe so. It's definitely where the father thinks they were going."

"Well, do you want to know what the sister was hiding?"

"Yes, please."

"Asa told her he would be coming back."

"He was lying to her. Giving her comfort."

"I don't think so," Joan said.

"Why?"

"He said he was going to 'fix it'—whatever trouble he was in, he was going to fix it."

"Not unless he can bring a man back to life," Gabriel said grimly.

They walked the rest of the way in silence.

"It's probably too late to catch them at the checkpoint," Gabriel said when they reached the drone. "So we'll follow their route with the assumption they're already in the Waste. It'll be harder to follow their trail once we're out there, but it can be done. Joan, come on."

Joan stopped, still standing in the middle of the field where they'd landed. She was looking at him as if she'd seen a ghost.

"Joan?" he said.

"We can't go into the Waste," she said. "I can't believe you're even suggesting that."

"At this point they're barely over the border," Gabriel argued. "We'll pick them up before they've gone a few miles."

"Gabriel, they're no longer our problem," Joan said. She set her jaw, nervously resolute.

"Eve could hold the key to bringing down the entire black market. And Asa is a *murderer*."

"Gabriel!" Joan looked shocked. "Are you listening to yourself? If they've gone into the Waste, they can never come back. You heard Hiram. We don't serve our purpose with the State by chasing them out there."

"I disagree." Gabriel shook his head. "He killed someone and she's a criminal lowlife. We can't just let them go."

"No one survives long in the Waste. You know that."

"But that's not justice."

"Our allegiance is not to justice—it's to the State. If the State says we can't keep going, then we shouldn't. They are no longer a danger to law-abiding citizens. Gabriel, if we go into the Waste, *we* can never come back!" Joan spread her hands in a helpless gesture. "I can't stop you," she said quietly. "But I won't go with you."

Gabriel sighed. Joan was outraged, her face tight and eyes wide.

"Then I won't ask you to," he said with a hint of kindness. "Will you be okay taking the drone back yourself?"

"Of course. All I have to do is press a button and sit there. But, Gabriel—"

"I'm going," he interrupted. "You won't change my mind. Just leave."

"I'm sorry, I just can't . . ."

"I should never have assumed that you would," he said shortly. He looked at her appraisingly. "You're good at this, Joan. Someday, you'll be great."

She swallowed, looking away. "Thanks."

Joan sighed and walked with purpose toward the drone. He pressed a button, and the door slid open for her. She got inside and keyed in the course back to Horizon but didn't close the door.

"You know how to start it?" Gabriel asked.

"Yes," she said flatly, meeting his eyes. "What am I supposed to tell Hiram?" she asked, a pleading note in her voice.

Gabriel smiled wretchedly. Joan bit her lip.

"Tell him I'm doing exactly what they taught me to do."

Before she could respond, he hit the close door button and stepped away from the drone, watching as it sealed itself. It lifted into the air without a sound as Joan gazed down at him, unanswered questions written across her face.

✦

Gabriel stopped the car he'd taken from the Rosewood garage and got out. He'd come to the last fork in the road—the bridge and checkpoint stood to his right, and the road continued straight ahead, running alongside the river. At the bend in the road, there was a streak of black on the pavement, and he knelt beside it and pressed his finger there.

Someone swerved—going too fast, unfamiliar with the road, almost missed the turn. Gabriel turned in a circle, taking a last look at the silent forest. *Into the Waste, then.*

He got back into the car.

Crossing into the Waste was anticlimactic. He had expected some kind of scan, perhaps, or at least to be given a final warning, but Gabriel simply drove across the bridge, through the gap in the wall, and out on the other side.

The terrain was the same, for a little while at least—a lush forest, broken only by the increasingly ill-paved road. As he drove on, though, the trees grew farther apart; the dirt becoming cracked and parched. Small scrubby bushes appeared, low to the ground with only a thin covering of leaves.

It's a little like traveling through time, Gabriel thought.

Asa and Eve had done little to cover their tracks—or perhaps they were unaware of just how much evidence they left behind. The paved road narrowed, then turned to dirt, and Gabriel spotted a clutch of broken branches where their car had swerved too close to a low-lying bush. As he left the last of the trees behind, the road vanished altogether into the arid landscape, and Gabriel stopped the car again and got out.

Before him lay a vast emptiness—more open space than he had ever seen, stretching into what looked like forever. The sun was sinking in the sky, streaking it gold and pink, and the air in his lungs was cold and dry. A little breeze scuffed up dust around his ankles, and far off in the distance, silhouetted by the setting sun, a jagged horizon hinted at mountains. Gabriel inhaled deeply, taking in the unaccustomed air, and felt a sudden, aching hollowness in his chest.

How can I be here to see this when you are not?

He closed his eyes, and for a moment he could feel her in his arms, the warmth of her body soft beside him. Longing jolted through him, and he gasped at the shock of it, covering his face with his hands.

Stop. Focus.

He suddenly opened his eyes, casting them in every direction for a sign of where his quarry had run. It took only moments— deep tire tracks showed their route, scored into the scorched earth like a beacon for him to follow.

Runners always leave a trail. Gabriel drove on.

CHAPTER ELEVEN

ASA'S FINGERS WERE BEGINNING TO CRAMP. He took one hand off the wheel and flexed it. Eve gave him a nervous look.

"What's wrong?" she asked. Her voice was tense; for the last hour she had been staring straight ahead, her lips pressed into a straight line.

Asa forced a smile, switching hands. "Nothing. Just holding on too tight," he said, but she was staring again, as if she'd forgotten the question as soon as she'd asked it. "Eve?" he prodded gently, and she looked out the window, away from him.

"It's like everything out here is dead," she said quietly.

Asa didn't reply. He had been trying not to think the same thing, gazing ahead as the forest vanished around them, giving way to this dry, cracked earth. The few plants around them were strangely shaped and low to the ground, as if the air itself weighed on them. From time to time, small creatures darted by, too fast for him to see what they were or whether they resembled animals he had seen before.

"Nothing is dead," Asa said firmly. "It's just a desert. There's a microclimate in the plaza in Horizon. I remember it."

Eve smiled weakly, then straightened her posture and gave him a sharp look. "I haven't been paying attention," she said. "How much time have we got?"

"Depends," Asa said grimly. "The car's eating up charge slower since the ground flattened out, but I'd say less than an hour."

Eve nodded, expressionless.

"I guess I assumed there would be . . . something out here," he went on. "People. A town. *Something* by now."

"Maybe there's nothing," Eve said. "Maybe everyone out here really is dead. Maybe all those stories about the Waste are made up. Maybe everyone just dies."

Asa laughed suddenly, caught by surprise.

"What?" Eve asked, looking annoyed.

"I don't know," he said. "You know, all I ever wanted was to get away from Rosewood and have some excitement. Now we're on the run, out in the Waste. I'm with the most beautiful girl I've ever met. And I feel like the world is ending." His heart sank, the brief moment of ironic mirth passing quickly. "I guess it's not that funny," he finished quietly.

Eve was smiling.

"What?" he said.

"You said I was beautiful."

Asa felt himself blush, but he kept his eyes fixed on the desert ahead. "I can't be the first person to mention it," he said stiffly.

"Stop!" Eve shouted, and he braked reflexively. The car jerked to a halt, and Asa's stomach lurched.

"What happened?"

"Sorry," Eve said breathlessly. "Look."

She gestured to her own window, and Asa leaned across the seat to look. In the distance lay a flat rectangular block, too neat to be a rock formation.

"It's a building," Asa said, hearing the doubt in his own voice.

"It has to be," Eve said firmly. "And where there's a building, there are people."

"Yeah, but what kind of people?"

Asa met Eve's eyes, looking for reassurance. They were tossing hope back and forth between them, each one holding on until overcome with fear again.

Eve gave him a quick smile. "I don't know. But you're out here, and I'm out here. Maybe the rest of the people out here are more like us than we think."

Asa shook his head. "No one survives out here but wasters— violent, antisocial criminals," he said with more vehemence than he had intended. Eve's face froze. "I'm sorry. I'm sorry, Eve, I didn't mean your brother." He scrambled to apologize, and she raised an eyebrow.

"Look, it doesn't matter who's out here," he said. "There's two of us. And we've got to charge the car or find another way to get across the Waste. We've got to go there." He nodded decisively and moved to start the car again.

"Actually, I don't think we do," Eve said slowly.

She was looking out the window again, and Asa followed her gaze. Something was moving toward them. He squinted and saw that it was a small group of people rapidly approaching from the direction of the building. They were running, and as they neared the car, Asa could see there were six of them, four men and two women.

Eve touched his arm. "Do you think we should get out?" she asked softly, and Asa hesitated.

"No," he said. "Not yet."

The group slowed to a walk, one man taking up the lead as the others fell back. Asa took them all in, aware that he was staring openly but unable to stop. The one who seemed to be the leader and one of the women were Panafrican. The three other men were dark-skinned, without markers for any one ethnicity. Only one of the women was Europan like Asa, her hair bleached pale white and her skin pink from the desert sun.

It was precisely the opposite mix of people that he was accustomed to, at least back in Rosewood. The strangers were all dressed in lightweight clothing—sleeveless shirts and long dark pants—except for the Panafrican woman, who was wearing pink shorts with ragged hems. All of them were muscular and hollow-cheeked, and they all had long black objects in their hands.

The group stopped, and the leader stepped forward alone, bending forward to see into the car. His eyes were dark brown and long-lashed, slightly incongruous with his sharply angular face and day-old beard. Asa shrank back instinctively, then steeled himself, straightening his spine.

The man came around to his door and stopped, hefting the stick in his hands as if he was testing its weight. Up close, Asa could see that it was not a stick but an oddly shaped object made of hard plastic, ending in a long tube. The man was holding it as if it were important. He bent over again and looked curiously at Asa, narrowing his eyes, then straightened and rapped the window with the butt of the object. Asa jumped. Beside him, he heard Eve's sharp intake of breath.

The man hit the window again, and Eve put a hand on his arm.

"They want us to get out," she said.

"Yeah, I got that." He glanced at her. "Wait here. Let me get out first," he said, summoning courage.

She nodded. "Okay."

Before he could respond, she opened the door and was out of the car. Asa rushed to follow her, shielding his eyes as he stepped out into the afternoon sunlight.

"Hi?" he said.

The leader flicked his eyes up and down, appraising. "Turn around," he said. "Lilith, search the girl."

The woman in the pink shorts stepped forward and took hold of Eve's shoulders. "Face the car," she said.

"Hey!" Asa protested, too late.

"Asa, it's okay," Eve called as Lilith began to methodically pat her body.

"You too," the leader said.

Asa complied warily, his face flushing as the stranger frisked him thoroughly, checking all of his clothing until there was no doubt that he wasn't hiding anything.

When the man stepped back, Asa spun around. "Look, we didn't do anything wrong!" he said, barely restraining himself from shouting.

The man didn't blink, turning to his cohort as if Asa had not spoken. "Aquila and Simon, search the car and drive it back."

The second woman strode forward, followed by a short, slim man. Forgetting himself for a moment, Asa stared at the man called Simon. His head was bald, and his face was half-hidden by a bushy gray beard, but there was no mistaking it from his face: he was old—far older than sixty, his skin wrinkled and thin as tissue paper.

Asa tried catching Eve's eye, but she was biting her lip, anxiously watching Aquila as she pulled a backpack out from under the passenger seat, slung it onto the car's hood, and unzipped it. Asa stiffened as she unpacked it, laying the contraband technology out on the hood carefully, as if she were decorating.

"That's yours?" the leader demanded, and Asa nodded.

"It's mine," Eve said.

"Cyrus, come look at this," Aquila said sharply.

The leader gave Asa a level look and signaled to Simon, who came trotting back from the trunk of the car, where he had been rooting through the emergency supplies.

"That's a nice water purifier," Simon said cheerfully.

Asa gave him a sidelong glance. "Thanks," he said.

His eyes fixed on Cyrus as he took the black rectangular thing Eve had packed out of Aquila's hands and examined it. He set it on the hood of the car and opened it.

The box, Asa thought, though he could not see inside.

Cyrus's face grew thoughtful. "It's ancient," he said to Aquila, again acting as if Eve and Asa were not present. "I don't even think we've got anything to scrap it for. The parts will be worthless."

"Ancient, yes," Aquila said patiently. "But who in there even has access to this kind of thing?"

She gave Eve a penetrating look. Eve stood her ground, staring back at her calmly.

"Are you with the State?" Aquila demanded.

"No, we're running from the State," Eve said.

"So, what's this?" Cyrus asked, closing the box.

"It's mine," Eve said. Cyrus and Aquila exchanged a glance.

"We have to take them back with us now," Cyrus said.

Asa kept his face carefully neutral. *Does that mean they were going to leave us here?*

Cyrus prodded Asa with the wide end of his stick and started walking. "Come on," he said shortly and gestured to the others.

Lilith touched Eve's arm, and Eve gave her a flat, deadly stare. But she complied as she was guided away from the car.

The two remaining members of the group took up the rear as they set off across the desert, heading toward the single building in the distance. Asa glanced back once; Simon and Aquila were patiently cataloging the last of his few possessions, laying his shirts out along the hood beside Eve's tech and the emergency rations, as if everything were of equal importance.

The walk took longer than Asa expected.

Cyrus strode ahead of him, and he kept his eyes on the man's feet, his heavy black boots kicking up the dust carelessly as they made their way through the arid heat. He glanced at Eve every few minutes; her expression was blank and immobile. She was staring at the back of Lilith's head as if she was trying to memorize it, and she never turned to look at Asa.

I've let you down, he thought.

✦

As they approached the building, Asa saw people outside; two men were shouting, talking over each other so that the argument was unintelligible. He glanced at Eve, who was still staring straight ahead, but she seemed to feel his eyes on her, because she turned her head for the first time since they had been accosted. She grinned quickly, but the smile did not touch her eyes.

"I'll kill you!" someone shouted, and Asa spun around, bracing himself.

The threat had not been directed at him. One of the men arguing lunged at the other, but before he could make contact, the second man reared back with a closed fist and punched him in the face. The first man stumbled back, then hurled himself at the other, knocking him to the ground. Something jabbed Asa in the back, and he jumped.

"Keep moving." The man behind him nudged him again with the wide end of the stick.

Cyrus was already at the wide metal door of the building, speaking with two large men who had been standing outside, either guarding the entrance or simply waiting.

"But . . ." Asa glanced around incredulously.

The two men were still fighting, struggling viciously in the dirt, and he could see that one was already bleeding from the nose. A woman and two men were standing a few feet away, shouting encouragement to one or the other—or both—while Cyrus and the others ignored the outburst. No one was rushing in to stop the fight. Asa looked to Eve, and he nodded toward their captors.

"Wasters," he said under his breath. "What do you expect?" But Eve still looked a little shaken.

"Come on." The butt of the stick jabbed him again, and Asa kept walking.

The hulking guard looked Asa up and down as they approached the door, then did the same to Eve. "The big man wants to see these two," he said.

"Big man?" Asa repeated.

Cyrus grinned for an instant, then his face turned stony again. "First among equals. He wants to see you," he said, starting forward, but one of the guards shook his head. "We already searched them," Cyrus said, but the guard eyed them skeptically.

"What about the girl?" he asked.

"I searched the woman," Lilith said, irritation in her voice. "They're clean. They had some tech on them but nothing dangerous."

"Anything's dangerous if you use it correctly," the guard muttered.

He stepped back, and his oversized companion heaved open the door. Asa and Eve stepped inside, flanked by their captors, and the door swung shut behind them immediately, closing with a loud bang and a rush of air.

The building was a single immense room, the ceiling high enough for a two-story house to fit under. It was empty except for two enormous rusting machines in the center; they looked a little like oversized tractors, though Asa knew that could not be their purpose.

Relics from the days before the Founding, he thought with a sudden jolt of excitement, and he nearly took a step toward them. Eve touched his arm, stopping him.

He heard a metal door creak open before he saw it—it was on the far side of the building, blocked by the machines. It clanked shut as three people strode briskly across the concrete floor, and Asa's stomach fluttered. *This has to be the third time today someone's going to decide whether or not to kill us.*

The small company passed between the machines, and as they emerged into the light, Eve screamed.

"Eve!" Asa shouted, reaching out for her, but she was already running. The new people were only ten feet away, and she crossed the distance in a blur. Before Asa could act, she flung herself at the man in the center, knocking him back, her arms wrapped around him. He pushed her away, grasping her shoulders and bending forward to peer at her face; then he gasped and pulled her to his chest. She clung to him as he stroked her hair, and in the vast, open space, Asa could hear the sound of her crying and the echo of the man's whispers, though he could not make out the words.

Finally, they separated, though Eve held on to his hand as if she were afraid to let go. She gazed up at him breathlessly, and Asa looked away.

First Daniel, now an outlaw—maybe she loves criminals, he thought.

"Saul," Eve said, and Asa jerked his head back up.

Saul. Suddenly, he saw the resemblance between them. It was unmistakable—Eve's brother looked just like her.

"Saul," Eve said again, "they told me you were dead ... I ..." Her expression changed, her eyes narrowing, and without warning, she hit him in the chest with an open hand. He jerked back, his eyes widening in surprise. "They said you were *dead!*" she repeated. "Did you know they told me that? You *jerk!*" she hit him again, as if for emphasis. "I thought you were dead. You were all I had, and you were *gone* ..." Eve hit her brother again, this time without conviction, and he pulled her close as she began to cry again.

"I'm sorry. Eve, I'm so sorry. It was for your protection," he said, and she lifted a hand off his chest and hit him again, this time lightly. She moved back from him and wiped her eyes.

"The next time someone lies to me for my own good, they're going to need protection," Eve said.

She smiled at Asa, and this time her face was radiant; she looked as if years of grief had been undone, and maybe they had. For the first time since Saul appeared, Asa took note of the rest of the group, who were all looking on warily, as if Eve were a snake who might bite at any moment. He eyed Lilith, who was standing closest to him.

"She's his sister," he explained quietly, and Lilith gasped.

"Eve?" she cried. Eve drew back, startled, and Asa watched the others as understanding dawned.

Saul laughed. "You're a legend out here, baby sister," he said and took her arm. "Come on, I'll show you our world."

Eve yanked her arm away. "No," she said evenly. "I want to know what happened first. You're going to tell me why I had to mourn your death while you were off playing in this sandbox."

"I thought you were happy to see me," Saul said, bewildered. "Now you're angry."

"I'm both. I'm complex," Eve snapped.

He frowned. "I don't understand—if you're here, Daniel must have told you everything."

"He didn't tell me anything. I didn't know you were alive until the moment I saw your face."

"What?" Saul stared at her for a second, then flicked his eyes to Asa. "Come downstairs," he said shortly.

He took Eve's arm again, and this time she did not protest as he started back across the cavernous room to where he had come from. Asa trailed behind them, flanked by the half-dozen guards.

The door opened to a dimly lit staircase. The steps were concrete, leading down in a squared spiral, turning every eight steps. Asa counted as they descended, keeping his hand on the thin metal railing. The stairs ended in a long, dark corridor, and Asa put his hand on the wall to guide himself as they traversed it, blinking in hope that his eyes would adjust.

Suddenly, light spilled out into the hall, and Asa realized Saul had opened a door and was ushering them through. He followed Eve, glancing back, but the rest of the group did not appear. They had vanished somewhere in the dark without his noticing. Saul shut the door, and Asa's heart skipped when he heard the click of a lock.

Maybe you can trust him, but can I? he wanted to ask her.

He watched her instead as she moved about the room, examining everything. There was a narrow bed with a thin mattress and a bookshelf that took up the whole of one wall. It was nearly filled with books, some so used their spines had worn away, the naked pages bound with rubber bands.

There were objects too—a little statuette of a cat and another of an enormously fat man, laughing; a little pile of shining silver tokens; a broken pot, painted bright blue; pieces of dark, flaky stone; and intricate metalworks that Asa peered at, uncertain whether they were made as art or for a different purpose. Eve picked up one thing after another, examining each with curiosity. Then she went to the desk on the opposite wall.

It was covered in strange things, the largest of which was a screen nearly the size of the ones on the trains. A second, smaller one stood beside it. There was a flat keyboard, a jumble of wires, and a small pile of objects that looked like the tech Eve had been carrying with her.

Asa looked at Saul, who was watching his sister with an expression of mild amusement, his hands in his pockets. He caught Asa's glance and cleared his throat.

"Eve," Saul said.

She ignored him and sat down in the desk chair, fiddling briefly with one of the wires before looking up. She sighed.

"Eve, tell me what's going on—"

"Daniel's dead," she said flatly, cutting him off.

"Oh." Saul cleared his throat. "What happened?" he asked, his voice sounding choked.

Eve picked up a small black box attached to a flat piece of green plastic by a dozen wires. "What's this?" she asked.

"Eve, tell me what happened to Daniel."

Saul sat heavily on the bed, and Asa shifted his feet, feeling suddenly obtrusive. He sat on the concrete floor, crossing his legs, and inched backward until he could lean against the wall.

"Ask him," Eve said with sudden hostility, jerking her chin at Asa.

Saul didn't look at him. "I'm not asking him, I'm asking you," he said patiently.

Asa smiled in spite of himself and ducked his head to hide it. *I hope I don't sound that patronizing to Hannah,* he thought. His smile faded. *I will see her again,* he vowed.

Eve was toying with the wires on the box. "Daniel killed himself," she said at last.

"Damn it," Saul said quietly. He leaned forward and clasped his hands, staring into nothing as he knotted his fingers together.

"You don't sound surprised," Asa said with a spark of hope.

Saul shook his head slowly, not looking up. "I'm not. He had nights . . . he always drank too much, and sometimes he talked like that. Once I stopped him from jumping off a bridge. We were walking home after a night out, and suddenly he was on the railing, talking about the abyss, teetering two hundred feet above the road. I jumped up and grabbed him, dragged him home, and let him sleep it off. But it was too close. After that, I was afraid it was only a matter of time. You can't talk someone out of doing something they really want to do. I figured one day he would get up on the bridge, and there would be no one there to stop him from jumping."

He sighed heavily. Eve looked stricken. Her hands froze on the wires as if she had forgotten how to move them.

"You don't think anyone could have stopped him?" she said, her voice sounding far away.

"No," Saul said. He looked up at her with a pained expression. "Eve, you couldn't have stopped him."

"He said he loved me with all the heart that he didn't have," she said, still as a statue.

"He always cared about you. It's why I trusted him to help you after I was gone. But, Eve, you were in no position—"

"He loved me." She shook her head slowly back and forth, the movement almost hypnotic. "I loved him too, but not like that. I tried. He gave me everything, but I wouldn't have his child, and I couldn't save his life."

"*What?*" Saul stood abruptly, his face red with rage. "His *child?*"

"He said he'd never had the procedure," Eve said, going back to the wires. She pulled one out of the box, then plugged it back in.

Asa got to his feet quietly, keeping his eyes on Saul.

"Eve," Saul said, his voice so tense it almost shook. "Did Daniel . . . were you . . . did he *touch* you?"

Eve dropped the gadget and looked up at him, her expression hardening. "I'm not a child, Saul."

"You were when I fled out here. I *trusted* him with you."

"He didn't . . . we didn't get involved until I was twenty-one." Eve stood, matching her brother's gaze. They glared at each other from across the room.

Asa cleared his throat. "Um, Saul?"

"What?" Saul didn't take his eyes off Eve, but Asa plunged onward.

"The reason we're here is that Daniel jumped out a window, and I tried to stop him, like you did. But I failed. And a drone got a really good image of what I'm sure looks like me pushing him, and probably Eve too."

"What?" Saul eased his posture. "You're on the run?"

"Why do you think we're here?"

"I thought . . ." Saul glanced at Eve, who turned away. She picked up the gadget she had been playing with and pulled out another wire, then replaced it. "I thought she came to find me," he finished without conviction.

"She didn't know you were alive," Asa said.

"She can hear you," Eve said icily from the corner.

"We have a plan," Asa said. "You might be able to help."

Saul sighed. "I'll see what I can do." He turned to his sister. "Eve."

"What?" she asked the wall.

"Come on," he said, voice soft. "Let's eat something."

"Fine." She set the gadget down and came to the door, not looking at either of them.

"Eve, I'm not mad at you. I'm mad at Daniel," Saul said with a note of pleading.

"Well, I'm mad at you."

"You're glad I'm alive though, right?"

Eve gave Saul a sardonic look, then took his arm again. "That line won't work forever, you know."

CHAPTER TWELVE

SAUL LED THEM BACK INTO THE HALLWAY and flipped a switch on the wall. Lights flickered above them for a moment, seemingly on the edge of dying, then came on, revealing beige tiled floors and dull greenish walls. They followed the corridor to another one just like it; Saul led them through a mazelike path of identical hallways, and Asa could not tell if this was really the way to something or if they were being deliberately disoriented.

"Nice place you've got," Eve said dryly, and Saul gave her an amused look.

"It may not be pretty, but it'll withstand just about anything," he said. "I'll give you a tour after dinner."

They eventually reached a heavy double door, and Saul shoved the bar at the middle of it, sending both sides swinging open. As they entered the hallway, it filled with soft noises.

Doors on either side were cracked open, light spilling out into the hall, where the harsh bulbs overhead had been dampened somehow. An aroma wafted from a door at the end of the hall: food, though the scent was unfamiliar. Someone was playing a stringed instrument and singing along in the distance. As they passed each room, Asa could hear the murmur of indistinct voices and, once, a crying baby and the hushed tones of someone soothing it.

Eve touched Asa's arm, and he noticed she had fallen behind her brother. She nodded her head minutely to their left, and he glanced in the direction she indicated. A little girl, no more than six, was peering through a crack in the door, her eyes wide. Asa smiled at her and bent down to say hello, but before he could speak, someone behind her pulled her back, whispering an admonition. The door closed firmly, and he heard the sound of a lock falling into place. Asa straightened, uncertain what he had done wrong.

Saul was waiting for them at the end of the hall, looking impatient. Eve and Asa hurried to him, and he threw open the door and grinned.

"Welcome to the dining room," he said.

Asa took three steps and turned in a circle to take it all in. The room was large and filled with a rank of perhaps ten long metal tables, each large enough for ten people or more. But the size was not what held his attention. There were no windows, but there was no need for them: the walls were hung with enormous paintings, and wherever there was space among the tables, there were marble sculptures, some of human figures, others abstract and unfathomable.

Saul ushered them to a table at the far end of the room, watched over by a painting of two red, vaguely human creatures making their way down a pink corridor. Asa sat facing away from it. Eve sat down beside him. As she sat, she took his hand under the table and squeezed it, and he smiled at her, surprised by the gesture. Her instant ease in this strange place was only serving to make him feel like more of an outsider, but he was surely grateful for her touch.

After a few moments they were joined by the welcoming party that had detained them in the desert—Cyrus, Aquila, Simon, Lilith, and the other two men, who were introduced now as Joel and Zachariah. More people began to filter in once they were seated, but they left the tables near Asa and Eve empty. No one acted as if it were unusual, and Asa wondered if it was because of his and Eve's presence or a deference always accorded to Saul. Asa looked for the little girl whose face he had scarcely seen on their way in, but no young children appeared at all.

A few teenagers emerged from a door at the other end of the room, with plates and spoons and large serving dishes for each table. The meal was a kind of stew, spicier than Asa was accustomed to but tasty. He thought it was best not to ask what was in it, thinking fleetingly of the small creatures that had darted in and out of view as they drove across the arid landscape.

"Did you build all this?" Eve asked, pointing her spoon vaguely at the room around them. "Not the decoration, the building," she added, and Simon choked on a laugh.

"Decoration, she says!" he said when he regained his breath. "These are masterpieces from the ancient world, young lady!"

"They're lovely," Asa said hastily as Eve gave the old man a cold stare, then turned back to her brother.

"Tell me about the building," Eve repeated. "Who built it? How long has it been here?"

"It's from the old civ," Saul said, and Asa shook his head, disbelieving.

"It would have rotted away," he said, "or been destroyed during the time of chaos before the Founding."

"Some things were made to last," Aquila said. "This was a military bunker, supposed to withstand a nuclear holocaust."

Asa glanced at Eve, then back at Saul. "I only understood about half those words," he admitted.

"It was built to survive a war, a storm, a flood—any disaster the world could create," Saul explained. "So far, it's lived up to expectations. I'll take you on a tour later. Everything we need, we produce within these walls, secure from the eyes of the State."

He said "State" like a curse word. He looked at Eve, who shrugged.

"The State leaves the Waste alone," Asa said. "You have nothing to fear from them. The only punishments out here are those inflicted by the Waste itself and . . ." *The men and women who inhabit it.* He stopped himself from saying the last part of the familiar phrase.

After a tense moment of silence, Cyrus burst out laughing, then the others joined him. Even Saul threw back his head and roared, his shoulders shaking. Eve raised an eyebrow and waited for them to finish. When they all calmed down, she turned her eyes on Cyrus.

"Tell us what's so funny," she said.

He set his spoon down carefully beside his empty bowl. "I'm not from your State," he said evenly. "No ancestor of mine ever set foot in that place. When the walls went up, my family stayed outside them."

"Why?" Asa gaped.

Cyrus gave him a searching look. "Can you really not imagine why someone might want to remain outside the shining walls of your perfectly planned society?"

"No," Asa said. "It was planned for a reason. The Founders wanted to protect us from the violence and greed that brought devastation and ruin upon the old civ!"

His face felt hot. Eve touched his arm, and he looked down to see that he was grasping his own spoon so tightly it was beginning to hurt his fingers. He set it down.

"Why did your family want to remain outside?" he asked, more calmly. Cyrus merely looked at him, and Lilith leaned over the table to answer.

"Asa, I was born inside the walls like you. I know all the things they say, but there's a cost to that well-run State you're defending."

"Like what?" he challenged.

"What are you doing out here?" she asked mildly, and he looked down at the table.

"That was a mistake," he said.

"Was it a mistake that you should pay for with your lives?"

"No," Eve said softly.

"They might as well know the rest," Simon said through a mouthful of food. "Tell them about the children."

Asa was suddenly alert. "The children?"

The others exchanged glances.

"Not just children," Aquila said. She sighed. "I'm not as convinced as Saul is that we can trust you," she said to Eve. "You may be his sister, but I have a sister too, and she'd sell me out in a heartbeat. So, if you're here spying for the State, we're not telling you anything."

174

"Okay. But we're not spies," Eve said.

"The State doesn't leave us alone," Aquila said. "Most people who run into the Waste, they do die of exposure or hunger or thirst within a few days. We help who we can, but it's not as if we get a weekly schedule—we never know who's coming out, or from where, and some people don't want our help. Besides us, there are some other scattered groups, but they're mostly living a rough life. At least, we think so."

"The State knows about us," Cyrus interrupted, his face harsh with anger. "They could destroy us if they wanted to, so why don't they?"

"Because the Waste is its own punishment?" Asa said, doubtful that this was the answer.

Cyrus smacked the table with the palm of his hand, making the dishes rattle. Silence fell in the dining room for a long moment, then conversation resumed, though people gave occasional sideways glances to their table.

"Even out here," Cyrus said in a low voice, "we see drones overhead from time to time. Sometimes they don't hide themselves because they want us to know they see us, that they're watching. Why do you think we keep everything underground?

"But we can't truly live underground. It's not right to raise a child totally hidden from the sun. So, we go up, walk around, trap game for food, and take cuttings to plant. Then every once in a while, the drones come in cloaked, and they snatch people.

"They do it so fast we can't stop them. We can't shoot them down without killing the people they've taken. All of us have lost people we love that way. Mostly they take children, so we learned to guard the children more closely. But if they can't get children, they'll take anyone."

Asa was speechless. Eve had her hand on his knee, and she was gripping it tightly; he put his own hand on top of hers, grasping it as if she could ground him.

"What's the matter? You didn't know?" Simon asked with a tone of bitter mocking.

"I've told you, Simon, they don't know about this on the inside," Lilith snapped. "Aquila, did you know? Zach?"

They shook their heads.

"I didn't know," Joel added, speaking for the first time. Cyrus made a noncommittal grunt.

"I knew," Saul said, speaking for the first time since they'd sat down.

"What?" Eve stared at him, shocked.

He grinned. "Finding out stuff like that is pretty much how I ended up here," he said. "Everyone finished? How about I take my long-lost sister on a tour? You too, new guy," he added, glancing at Asa.

The three of them stood, and Saul led the way out of the dining room and down another staircase. This one had more paintings on the walls—mostly landscapes—and at the bottom of the stairs was another statue, this one a creature—half-man, half-horse—chasing a human woman.

"Where does all this come from?" Asa asked as they passed it, making their way down another narrow hallway.

"The sculptures? Most of the art comes from a vault we found under the city ruins a few miles away. Some of it we make—not me, but some of the others."

"There was a city here?" he asked.

He was suddenly fascinated by the prospect of such a real, tangible connection to the years before the Founding. He had known in a vague way that some traces of the old civ must exist, but the idea that real people had found them and brought the artifacts into their present lives was somehow both obscene and enchanting.

"Nearby, anyway. The wreckage of the old civ is everywhere. I send parties out, the people who want to explore. They search for tech and materials and for others who have run away into the Waste—not everyone wants to live among us, and not everyone wants us to live, but many do, and those we bring home. But there are those who want to discover the treasures of the old civ, and I encourage it. They kept much of their artwork in climate-sealed, underground storage vaults. I suppose not all of the art survived, but enough did that we've built up what I imagine is quite a collection."

"Impressive," Eve murmured, looking back at the statue.

"Not as impressive as the rest of what we've been able to do. The ruins of the old civ are what allow us to survive. Our water treatment is upstairs. It started out as a cobbled-together mess, but now I'd put it up against anything you've got on the inside. There's no shortage of materials and parts out here, so if you've got someone who knows what they're doing, there's no limit to the tech you can create."

Eve was smiling. "And by 'someone who knows what they're doing,' you mean you?" she teased.

Saul grinned. "Not just me. Look, there are generations out here. People like Cyrus whose grandparents stayed outside when the walls went up. People whose parents left or were cast out before they were born. It's a real society. People have handed down knowledge that I had never heard of before I got here.

"And, yes, there's me. I was able to upgrade a lot of their tech. I taught some boys and girls programming and plumbing. Meanwhile, I've learned some things myself."

He threw open a door, and Asa and Eve gasped in unison. Before them lay a vast expanse of greenery and light from above as bright as the sun. It took Asa's eyes a moment to adjust before he could figure out what he was seeing.

"Hydroponic greenhouse," Saul said. "You can't plant much in the desert, and we don't want our food supply aboveground— vulnerable to the drone raids."

Asa nodded, trying to catalog the plants—some were familiar, tomatoes and beetroots, while others were mysterious, leafy greens and budding berries he could not have named. A squawk came from the far side of the greenhouse, and Eve jumped.

Saul laughed. "Fowl," he said, beckoning them toward a fenced-off area where a couple of small fat brown chickens were scratching and pecking at seeds scattered in the dirt that covered their patch of ground. There were a few more behind them, and in a little hutch by the wall, Asa could just make out a few more, sitting on nests.

"Mostly we keep them for eggs, sometimes meat," Saul said. "Come on, there's more."

On their way out of the greenhouse, they passed three women going in, chatting enthusiastically until they noticed Saul and his guests.

"Don't mind us," Saul said, watching amusedly as they stared at Eve. "Just my little sister."

One of the women flicked her eyes over Asa. He shrugged.

"Eve, welcome," the woman said, smiling. "We heard you'd come. Mary, stop staring at the poor girl."

They walked down the hall a few yards, and Asa could hear music again. Saul opened a door to let them into another room. The music expanded outward like a physical force, a pounding beat so loud Asa could feel it in his chest. He looked at Eve, who was covering her ears. There was a young man sitting at a table, a wide array of tech spread out in front of him. After a moment he looked up, saw them at the door, and turned a knob on the box beside him. The music faded into the background, and Asa felt his shoulders relax. Eve took her hands away from her ears.

There were half a dozen tables scattered around the room, each one covered in what looked like a messy tangle of wires and parts, though Asa suspected they were all in fact precisely arranged. A gray-haired woman was standing over the farthest table, engrossed in her work, and behind the young man who had turned down the music was a large screen, perhaps four feet across, where animated figures ran across painted terrain. It was some old civ movie, discovered and restored. Two children were sitting in front of it, their ears covered by large black devices, their hands manipulating small gadgets. Asa moved closer behind them, watching, and determined that the children were controlling the animation onscreen. The children did not seem to notice him, their attention absorbed.

"Asa?" Saul was standing at the door; Eve was already in the hallway. "I have one more thing to show you," he said.

Saul led them back to the staircase and opened a door Asa had not noticed, leading to yet another set of stairs. They descended yet again, and Asa began to wonder how far into the earth they were—a hundred feet? Two hundred?

Each staircase seemed to take them farther than the space from one floor to the next, as if something were hidden in the space between, but he was disoriented. At the bottom of the stairs, Saul looked nervously at Eve, then threw open the door. Eve took a step inside and gasped.

Asa moved closer to see what lay inside, then stopped when

he saw the look of shock on Eve's face. The room was domed, the walls deep brown and uneven. Light streamed in through the thin places. It cast a dim amber glow, crossed with shadows. At the center was a column that stretched to the ceiling, and Eve walked slowly toward it. Asa came into the room, and Saul followed, closing the door quietly behind them.

Saul watched his sister with a slight, almost reverent smile on his face as she walked to the column at the center and fell to her knees in the latticework of light, the look of shock still on her face. Saul broke the silence with harsh, guttural words Asa did not understand, and Eve covered her face with her hands.

He heard her whisper something in response, and Saul went to kneel beside her. He took her hands from her face and held them, and Asa could see that her cheeks were wet with tears, glistening in the artificial sunlight. Saul said something to Eve that sounded like a question, in the same unfamiliar language, and she answered immediately with the almost child-ish cadence of ritual. They exchanged three more questions and answers, then Eve bent her head again, and Saul brought her hands to his cheeks.

"I can't believe you're here," he said softly.

"How do you have all this?" Eve asked, pulling away from him gently and standing.

She put her hand on the column and ran her palm up and down it, looking up. Asa followed her gaze and saw that the top of the column became a stylized tree, the branches interweaving and reaching out to form the whole ceiling of the small room, then bowing down to the floor to make the walls.

"We made it," Saul said. "Not everyone, I mean—just me and a few others. Not everyone believes, but it's allowed here. Some people have other beliefs I had never heard of before coming here. We're all free to worship as we wish. There's no one in this world to stop it."

Eve nodded, almost dazedly. "I gave you my necklace," she said. "When you went away."

Saul smiled. "You want it back?"

"No. I wanted you to have it. But can I see it?"

He took something from his pocket and handed it to her; Asa was too far away to see it in detail, but Eve gazed at the small thing in wonder, turning it over in her hands.

"Eve," Saul said gently and held out his hand. She gave it back. "Turn around and get all that hair out of the way." Eve obliged, lifting her long hair up so Saul could fasten the chain around her neck. "It's always been yours. Mom gave it to you."

"Mom would be disappointed in both of us," Eve said, picking up the charm and looking at it upside down.

"Oh, that would have been true no matter what we did," Saul said cheerfully. "Come on, you'll have all the time in the world to pray later. Let's show your friend the rest of this place."

He led the way back to the staircase, and Asa followed behind Eve, still seeing her aglow in the strange underground tree room.

She's a believer . . .

It was the last thing he would have guessed of Eve, that she would place her faith in myths and stories, holding fast to one of the great destructive forces of the old civ. *Worship begins war*, he thought, recalling a phrase from childhood, though he could not remember where he had heard it. It was like *The sun always rises* or *We're all in this together*, bits of truth that everyone just knew.

"*We are all free to worship as we wish*," Saul had said.

"No wonder the Waste is so brutal," Asa said under his breath, too quietly for Eve to hear him.

✦

The rest of the tour took them past variously arranged living quarters—some people apparently lived alone, like Saul, or in couples or families, and others were ten to a room, bunk beds lined up against the walls in rows.

"How is it decided who shares?" Asa asked, and Saul gave him an odd look.

"People just do what they want," he said.

They passed an open area, where a few people were lounging in chairs and on cushions, reading books, and others talked quietly in small groups. On a bright blue carpet in the corner, two men were helping a toddler build a tower of blocks. Asa paused for a moment to watch them. One of the men looked up and smiled; the other moved closer to the child, his face guarded.

"I used to do that with my dad," Asa said. "Building towers. I'm Asa," he added hastily.

"I'm Judah," said the man who had smiled. "That's Abe, and our daughter, Claudia." He put a hand on her shoulder. "Claudia, say hello," he said gently, and the little girl threw the block in her hand onto the rug.

"No!" she declared, then collapsed in a fit of giggles. Abe shook his head and gave Asa an apologetic smile.

"She just learned how to say no," he explained.

Asa smiled back, then gave a short nod and hurried to catch up with Eve and Saul, who were already several paces down the hall.

Saul rolled his eyes good-naturedly. "Abe and Judah spoil her," he said in a low voice. "If they don't start teaching that girl discipline—"

"She'll be a regular, happy kid?" Eve interrupted.

Saul shook his head, his face growing serious. "Not out here," he said. "They're good parents, as far as I know anything about that. But if you're going to raise a child out here, you have to make sure they'll run when you say run and stop when you tell them to stop."

"The drone raids," Eve said, comprehending.

Saul nodded. "We don't teach them blind obedience, but a kid who can't follow orders is a kid we'll never see again."

Asa glanced back, still feeling a step behind. "Do you raise the kids, um, collectively?" he hazarded at last. "Judah said, 'Our daughter.'"

Saul barked a short laugh, and Eve glared at him, then looked hesitantly at Asa. "Asa," she said, "I think he's . . . *their* daughter. His and Abe's."

"They adopted her after her mother was taken in a raid," Saul said a little coldly. "She's a lucky kid."

He strode ahead down the hallway, and Eve picked up her pace to match his. Asa let himself lag behind, a bit disturbed. Everyone knew there were men and women whose sexual appetites ran against nature; it was a defect they were born with. No one judged them for something they could not control. But to allow two men to live like a married couple or—worse—to raise a child together that way? What would young Claudia see as she grew up? What would she come to believe was right?

"Asa?" Eve was waiting for him; she and Saul had stopped at the door to a staircase.

"Coming," he said, picking up his pace to join her.

They wound through the mazelike halls of the building again, ending up this time in a bedroom meant for a half-dozen people. Three bunk beds lined up neatly to fill the space. Asa's and Eve's bags were piled on the one nearest the door, and Eve went straight to them and picked up hers, the one she had filled with Daniel's devices.

"There's no one else staying in here," Saul said quickly. "We have more space than we need, really."

Asa glanced at Eve, his pulse rising as he considered the possibilities for where they both might sleep. Eve sat down on a bunk and leaned back against the metal headboard, crossing her legs and swinging the bag up onto her lap.

"I know it's not much," Saul said. "But it's just for tonight while we make a proper room for you. We've got a wealth of old furniture, artwork, things to make the place more comfortable . . . and another room for you," he said hurriedly, looking to Asa. "If you want one. Or even another room for tonight . . . Sorry, I guess I assumed . . ." He looked sheepishly at Eve. "Baby sister, is he with you or what?"

Eve smiled. "Or what. We can share for tonight at least. Thanks, Saul."

She'd unzipped the bag partway but had not begun to examine what was inside, and now she took out a single item, one of the metal strips she'd used to buy the rail tickets, and began to toy with it, bending it one way and then the other as if testing how far it would go before it broke.

"Wait," Asa broke in. "Thank you, Saul, really—you've saved our lives, I think literally, but we're not staying after tonight."

Saul laughed briefly, then stopped when Asa did not smile. "You're serious? What, do you have another congregation of outlaws you'd rather stay with?" He looked from Asa to Eve. "Kids, I'm sorry, but you're looking at the only city in the Waste. It's not so bad once you're used to it, Eve, I promise. We do some great things down here, stuff Daniel and I dreamed about but didn't dare attempt on the inside. It's not a paradise, but it's my home, and it can be yours too. I promise."

He sat beside Eve and held out a hand. She didn't take it, so he patted her foot awkwardly. She kicked him halfheartedly, but she smiled.

"We're not staying," Asa repeated. "We've got a plan."

"What's your plan?" Saul asked.

Asa sat on the bunk facing them. "You must know what's in that bag," he said, gesturing to it. Eve's hands tightened on the canvas, and Saul nodded.

"We have to be very careful what comes in here. Everything in those bags has been returned to them, though I hope you'll let me take a closer look," Saul said to Eve, who hesitated, then relaxed her grip on the bag.

"Of course."

"It's Daniel's stuff," Asa said.

"I assumed as much."

"Daniel always talked about how he had a backdoor into the system," Eve said. "He said it was how he got you off that transport before you could be . . ."

"Terminated," Saul said. He nudged her gently. "Saying the word won't make it happen," he added.

Eve gave him a cold look. "Yes. Thank you. Anyway, we had hoped we could get across the river to Sanctuary, to Daniel's grandfather, David. He built the Network. He built the back door . . . and we thought he could help us."

"Expunge our records, call off the stalkers," Asa explained.

Saul nodded, but his face was grave. "Do you even know if David is alive?" he asked.

"No," she admitted.

Eve was beginning to look exhausted, and Asa straightened his spine, warding off fatigue of his own. He realized that he was not exactly sure when he had last slept. Not the last night, certainly, and very little the night before—and that was in the stalkers' cell.

"Saul," Eve said slowly. "I know it was a long shot, but it was the only chance we had. You worked with Daniel. He trusted you with his life—"

"I'm not sure how much that counted with him," Saul said dryly.

Eve glared at him for a moment, then went on. "He trusted you. Do you know how to access his back door? Can you get into the system? I have his computer, the one he kept everything on."

"No," Saul said and sighed. "I'm sorry, Evie."

"Don't call me that," she said—it sounded like an automatic response, ingrained from years of habit, and Asa hid a smile.

"*Eve,*" Saul said with emphasis. "Daniel never showed me how to get into the system."

"Could you try?" There was a note of pleading in her voice.

"Maybe I could figure it out, sure, but . . ." He grasped for words. "You want me to change your records in the State system? Make it look like none of this ever happened?"

"Yes," Asa put in quickly.

"Right. So, the problem is, the Network is *live*. It's constantly monitoring itself for anomalies, break-ins, that kind of thing. If I try to get in there and change something, not knowing what I'm doing, three things will happen: I'll be spotted almost instantly, my access will be cut off, and whatever I was doing will be scrutinized. If I wanted to break in and shut down Horizon's drone system for a minute, I might be able to do that. But I would never be able to access it again, because whatever crack I found my way through would be found and sealed. Does that make sense?"

"Yes," Asa said, though he had understood only about half of it.

Eve hugged the bag of Daniel's things to her chest. "Why could Daniel get in, then?" she asked.

"Because he had whatever pathway his grandfather built in when he created the Network, and I don't know where it is. It's like a secret passage in a house. If you know where it is, you can get straight from one room to another without anyone knowing you're there. Me, I don't know where it is. I'd have to start by breaking through the walls with a hammer. People notice that kind of thing. Just by looking for it, I would give myself away."

Eve sighed and rubbed her eyes. "So, we have to get to David in Sanctuary after all," she said wearily.

Saul frowned. "Why do you have to go back at all? Now that you know we're out here, why not stay? I know it's a different life, but it's a good one, and Eve . . . I don't want to lose you again."

Eve pulled a little coil of red-coated wire from the bag and began twisting it back and forth but did not answer.

"*I* have to go back," Asa said firmly. "I can't stay out here, cut off from my whole family—from the whole world." He glanced at Eve, who was fixated on the wire, lacing it through her fingers, then undoing it, over and over. "Can you help us get to Sanctuary?" he asked.

Saul leaned back, looking up at the bunk above his head as if the answer might be written there. "I can," he said at last. "The river isn't far from here—a few hours' drive, and we have solar cars, so you won't get stranded in the middle of the desert."

"The electric car was all we could get," Asa said defensively.

"Well, it's going to make a very nice scrap vehicle for parts," Saul said. Asa was about to protest but thought better of it. "The problem is the river," Saul said. "Are you really going to cross a

whole river full of water? It's not some little stream in the countryside, it's massive, and it's fast-moving. You can't just paddle
across. You could fall in or get exposed."

He glanced at Eve, who was still toying with the wire,
though now she was staring into space as if the men beside her
were not there.

"Is there a way across?" Asa asked, letting his voice grow steely.

He had spent the day bewildered by their new surroundings,
but now someone was trying to convince him not to do what he
wanted to do. Asa was used to that, but he was also accustomed
to eventually getting his way.

"It's not safe," Saul repeated. "This is crazy—I can't send my
baby sister off to get her brain eaten by the Bug."

"What do you know?" Eve snapped, and Saul jumped. She
set the bag aside and stood up, crossing her arms. "I'm not a *little
girl*. You don't know anything about me. My parents died, then
my brother died too. I had to get tough." Saul stared at her. She
looked as if she wanted to say more, but instead she smoothed
her hair, brushing it back, and sat down beside Asa. "Is there a
bridge?" she asked calmly. "Or a boat?"

Saul looked from her to Asa and back again. "There's a boat."
He paused. "Tomorrow morning, I'll take you to the old boathouse at the river's edge. You can go from there."

"Thank you," Asa said fervently. Eve simply nodded.

Saul stood. "I'll see you in the morning," he said and walked
out, closing the door behind him.

Asa turned to Eve, but she had already curled up on the bunk,
facing away from him. *Oh well,* he thought and got up to turn off
the light. He felt his way back through the dark to the bunk next
to Eve's, aided by the faint glow of a small night-light on the far

side of the room. He was settling himself on the bed when she muttered something only half-audible.

"What?" Asa whispered, and she turned to face him.

"I said there's room here." Her eyes glinted softly in the shadows. She gave Asa a tentative smile. "I'm so tired," she whispered, "and I don't want to sleep alone."

"You don't have to," Asa said quickly.

He grabbed the pillow from the second bunk, then carefully got onto the narrow bed beside her. She took his arm and pulled it around her waist, holding his hand against her chest as he wrapped himself around her smaller body. He brushed his lips against the back of her neck, and she sighed contentedly, resting beside him as if he could protect her from the world.

You will never have to sleep alone, he vowed to her silently. She stirred, her body swaying against his, and he wondered, with a sharp longing, if he would ever be able to sleep again.

✦

In the morning, a teenage girl came to wake them. She shouted, "Breakfast!" and pounded on the door before flinging it open, and Asa hastily stood up, disoriented. The girl stared at him for a moment, then repeated, "Breakfast."

"Thanks," he said awkwardly.

Eve sat up. "Can you show us how to get there?" she asked, and the girl nodded.

"I'll wait outside," she said after a moment's thought and closed the door behind her.

Saul was already in the dining room when they were led in,

and Cyrus, Lilith, and Simon joined the group when Asa and Eve sat down. They ate quickly.

"I'm going to have Cyrus and Lilith take you to the boathouse," Saul said briskly. "From there, you're on your own. You'll have to cross the river, get into Sanctuary, find David, get back out, and cross the river again." He looked as if he was about to say more, but Eve stopped him.

"We already know what you think, Saul. We're still going," she said firmly.

Simon had a small gadget on the table beside his plate and had been neglecting his breakfast as he tinkered with it. Now he made a small, satisfied sound and held it out to Saul, who inspected it briefly, then nodded. Simon gave the thing to Eve, who pressed a button experimentally.

She's probably seen it before, Asa thought, slightly envious for the first time of her apparent ease with this strange society.

"Once you're ready to leave, you can radio us," Saul went on. "Someone will come back with a car to get you, but don't use the radio before you reach this side of the river again. The State monitors the radio waves, and there's a chance they'll pick up the signal and find you before we can." Eve nodded soberly, and Saul stood. "There's one more thing you should take," he said.

"I don't think that's a good idea," Cyrus said, and Saul held up a hand.

"We talked about this. I'm not sending her out there unarmed."

"She doesn't know how to use it," Cyrus argued. "She could hurt herself, or one of us."

"What are you talking about?" Eve asked sharply, and they looked at her as if they had forgotten she was there.

"A gun," Lilith said. "Saul wants to give you one, and I agree.

You don't know what you're going to face out there. Something like this."

She took two strange metal objects from her belt and laid them heavily on the table. Asa glanced around the dining room. Earlier he had noticed people wearing what he had assumed to be cumbersome belt decorations of some kind, but he had not considered whether they had a purpose. Now he looked around and saw, appallingly, that almost every person there was wearing a weapon. He looked at Saul; Eve's brother wore two, almost identical to the ones Lilith had just set on the table.

"We're not taking *weapons*," Asa said, not attempting to hide his disgust.

"It would be for your protection," Saul said.

"No," Eve said. "No. I know things out here are . . . different. But no." She watched Lilith's weapons, inert on the table, as if they might suddenly spring to life.

"Eve, you don't even know what they do," Saul said.

"Saul! I said no."

Lilith slowly took her weapons off the table and reattached them to her belt. "I think it's a mistake," she said mildly.

"I think all of this is a mistake," Cyrus said, giving Asa and Eve a dark stare.

"Maybe," Asa said. "But it's what we're going to do."

"Time to go," Saul said, picking up one of Eve's bags as he stood.

They followed him out of the dining room and up the many sets of stairs to the enormous room at ground level, Lilith and Cyrus taking up the rear like guards—which, Asa realized, they actually were.

Asa shielded his eyes as they emerged into the sunlight,

blinking as his vision adjusted. He looked at Eve, who smiled at him.

"Nice to be outside again," she whispered, and he nodded.

"Asa Isaac Rosewood! Eve Layla Ashland!" someone shouted from a dozen feet away.

Asa looked around wildly and spotted the stalker who had arrested him in Horizon emerge from behind one of the cars parked beside the building. He strode toward them almost mechanically.

"By the authority of the State, you will be questioned, judged, and sentenced—"

Cyrus lunged at the stalker, then was thrown back by an invisible force. He collapsed on the ground, writhing in pain, and as the stalker kept walking, Asa saw the stunner in his hand.

"Asa Isaac Rosewood," the stalker repeated. "Eve Layla Ashland. By the authority of the State—"

A bang went off, like a small explosion, and Asa grabbed Eve instinctively, pulling her toward him. The stalker jerked his head back as something whizzed by him unimaginably fast, then embedded into the concrete wall of the building with a resounding crack.

The stalker stared at the wall, where a hole had appeared, and raised a hand to his ear. His fingers came away bloody. He looked around slowly. Saul and Lilith had leapt into protective stances on either side of Eve and Asa, and behind him were several of the guards. They were brandishing the small metal weapons they all carried on their belts, but no one used them. Instead, they began to gather from all sides in a trained formation, moving to capture their prey. Just as they closed in on him, the stalker jumped between two of the guards with lightning speed, then took off at a run. He clipped against Cyrus without slowing as Lilith and the other guards discharged their weapons.

"He's got my gun!" Cyrus shouted, scrambling to his feet.

He reached for his other weapon and took off chasing the stalker. Two of the guards followed. Asa gripped Eve's hand, his heart pounding; the stalker was faster than anyone he had ever witnessed, and he had seemed to vanish almost instantly, disappearing into the vast expanse of a desert that offered nowhere to hide.

Minutes passed, then Cyrus and the others reappeared, exhausted. "I don't know how, but he got away," Cyrus said grimly as he tried to catch his breath.

Lilith turned on Eve with a fiery glare. "This is all your fault," she hissed. "You've brought the State down on us. You both have to get the fuck out of here!"

"Back off her. We didn't do this on purpose!" Asa yelled.

"It's not their fault," Saul said curtly. "Asa, get in the car. I can't send my people with you now. Leave it by the river."

Asa nodded and opened the passenger side door as Eve went to the driver's side.

"Eve," Saul said, grasping her arm. "Don't do this. Stay with me. Don't risk your life to go with him."

"I'm not going for him!" Eve wrested her arm free, then took her brother's hand. "I'm going for me. I have to know what happened to Daniel—why he was the way he was. What could have made him despair so much that he would take his own life. I thought it was me who failed him, but now you say he was always like that, and I . . . I want to know why. I didn't want to spend the rest of my life with him, but I loved him. He loved me—he loved *us*. He was a good man. I know his grandfather has answers, and I need to hear them."

Saul sighed. He started to say something, then just shook his head.

"Can't you come with us?" Eve asked.

"No," he said sadly.

"Okay, then." She opened the car door.

"Eve. I'll see you again," Saul said with sudden confidence. "Believe and it will be so."

She nodded. "You will," she whispered and hugged him fiercely. Asa got into the car, and a moment later she joined him, slamming the door behind her as she wiped her eyes.

"Are you ready?" Asa asked, and she smiled at him, her eyes still red.

"I better be," she said and started the car. In the rearview mirror, Asa saw Saul and his people watching their departure resolutely. Eve glanced back once, then sped up as they drove toward the river and Sanctuary.

CHAPTER THIRTEEN

GABRIEL WAITED, CONCEALED BEHIND AN outcropping of rock, until the last voices and sounds of movement had faded. He carefully pulled the balled-up cloth of his shirt away from the wound for a moment to check it. The blood was still flowing freely, but as far as he could tell, all that was damaged was his earlobe. He looked down at his chest, already pink from the blazing sun overhead.

It seemed brighter out here in the Waste, as if the air were thinner and the atmosphere less protective—though that must have been because there were no buildings or trees to give the respite of shade. This rock was the best he'd found so far.

There'll be an emergency kit in the car—and hopefully an extra shirt.

Gabriel took steady breaths. He was beginning to feel light-headed, but he had not lost enough blood for that to be the reason; he was only feeling the aftereffects of adrenaline.

Wait fifteen minutes. If they don't come back, get to the car. One, two, three . . .

He began to count the seconds, tracking the time as they had all been trained to do when they learned to count. Thirty years on, he could do it in the back of his mind, scarcely paying attention. He sometimes thought he was always counting, even when he didn't mean to, tracking the moments as his life ticked by, just in case someday someone showed up to demand an accounting.

As he tracked the seconds in the back of his mind, he turned the rest of his attention to the strange weapon he had snatched from the man who had attacked him. It was an L shape, about eight inches in length, with a little loop and tab at the bend.

That's the trigger mechanism, he thought, envisioning his attacker's movements in the split second before the projectile had struck him.

He ran his hands over the smooth metal, then picked the thing up carefully and held it the way the outlaws had, keeping his finger outside the trigger loop.

The thing that hit me—it went an inch into a concrete wall. It was meant to hit me. The thought sent a cold sensation down his spine, but he brushed thoughts of his own mortality aside, more interested in the meaning of what he had witnessed.

So that is the brutality of the Waste. Men and women with weapons that will rip a human being apart, dispatching them without even a question.

Ten minutes left; he noted his internal clock.

Something nagged at him: the insight was incomplete. He closed his eyes and pictured the scene again.

They came out of the building with the wasters. I shouted their names. That man approached, and I knocked him down with my stunner. The weapons were not their first choice—no one fired on me until I had harmed one of theirs. They were organized—they had rules of some kind. Discipline.

Seven minutes.

They came out of that enormous building—it's big enough to house a whole community. There were men and women. They were all well-fed, healthy looking. Not desperate, not scrabbling to survive. They defended that place like it was their home.

Five minutes.

Gabriel leaned back, letting the sun beat down on his face. *Wasters are scattered, indiscriminately violent—almost inhuman,* he thought, recalling the common wisdom everyone knew. *That's the problem with something everyone knows—no one ever bothers to find out if it's true.*

One minute.

Gabriel opened his eyes, hefting the weapon in his hands again. He itched to try it, just once, but the sound it made had been deafening, like fireworks at close range. It would bring the wasters running to him.

Time's up.

He leaned on the rock for support to stand but found that he was steady on his feet; the blood loss was not as bad as it looked. Gabriel glanced around cautiously, then hurried across the sand to the place where he had left the solar car he had taken from the Rosewood garage. He threw open the trunk and found the first aid kit; there was a large tube of wound glue.

Dropping his bloody shirt into the bed of the trunk, he took the tube, along with a spool of gauze and a small bottle of disinfectant, around to the side mirror. He stared at himself for a second in shock. The left side of his face and neck were drenched in blood, and it was still coming, making rivers on his bare chest and trickling down his spine now that he had removed the cloth from it.

It's just because it's a head wound. Head wounds always bleed.

Gabriel put the first aid supplies on the roof of the car. He opened the disinfectant, clenched his teeth, and poured it over his ear.

He nearly shouted in pain but clamped his jaw shut, forcing himself to breathe through his nose until the sting faded. He checked the mirror again. The disinfectant had cleared the blood, and he could see that his earlobe was gone, the edges of his skin ragged.

I've still got the important parts—that's all that matters.

He took a strip of gauze and patted the area dry as best he could, then squeezed out the glue along what was left of his ear. The bleeding stopped, the glue sucking the skin together and drying instantly. Gabriel closed the tube and wet some gauze with disinfectant to wipe away the rest of the blood.

A flash of light in the distance caught his eye, and he stopped what he was doing to peer across the desert. The light bobbed up and down; something was reflecting sunlight as it moved away from the concrete building.

It's them. They've got a car.

Gabriel tossed the first aid kit onto the passenger seat and got in. His skin was still sticky with blood, but he ignored the itchy sensation and started the car, speeding up as he drove toward the gleam ahead.

I will bring them back to justice.

When he drew close enough to see the car, Gabriel tracked their course for a moment, then dropped back and veered away. He would have to take another route, circling away before coming back to check that he was still on their trail—otherwise, in this wide-open space, they would see him easily. Still, his disadvantage would be theirs as well: while he fell behind, there was nowhere for them to hide. Eventually, inevitably, Gabriel would find his prey.

But where?

He had assumed their flight into the Waste had been driven by panic, their only aim to evade capture and judgement. It was a stupid choice, for the punishments of the Waste were known to be far worse than the measured justice of the State, but people did it now and then nonetheless.

Gabriel hung back, circled around, came close enough to spot their tracks, then turned away, each time marking their direction and location in the small notepad he always carried. After the third cycle, he was certain: Asa and Eve were heading in a straight line.

They're not just running; they know where they're going. He turned the car toward a cliff in the distance and set it to autopilot for a moment to write down the fugitives' trajectory. *Where are they going? Where is there to go?*

They had contacts among the wasters, that much was clear—maybe Eve's brother, Saul, had been in communication with her before he died; maybe she still had a contact. Perhaps there were other groups like that, scattered across the Waste.

How big is the Waste?

It was not a question that had ever interested him, not because he was incurious but because it did not matter. The Waste had never been his domain—his mandate was justice for the people of the State, and the Waste was out of his jurisdiction.

Until now . . .

He thought briefly of Joan; it felt like days since their argument. *Our allegiance is not to justice—it's to the State,* she had said with such perfect assurance that she sounded as if she were quoting something.

Gabriel searched his memory perfunctorily. It sounded familiar, but if she was quoting, he hadn't read the book. *Our allegiance is to the State.* That was the quote he knew, the words he'd learned to say before he could write his own name.

"Our allegiance is to the State," Gabriel echoed to the empty car, feeling for the first time in decades as if he had somehow been naive. It had never occurred to him that allegiance to the State and allegiance to justice could be different things.

What does she know? Barely out of training. Quoting textbooks because she has no experience of her own to draw on.

Checking his direction and mileage, Gabriel turned back toward the path his runners were on. As they'd journeyed, the desert had slowly receded, and now they crossed fields of tall grasses and lengths of forests. There were worn-down places, almost roads, that Asa and Eve were following—more evidence that the Waste held more than Gabriel had realized.

Our allegiance is not to justice but to the State. He remembered where he had heard the words: there had been a crime.

A little boy in Clearview was killed by a man from another community. There had been something wrong with the man—he was defective and should have been found sooner, his behavior flagged by the drones as potentially dangerous so that he could be removed, sent to Work or terminated, depending on the severity of his problems.

But he had been missed.

He killed a boy, strangled him with bare hands in his own backyard, and the boy's mother had arrived on the scene before the local Contract Enforcers. She had taken a kitchen knife and stabbed her son's killer to death.

Gabriel and Naomi had been sent to sort it out. The local Contract Enforcers were holding the mother—her name was Caroline. They were keeping Caroline under guard in her home, and every hour someone from the community came to the door to sit with her, to offer comfort, to bring food for her and her husband, Abe.

When Gabriel and Naomi arrived from Horizon, there were a dozen neighbors at the family's house: a few were tending the garden, two men were repairing a broken railing on the porch, and others were gathered in groups of two and three, talking quietly. Everyone watched them closely as they landed the passenger drone and walked up to the door, but there was more curiosity than worry on their faces. Gabriel saw that the community assumed their presence was only a formality and that, of course, nothing would be done to Caroline.

When Gabriel and Naomi walked into the house, they were greeted by the local Contract Enforcers, a man and woman in their mid-forties who had been looking after the community for the better part of their careers. In hushed tones, they explained what had happened.

From the corner of his eye, Gabriel saw Naomi's eyes brighten with unshed tears, and he knew she was picturing the scene, feeling the mother's devastation as a physical pain in her chest. He wanted to comfort her, take her hand, stroke her hair, and whisper sweet lies about the future, but it was the wrong impulse, and he shoved it away.

Empathizing the way she did was part of her job—her specialization—and besides, that was back before she loved him.

Naomi and Gabriel listened to Caroline. They spoke to her husband—they watched and listened as the parents choked on their grief. They had already seen the drone feeds; there was no uncertainty as to what had happened, no question that Caroline was telling the truth. Several hours went by as they listened to witness after witness tell their stories. Then Naomi met Gabriel's eyes. There was no need for them to confer—they had known what they would do since before they left Horizon. Naomi gave him a tiny, sad smile, encouraging him to do what neither of them wanted to. He nodded, an imperceptible movement to everyone but her, and then stood.

The whole room drew back, even Naomi, though a split second later she was on her feet beside him.

"Caroline, please stand," Naomi said quietly, and Caroline did, her face a mask of confusion and grief.

"Caroline Anne Clearview," Gabriel said grimly, "by authority of the State, you will be questioned, judged, and sentenced."

"*What?*" Caroline's husband was on his feet, his fists clenched, his face red. "What are you talking about? Don't you see what she's been through? What we've all been through?"

Gabriel ignored him. His eyes were on Caroline, who was staring off into the distance as if her mind were elsewhere.

"Caroline Anne Clearview, please come with me," Gabriel said.

She nodded absently and followed him to the door.

"You can't *do* this!" her husband shouted as they all walked out the front door.

It looked as if half the town had gathered outside the house, and probably they had. Gabriel had not attempted to restrain Caroline, and now he was glad of that decision—if she had come out with her hands tied, a riot might have broken out.

"Caroline, what's happening?" a woman cried from somewhere in the crowd.

"They're taking her away!" Abe snarled. "Our little boy is *gone* and they're taking her away!"

The local Contract Enforcers looked nervously at one another. Gabriel marched the woman toward the drone without response and then felt Naomi's hand on his arm. He stopped and looked at her.

Tell them something, she mouthed, and he turned to face the unsettled crowd.

"Violence is a severe violation of the Social Contract that grants us all safety and community. No matter how much we may empathize with Caroline's distress, her actions were unspeakable. A man is dead."

"Our *child* is dead," Abe said brokenly, and Gabriel nodded.

"I know," he said.

Naomi stepped forward and put a hand on Abe's shoulder. She whispered something to him, and he began to weep. Two men stepped forward, gently pulling the grief-stricken father back into the fold of the crowd, where others crowded around to comfort him. Abe was quiet for a moment, then surged forward again as the crowd parted to let him through.

"This is wrong!" he shouted, striding toward them, and Gabriel caught the man's eyes and gave him a deadening stare.

"This is for everyone's protection," he said with quiet intensity.

Abe stopped moving, but he did not break away from Gabriel's gaze. When he spoke again, his voice had an eerie calm.

"This is not justice," he said, and Gabriel thought for a moment before answering. He didn't look at the crowd, but he could feel the tension all around them, ready to break at the wrong word. He glanced at Naomi; she was looking expectantly at him.

"You're right," Gabriel said slowly. "But our allegiance is not to justice. Our allegiance is to the State. Our allegiance is to the safety and security of all our communities. Another word for the justice you want is vengeance, and our allegiance can never be to that."

There was a hush, and before it could break, they walked Caroline the rest of the way to the drone, careful to keep a steady pace. He settled her in the back seat and sat beside her, respectfully, as if she were not a prisoner. The crowd watched quietly as the doors closed. The drone rose into the air, and then to the onlookers, it seemed to disappear. Naomi was sitting in front, and as she bent forward to enter their destination, Gabriel could see that she was crying. Caroline stared out the window, her eyes still fixed on a point no one else could see.

"You're right, you know," she said an hour later.

Naomi turned in her seat, her eyes wide. "What do you mean, Caroline?" she asked in a whisper, and Caroline gave her a faint smile.

"I wanted vengeance," she said. She sounded as if she were saying "I wanted breakfast," and Gabriel felt something wrench inside him.

Naomi nodded. "I think I would too," she said.

She reached out, offering Caroline her hand, and the other woman took it. She held on to Naomi's hand all the way back to Horizon.

Eventually, Caroline was sent home; Naomi insisted that she was unlikely to commit violence again, and Gabriel reluctantly agreed. She was sterilized even though she was only twenty-nine, her trauma rendering her unfit to be a parent again. She faced no other consequences.

Gabriel's brief address to the Clearview community was probably misquoted in a training text. *Our allegiance is not to justice but to the State.* Joan had read it in a book, after all.

Gabriel came back to reality as he circled around again to the runners' trail, and began to hear a steady, rushing sound.

A river, he thought, recalling the rapidly flowing water that separated their world from the Waste.

He crested a hill surrounded by tall, thin trees with lush, draping branches, and both the river and the other car came into view in the distance. Gabriel stopped, forgetting momentarily to pull out of sight. Lying below him was a river wider than any road. Its water flowed quietly, unlike the churning rapids before entering the Waste, but it was moving fast; he spotted a stick bobbing at the surface and watched as it sped downstream.

Gabriel slowly backed the car down the hill, out of sight, and got out. He grabbed his jacket, leaving behind the blood-encrusted shirt, and rummaged in the trunk's emergency kit, coming up with a flashlight, a pair of binoculars, and more of the wound glue. Those he tucked in his jacket pockets, and the stolen weapon he secured with his belt at the small of his back, wishing he could be sure he was not about to strike himself accidentally with one of its projectiles. He crept back to the top of the hill, concealed himself among the odd verdant trees, and focused the binoculars on the car below him.

They were driving alongside the river, and as he tracked them, they slowed, then came to a stop. They got out of the car, and he saw that they were beside a small stone building, not big enough to be a house of any kind. It was built so close to the river that it looked almost ready to fall in. There was a single tiny window on one side, and on the roof was a lone old-fashioned solar panel.

Gabriel moved carefully down the hill. He could make it almost to where they were under the cover of trees, but he would have to cross an open field to make it to the building. When he reached the foot of the hill, he crouched behind a tree trunk, watching as Asa came out of the building and retrieved something from the car. Gabriel waited, and when Asa did not emerge again, he made a run for it, sprinting across the grass with one eye on the half-closed door. He ducked behind the structure, and through the open door he could hear them speak in low voices.

Eve muttered something indistinct, but Gabriel clearly heard her say, "Do you even understand any of this?"

"Yes," Asa said firmly, then sighed. "Well, I think I can figure it out."

Gabriel crept around the far side of the building, to the filthy window. He peered through it, careful not to smudge the dirt, and was just barely able to make out what was inside: *A boat. They're going to try to cross the river.* Eve glanced back toward him, and Gabriel ducked out of sight. *I could stop them right here; there's only the two of them.* But something kept him where he was, crouching in the dirt instead of making the arrest. *Why are they crossing the river?* He smiled briefly, reminded of an old joke. *To get to the other side.*

"What's on the other side?" he whispered, barely hearing his own voice above the rushing river.

He had told Hiram and Omar that Eve could be the key to bringing down the underground banks. Whatever *was* on the other side, it was important enough to cross moving water, putting both of their lives at risk. All it would take was a single misstep for the boat to capsize, for one of them to fall overboard and become infected. Whatever they were heading for, Gabriel wanted to see for himself.

Gabriel crept around to the front of the building, which opened directly onto the water, revealing the boat. It looked familiar, like something out of a history book, from the time before water travel became too dangerous. It was white and brown, though the paint was faded and cracking, and it was a little larger than a car, with a deep base that came to a point at the front. There was a short deck at the back and a small square cabin in the middle. Craning his neck, Gabriel could see controls through one of the large side windows. The boathouse floor was cut out in the middle, and the boat was suspended slightly above the water, held aloft on two rusty beams that connected to the ceiling with hefty chains. At the top, he could see some kind of pulley system, though how it worked was not clear.

Asa and Eve were on the other side of the boat, conferring with their heads together, and Gabriel crouched and crept in a little farther. The walls of the small building were lined with shelves of neatly stacked labeled containers of varying sizes, though Gabriel could only read a few of the labels from his position: "H2O 5GL," "RICE," "CORN SYRUP," "MRTE." Only the second of these made sense to Gabriel.

The back wall was lined with plastic tanks labeled "DIESEL FUEL," and in a corner he could see the square black battery that connected to the solar panel on the roof. *Whoever lived here was preparing for something, anyway.*

Asa turned, coming around the side of the boat, and Gabriel pulled back into the dark corner of the building, concealing himself behind an enormous black plastic crate marked "5 AR-15 10,000 RDS."

✦

Asa stepped onto one of the beams supporting the boat and crossed it with his eyes on the water below. The door to the cabin was unlocked, and he ducked his head to enter it, settling into the captain's seat to examine the control panel; everything was clearly labeled, but only half the words made sense to him. The steering wheel seemed straightforward enough, though it was straight upright and had spokes sticking out in every direction. The array of dials was a mystery. He pressed buttons and raised levers as Eve watched anxiously from the side.

"Can you figure it out?" she called, as if he were farther away than he was.

"I think so. Everything is labeled," he said. "The thing is, it has a fuel gauge—it's not even electric."

"Do you know how to do it?" Eve asked.

He smiled at her. "Well, no, I mean who does? But I know you have to put fuel in the boat somehow. There should be somewhere to do that, like a tank or something. I don't see anything in here, so maybe it's where the engine is."

"Where's that?"

"Eve!" Asa said with mock exasperation. "I know exactly as much as you do. I'll check the boat for somewhere to put fuel, and you see if you can find any."

"All the tanks back here say, 'Diesel Fuel.' Is that what you need?"

"Let's hope so. See if you can figure out how we get this thing into the water." He gestured to the beams and pulleys. "There's got to be a lever or a crank or something."

Eve nodded, and Asa went to the back of the cabin, where a door led out onto a small deck. It was empty, but on the floor, right behind the cabin, was a small trapdoor. Asa pulled it up and grinned. A tank filled the space, with a cap labeled "DIESEL ONLY" in the center.

"Found it!" he called. He climbed off the boat and crossed the support beam to where Eve stood examining a large lever.

"This connects to those chains," she said as he reached her side. "I think we just pull it."

"Worth a try," he agreed.

Asa went to the wall of yellow fuel tanks and grabbed one; it had a place for a spout, and after a moment he found one in a box labeled "SPOUTS" on the nearest shelf.

"Whoever set this place up was definitely organized," he murmured as he returned to the boat with the can of fuel.

He fitted the spout into the small opening in the boat's tank and poured the fluid in slowly. When the yellow can was empty, he righted it, and the slick substance ran down from the spout onto his hands. He dropped the can and wiped his hands hurriedly on his pants, but the fuel did not burn or hurt as he had expected it to. Carefully, Asa screwed the cap on again and closed the trapdoor.

"I think it's ready," he called to Eve.

"We've still got to get our bags from the car," she said and headed out the door. He climbed out of the boat and followed her.

✦

Now or never.

As soon as Eve and Asa were out of sight, Gabriel crept out of his hiding place and across the beam suspending the boat over the water, then crawled in through the open cabin door, searching for a place to hide. There were two seats in front of the control panel, and a bench behind them, built into the wall. Gabriel smiled and flipped the top of the bench up, revealing a compartment.

It held three square blue cushions. He took them out, shoved them under the seats, climbed into the compartment, and pulled the top down. He found himself in complete darkness as Asa's and Eve's voices rose again, coming back into the building.

The planks creaked as Asa and Eve climbed into the boat, and he heard murmured voices as they talked. Gabriel relaxed into stillness, deliberately slowing his breathing.

I hope they know what they're doing, he thought, though of course they didn't. *I hope they're not complete idiots,* he amended.

✦

"Ready?" Eve shouted.

Asa answered something indistinct. Then, with a screech of grinding gears, the boat began haltingly to lower into the water. Gabriel braced himself against the sides of the storage compartment, clenching his teeth as the platform shuddered on its long-unused pulleys. There was a soft splash; then the whole boat was buoyed up, rocking for a moment nauseatingly. The ancient engine began to roar, and Gabriel closed his eyes.

I hope this thing doesn't leak.

CHAPTER FOURTEEN

ASA COULD FEEL EVE'S EYES ON HIM AS HE stood in front of the wheel with his hands light on its spokes, steering the boat with ease. She was tracking each movement he made like a hawk watching a field mouse. He glanced back at her and grinned.

She shook her head in disapproval, her face grave. "Watch where we're going," she said tightly.

She was sitting cross-legged on the seat beside him, holding on to both arms of the chair, and every time they rocked side to side her grip tightened. They were barely halfway across, and already her knuckles were so white Asa imagined he could see the bones through her skin. He turned back to the wheel with haste.

"The boat's covered—we're not going to fall out," he said matter-of-factly, trying to suppress his own excitement. *We're crossing a river!* he wanted to shout. *On a boat! Who have we ever met who's done that?*

After days of running, the violence they had witnessed, the fear that had followed them from moment to moment, they were finally having the kind of adventure that he loved, boldly taking on something no one else would dare to do.

He glanced back again at Eve, who had her eyes screwed shut now, then fixed his gaze on their destination. The water moved smoothly, but it moved fast: in the little mirror beside the wheel he could already see the boathouse was well upstream, although he had aimed to go straight across.

Asa turned the wheel cautiously, and the boat tipped a little; beside him Eve inhaled sharply.

"It's okay," he said, trying to sound confident. "I'm just making sure we don't go too far downstream."

"What? I thought you could drive this thing!"

"I can! Eve, it's fine."

Asa held out a hand, and after a second Eve took it, squeezing it briefly, then stood and crossed the few steps between them unsteadily. She put an arm around his waist, clutching him tightly, and stayed there, watching as he steered them toward the shore. Asa kept his eyes on the water, his pulse quickening as she held on to him, the line of her body pressed close against his.

"Have you ever seen so much water?" she whispered, so close he felt her breath on his neck.

He swallowed and shook his head. "Never."

They were fast approaching the riverbank. Asa had been scanning it for another boathouse since they set out, but there was nothing like the little structure they had come from, only a solid-looking concrete wall standing about as high as the boat itself and above that a fence.

"I don't know where to stop," Asa said, worried. Eve bit her lip.

"I think we have to tie the boat to that fence," she said faintly, and her grip on his waist tightened, her fingers digging into his side.

Asa nodded. "I'm going to need you to take the wheel," he said. She didn't answer, and he went on before she could protest. "I'll get out on the deck in back, and I'll tie the boat off to the fence. Then we'll just have to climb over it."

"Over the fence?" Eve asked, looking at him as though he had just suggested they swim the rest of the way.

"It's not high," he said. "Look, the wall isn't any higher than the top of the boat. It won't be hard to climb up."

"If it's so easy to get past, why is there a fence at all?" Eve countered. "What if it's more dangerous than it seems?"

Asa let out a long, slow breath; he had been considering this as they crossed. "I think it's like how there's nothing really stopping you from going out into the Waste," he said. "People probably aren't trying to get into Sanctuary because no one really knows where it is—they get brought here somehow, and it's not like they have any reason to leave. I bet that fence is just there so no one loses their balance and falls in."

He lowered the boat to the slowest pace he could without stopping.

"Maybe." Eve didn't sound convinced, but she let him guide her hands to the wheel as he stepped aside. "What do I do?"

"Just keep it aimed at the wall, and when I give the signal, pull that lever down into neutral." Asa pointed to the neatly labeled engine controls.

Eve forced a smile as he went out onto the deck. He picked up a rope that was tied off to a small piece of metal attached to the boat's side. He pulled against it hard to test its strength; the rope held. He waved at Eve through the window, and she nodded curtly and pulled the lever into neutral. The boat drifted for a moment, then rammed into the concrete wall.

Asa lurched forward, catching himself just before his head hit the wall as the boat began to drift downstream. The fence atop the wall was the height of his shoulders, and Asa reached out with the rope and grabbed a thin metal fence post. His fingers slipped immediately from it; the boat was too heavy for Asa to hold, but he looped the rope around the post and held on to that for dear life.

Slowly, the boat came to a halt, and he began to pull on the rope, dragging them along the wall back to where they had first tried to stop. After a moment, Eve emerged from the cabin and walked over behind him to help. They pulled on the rope in concert until they made it back to the fence post. He tied off the rope in a series of knots, then turned to Eve and hugged her impulsively. She made a startled squeak, but she hugged him back fiercely.

"What was that?" she asked breathlessly when he let her go.

He shrugged. "I think I like boats," he said. "Come on."

He held out his hands to give her a boost, but Eve ignored him; she grabbed the fence post, stepped on the railing, and smoothly lifted herself onto the concrete wall and over the fence. Asa blinked.

"Toss me the bags," Eve called softly.

He retrieved the bags from the control room and handed them to her, one by one, then scrambled up the wall and over the fence. She took his hand when he landed beside her and stood on her toes to kiss his cheek.

"I hate boats," she whispered in his ear, then laughed in that frantic way she had.

They were on an open path that seemed to run along the riverbank, edged by the fence, and what Asa suspected had been right; the barrier was only there to prevent accidents. From their path, other, narrower paths branched out, leading to open grass. Off in the distance, Asa could see houses and a few scattered larger buildings. Before them lay a large field where crops were growing: corn, wheat, and some he did not recognize.

As they watched, white drones swooped over the field and sprayed a fine mist of water over the crop, then dropped almost to ground level, disappearing among the various plants. Asa went to the edge of the field and crouched. The drone opened a panel in its side, and dozens of tiny white ants came spilling out. Asa crawled closer.

"Asa, what are you doing?" Eve was standing behind him.

"Just a second."

He watched as the ants formed into a phalanx and began to march through the dirt. Pairs split off as they passed each stalk of corn and began to climb, and Asa stood, watching the progress of two ants as they made their way up. They moved in concert, circling the stalk as they climbed it, then reached the first ear, where Asa spotted a little green beetle with black spots, sheltering on a leaf.

"Eve, watch," he whispered, and she bent down beside him to see.

On the opposite side of the stalk, the ants stopped and came together, almost seeming to confer, then they set off marching side by side toward the beetle.

The insect scarcely roused to move before one ant had it by the wings, the other at its head. They were swift and brutal, using legs and mandibles to tear the beetle apart, letting its remains fall to the ground below. When the beetle was destroyed, the ants seemed to confer again. They marched back and forth where the insect had been, their tiny heads down as if inspecting the space. Asa leaned closer, trying to see them better.

Even for ants this is weird, he thought, and then the creatures stopped moving, and the tips of their antennae began to flash rapidly with green lights, sending an almost inaudible series of high-pitched beeps. Asa pulled back, stunned.

"What did I just witness? A tiny insect murder?" Eve asked.

Asa nodded. "I think so. Look."

He pulled her along and crouched to look at the crop of wheat, where more ants were marching along each stalk. From somewhere inside, he could hear a soft rustling as individual stalks of wheat swayed, followed by the quiet beeping. He cupped his hands around his eyes, and from a dozen points among the crops, he saw flashing pairs of bright green lights.

"What is that?" Eve asked.

"They're automs—the ants are all automs. They're ... pest control."

"What?"

"They're searching each individual plant for pests, probably for disease too—that beeping and flashing, they're signaling something."

"Isn't that a waste of tech?" Eve asked, moving them back to the path where they had started, but Asa shook his head.

"I mean, it depends on your priorities. If you want to make sure you never lose a crop to blight or bugs ... then no, it's not a waste at all. At home we spray crops with a solution that kills the bugs, but they can become resistant. There's always a risk that something will come along that you can't stop. But this? You're not going to run across a strain of beetle resistant to ant-sized automs tearing them apart."

"Unless you get really big beetles," Eve said, and Asa gave her a distracted smile.

"Then you'd just send more ants."

He started back toward the field, and Eve caught his hand.

"Asa, what's wrong? Why are you so focused on these things? This isn't what we're here for," she reminded him.

He stopped and looked at her; she had a genuinely puzzled expression. *She doesn't understand.* He reached out and touched her cheek.

"City girl," he said, then met her concerned gaze. "I'm a farmer, Eve. Look, there's been no shortage of food since the Founding. If one community runs low, another always has a bumper crop to help out. We really are all in this together, right?"

"Of course," she said slowly.

"But we've been lucky too—there could be a blight. There could be some infestation we're not prepared for. It's *always* possible."

"Okay," she said, still uncomprehending.

Asa sighed in frustration. "These ants—they're not just pest control. They're an early warning system. I bet they detect signs of disease ages before human eyes could. They could take down a resistant infestation one by one without damaging the crop. They could detect disease and probably sort which plants should be destroyed and which can survive. They could prevent a famine."

"Oh," Eve said, her eyes going wide. "That's incredible."

"Yeah," Asa said. "So why aren't they everywhere? Why don't *we* have them?" They stared at each other for a moment, wordless; then Eve grabbed his arm.

"Look," she whispered, and he turned around.

Less than fifty feet away, a perfectly round cloud slowly descended from the sky. As it touched down, the mist around it dissipated, revealing a large round passenger drone. Asa's heart skipped a beat.

"Contract Enforcement," he said so quietly he could barely hear himself. "They tracked us."

There was nowhere to hide, unless they went in among the crop, but it was too late; they would be spotted by now. Asa took a deep breath and squared his shoulders, stepping protectively in front of Eve as the door to the drone opened.

Three people clambered out in an excited chaos, laughing and shouting as they gathered bags and parcels from inside. Eve and Asa exchanged a glance; then Eve gave him a quick smile and strode toward them. There were two women, one extremely thin and pale, with iron-gray hair, and the other plump and brown with a puff of hair that was a pale pink. The third person was a Panasian man without a shirt. Asa tried not to stare at his chest; it was defined and muscular, but his skin appeared thin, hanging off the muscle as if it was too loose.

"Hello," the man said, waving as they approached. "We're just on our way to have lunch in the park." He held up a basket as proof.

"You must be with the State!" the pink-haired woman exclaimed, then laughed at their expressions. "Don't look so surprised, kids. I hope you weren't expecting to blend in."

"What are you here about?" the gray-haired woman asked tensely, and Asa looked at her in surprise.

The other woman laughed. "Claudia! You can't ask that. It's none of our business." She shook her head exaggeratedly and smiled at Eve. "I'm sure they're very good at whatever it is they're doing," she said firmly.

"Thanks," Asa mumbled uncomfortably, and Eve caught his eye.

"We're here to speak with David Micah Founder," Eve said with smooth assurance. The group stared at her for a moment, then the man laughed. "Can you tell us where to find him?" she asked, her voice tightening, and the man nodded.

"He's in his old cabin past the City Block," he said, pointing.

Off in the distance were large, brightly painted sculpture buildings like the ones in Horizon, all clustered together, though spread out along the narrow roads. Asa could see houses that looked like the ones back in Rosewood.

Something for everyone, he thought.

"He's as close to the ocean as anyone dares to be," the man added.

"Why did you laugh?" Asa asked suspiciously. "When she asked about David, why did you laugh?"

"Oh, everyone's always looking for David," the pink-haired woman said. "But good luck getting him to talk to you!"

"Thanks," Eve said wryly.

She glanced at Asa, and they started down the path toward the buildings in the distance.

✦

It didn't take long to get to what the man had referred to as the "City Block," which was indeed about the size of a city block in Horizon. The unique sculpture buildings stretched up and out in strange proportions, each one decorated without any thought to how it might look next to the others. Asa marveled briefly at a black dome, shimmering like a dark stone in the sun, set next to a jagged tower painted in orange, pink, and yellow stripes.

"It looks like they just picked up a chunk of the city and set it down in the middle of this place," Eve whispered, echoing his thoughts.

"Do you feel right at home?" he asked lightly, and she laughed and shook her head.

"No. It feels strange. I think I'd feel more at home in a place where everything is new to me. This just looks like they've tried to make a copy of my home." She gave him a curious look. "Does that make sense?"

"Yeah," he said thoughtfully. "I kind of imagined Sanctuary would be . . . unimaginable. But if you're going to spend the rest of your life somewhere, it makes sense that you'd want it to be familiar."

"I guess," Eve said.

Asa glanced at her. Her face was placid, but he had the feeling of something else beneath the surface—some conversation she still wanted to have.

Without discussion, they took the path that circled around the City Block instead of going through it. When they made the first turn, Asa realized that what he had assumed to be one of the buildings was actually an immense concrete wall, rising as high as the tallest of the Horizon-style sculptures. It ran along the path ahead of them, and when he looked back, he saw that it stretched a little beyond the farms they had first passed. At the end he could just make out a low, round building that resembled the water treatment plants back home.

There was an odd noise coming from somewhere nearby. It almost sounded like the boat engine running, but not quite; it was softer and more soothing, but still it roared on the other side of the wall.

"Asa, look," Eve said, picking up her pace.

Catching up to her, he squinted into the distance, then saw it:

a small house backed up against the concrete, almost as if it had been built into the wall.

"That must be David's cottage," she said in an excited whisper. Asa put a steadying hand on her arm.

"We have to stay calm," he whispered. "They all think we're with the State, but what if someone checks?"

"Right." Eve slowed. "Asa, what am I going to say to him?"

There was a note of panic in her voice, and Asa stopped, guiding her off the path for a moment to stand beneath a pair of tall, leafy trees. Eve looked as if she were about to cry.

"What's wrong?" he asked in a low voice. "Eve, we're almost there. You still think David will help us, right?"

She met his eyes, and for a moment the few years between them felt like a palpable lifetime.

"But what will I tell him about Daniel?" she whispered.

Asa felt a thud of shock in his chest; he had almost forgotten about Eve and Daniel, or at least he had not considered what this moment must mean for her.

"We'll tell him the truth," Asa said, and she looked at him helplessly.

"What's the truth? That he loved me and I couldn't save him?"

Asa hesitated, searching her face for a hint of what she wanted him to say. At last he gave up. "Yes," he said. "No one could. Even Saul said as much. You can tell David that he loved you, and you tried to help him, but you couldn't save him."

She nodded, but her gaze was distant, as if she hoped still for another answer. Asa waited, and finally she sighed and adjusted her backpack, gripping the straps tightly. Asa kissed her cheek, and she put her hand on the back of his head, holding him close for a moment before stepping away.

"Let's go, then," she said grimly and nodded toward the path.

✦

The cottage was small. As they walked to the door, Asa thought it could hardly hold more than a single room. The building itself was made of large irregularly sized stones, held together with pale, sturdy-looking mortar, and the roof was tiled with gray slate shingles. It was cheerful-looking and reminded Asa of a picture book he'd had as a child. Eve raised her hand to knock on the wooden door, then hesitated, glancing at him as if for encouragement. He nodded and gave her a smile. She knocked.

The door opened almost instantly, and Asa and Eve drew back in surprise. A tall, gray-haired man who looked more weather-worn than elderly glowered down at them, his jaw set and his dark eyes hard as iron.

"We're looking for David Micah Founder," Asa managed to say, and the eyes swept up and down him like a scanner.

Asa shivered with the fleeting sensation that everything he had done, good and bad, had just been seen and judged. The man turned to Eve and did the same to her, assessing her in an instant with an impassive expression. He said nothing. Eve straightened her shoulders, steeling herself.

"It's about your grandson, Daniel," she said shakily. The man's eyes widened with a hint of surprise, then he stepped back and held the door open.

"Yes, I'm David," he said roughly. "You'd better come in."

They obeyed, and when they were inside, he closed the door behind them. The cottage went dark. Eve gasped, and Asa moved protectively closer to her.

"Sorry. Let me open a window," David said.

There was shuffling in the darkness, then the click of a switch, and a screen on the back wall began to rise, flooding the room with daylight.

"I was working with ... something else," David added by way of explanation, gesturing at the adjacent wall, which was spanned by a long workbench and a half-dozen monitors, their screens blank.

"Oh," Eve said softly, leaving Asa's side, and he turned away from the impressive private collection of technology.

She was staring at the back wall of the cottage. It was now a huge window, and beyond it lay an immense landscape of water, undulating like a field of wheat in the wind. Asa hurried to join her, staring down; the concrete wall plunged all the way down into the water, which crashed against it rhythmically, sending up sprays of white foam that almost reached the little house.

"Is it real?" Asa asked, and David chuckled.

"It's the ocean."

Asa and Eve stared at each other, then back at the window and the waves below.

"It can't be," Asa whispered, but it could be nothing else.

There was nothing else but water, as if it had taken over the world. He had known the ocean existed, but in the way he'd known the stars and the void of space existed: he didn't expect to walk into someone's house and find them out the back window. He watched the crashing waves, mesmerized by the constant motion.

"Is it safe?" Eve asked faintly, taking careful steps back from the window, and David shook his head.

"No," he said firmly. "It's no safer than freshwater. Don't get any ideas."

"I meant, is it safe to live so close to it?"

"Oh." David peered past her, looking down at the water as if considering the question for the first time. "So far, no one's died while visiting."

Eve laughed.

"What?" he growled, and Asa spun around to see him glaring again at both of them.

"You're just like him," Eve said.

David's face hardened. "Yes, well. Maybe you'd better have a seat and tell me whatever it is you have to say about Daniel, and why you want to tell me about it."

He grabbed the chair from the workbench and flipped it around to face them, sitting and crossing an ankle over his knee. He moved like a man Asa's own age, hinting at the answer to one of the rumors about Sanctuary. *They make you young again.*

"Asa," Eve hissed, tugging at his sleeve.

He sat beside her on a couch he had not noticed before, a well-worn piece of furniture that sagged in the middle, pushing them together. Eve looked down at her hands in her lap, fidgeting for a moment, then looked up to meet David's hard gaze.

"Your name is David Micah Founder," she asked. "Is that right?"

David nodded, then smiled sadly. "It used to be Pasternak," he said.

"What?"

"Before the Founding, the names were different—I couldn't be called 'Founder' before anything was founded, could I? I was David Pasternak." He looked at their faces amusedly. "It means 'parsnip.'"

Eve shook her head, her mouth slightly open; then she swallowed, regaining her composure.

"I'm sorry, I . . . I don't think I ever quite believed him."

"Daniel," David said quietly.

"Daniel, yes." Eve said. "He told me you were one of the Founders, and I . . . well, I believed that *he* believed it." She laughed, and her face turned grave. "David, I'm so sorry." Asa saw her eyes shine with tears. "Daniel's dead."

The tears spilled over, and she covered her face with her hands, wiping them away. Asa started to reach out to her, then stopped, aware that it was not his place, not here. He shifted on the couch and turned his attention to David, whose expression was stony and illegible, his eyes fixed on Eve as if Asa were not even there.

"Who are you, that you've come here to tell me that?" he asked, all the warmth gone from his gravelly voice. His frozen tone seemed to shock Eve back into a kind of calm, and she straightened, folding her hands in her lap.

"I'm the closest thing Daniel had to family, apart from you," she said with calm assurance, as if, having said the worst thing, the rest had become simple. "My name is Eve. We were a couple when he died—for the last four years—and I knew him much longer than that. My brother, Saul, used to help him with . . . honestly, I don't know what they did. Daniel was always careful not to tell me too much."

David was watching her keenly, and now he narrowed his eyes. "What do you think they did?"

"Plenty." Eve smiled suddenly. "You know he was brilliant, don't you?" David's face remained immobile, but something sparked in his eyes. "He was always playing with something. I know most of the tech he dealt in was illegal, but it was more than that."

"You tell me," David said quietly. "I haven't seen the boy since he was very young."

"He used to go off on these rants," Eve said, a faint smile still on her lips, and Asa felt a rush of jealousy. "We would go out—or sometimes not—and he'd, well, have too much to drink." She glanced at David, looking embarrassed, but he showed no reaction, and she went on. "Daniel would start talking about personal liberty, about abolishing the security protections on scientific research outside the State apparatus, about ending the safety restrictions on childbearing—he scared me. He didn't make any sense. But from what I saw, all it was all about, really, was these."

Eve unzipped the backpack at her feet and pulled out one of the metal strips she had used to purchase the train tickets out of Horizon. She handed it to David, who gave it a passing glance, then reached behind him and pulled on his workbench. Part of it separated from the rest and glided out across the floor on wheels. There was a large screen on top and a keypad. Asa decided it looked like something a State Bureaucrat would most likely have, the kind of tech desk he had only seen in the background of broadcasts.

David pressed a few buttons on the keypad, then fitted the strip into a slot on the side of the desk. A string of incomprehensible symbols appeared on the screen, and a faint smile crossed his face. Then he yanked the metal strip out, and the screen went blank. He pushed the desk away, and it drifted a few feet across the floor as he turned his attention back to Eve, absently rubbing the metal strip with his thumb.

"I see," he said dryly.

"He called them mayflies," Eve said.

"So, Daniel was making money," David mused. "I did teach him to take a direct approach." He chuckled to himself, then sobered. "Is that what got him killed?" he asked Eve.

She shook her head, tears spilling over again. "It was my fault."

"That isn't true!" Asa half rose from his seat, realizing as they turned that he had nearly shouted. "It's not true," he said more calmly.

David looked at him as if just recalling that he was there, and Eve had covered her face again, her shoulders shaking as she cried silently. Asa took a deep breath and addressed Daniel's grandfather.

"David, Eve feels guilty because she thinks she should have been able to help Daniel. But the fact is, he killed himself. The three of us had dinner in their apartment. It was at the top of one of those tall buildings, and that morning he jumped from the window. I tried to stop him, but I just . . . couldn't. I'm sorry. But you can't think it was Eve's fault," he finished.

David stood abruptly and came toward them. Asa stood belatedly, and David gave him a curt nod, then sat where Asa had been beside Eve, who sat up straighter, wiping her eyes.

"Of course it wasn't your fault, my dear," he said softly. "Daniel struggled all his life. I have feared this moment for years." He took her hand. "Daniel and I have not seen each other in a long time, but we did communicate, as I suspect you already know. He spoke to me several times about you. The light in his abyss. Eve Layla Ashland." David looked away, stifling a cough. "He was unhealthily poetic, I think, but the sentiment was real. You meant a lot to him."

Eve smiled briefly. "I know," she said. "I'm glad I gave him at least some happiness, anyway."

"I believe you gave him a great deal." He reached up to brush a tear from her cheek, and Asa cleared his throat nervously. Eve looked up at him, and David stood, giving Asa a small ironic smile, and gestured to the couch. "I believe I've taken your seat," he said, returning to his chair.

Asa sat, flustered. David gave him a cool, appraising glance, and once again Asa had the unpleasant sense of being measured.

"I don't think you are here only to tell me this news and share in my grief," David said sharply, startling them both.

He gave Eve a kind look; then his demeanor changed again, his face as harsh as it had been the moment they entered the cottage. Asa shifted in his seat. The man's quick changes, from hard indifference to compassion and sorrow and back again in fractions of a second, were unsettling.

David went on. "There are no easy ways to get to Sanctuary for you two, other than waiting for about forty years, so I have to believe you endured a great deal to come here. Why?" He settled back, waiting for an answer.

"You said you have been afraid Daniel would kill himself for a long time," Asa said slowly, and David nodded. Asa took a deep breath. *Please believe us.* "When he jumped, I tried to grab him. I leaned out the window and reached for him. Eve was right beside me, and then we realized there was a drone watching the whole thing—from the angle it was hovering, I know it looked like I pushed him."

David frowned, his thick eyebrows furrowing almost comically. "There are drones everywhere. There must have been three more that saw it from other angles. The Contract Enforcers will have seen every feed. You have nothing to worry about." He looked at them perplexedly.

Eve shook her head. While Asa was talking, she had pulled her backpack up onto her lap, and now she was hugging it to her chest as she had when they first boarded the train to Rosewood. "Daniel limited the number of drones near our building," she said.

David made an exasperated sound. "Of course he did. I can't say I blame him, but things like this are exactly what the drones are for. Still, with only one feed, it's got to look inconclusive, at least."

"The night before, Daniel and I got into a fight at some night-bar. We were both arrested," Asa said miserably. "We'd worked it out, honestly, but . . . it wouldn't make things look good. The dots would have been connected, and there's little doubt the State would have passed swift judgement, charging me with murder. We had to run. We escaped into the Waste, then crossed the river to get here."

"I see." David gave them each a wary look. "What is it you think I can do to help?"

"Daniel said you had a back door into the system," Eve said. "He used it once, that I know of—to help my brother, Saul."

"I know of this as well," David said curtly. "Saul is a good man."

"We thought you could help us change our records," Asa pressed. "Rule Daniel's death officially a suicide, take away any marks we've been given so we can go home."

David looked thoughtfully at Asa, then sighed. "If I had any doubt of your innocence, I would send you back into the Waste with no help whatsoever. But I happen to believe that you did no harm to my grandson. So I will help you."

Relief washed over Asa, dizzyingly, and he closed his eyes for a moment, steadying himself.

"I have Daniel's computer," Eve said.

David looked as if he heard it from far away. He opened his eyes as she handed over the thin black box. He put a hand to his temple, and for a moment he looked ancient, the years settling on him all at once. Then he opened the object, revealing a screen and keypad.

"I gave this to Daniel when he was a child," David said

quietly. He placed his hands on the keypad lightly, then sighed and closed the computer.

"David . . . would you tell me more about Daniel?" Eve asked hesitantly, and Asa raised his eyebrows, then quickly smoothed his expression.

It's her only chance, he reminded himself. *They knew each other a long time.* David was staring down at Daniel's computer, rubbing the edge of the screen with his thumb.

"You knew him better than I did, Eve," David said in a hollow voice.

"No, I didn't," she said insistently. "Daniel was so absorbed by all his secrets—*those* were his life—and he never told me anything important, just hints when he was drunk. Then he'd catch himself and stop. I wanted to know more, but he said I'd be in danger. He wouldn't even tell me from what. David . . . I want you to tell me about him. I want to understand why . . ." She closed her eyes for a moment. "I want to know why he was so sad."

David reached out and grabbed the edge of the desk, dragging it back toward him. He switched it on and pressed a series of buttons, hunching forward over the keys; Daniel's computer was still balanced on his lap. Asa glanced at Eve, and she gave him a distressed look and held out her hand. He grasped it briefly, then let go as David snapped his head up to look at them.

"What's your name, young man?" he asked, and Asa was startled.

"Asa Isaac Rosewood," he said.

David started typing again. A moment later he sat back and sent his desk rolling away again. "You're no longer fugitives," he said.

Asa and Eve exchanged a glance.

"Wait—really?" Asa asked.

David shrugged. "It's a simple, rather elegant system, if I may say so myself. User-friendly."

"What-friendly?" Asa repeated.

"You built it, didn't you?" Eve said, and David gave her a hint of a smile.

"I did indeed. Every computer system the State depends on, it's all the work of one poor old man who used to be called David Pasternak."

"And is that what Daniel was doing? Interfering in the State system?" Eve asked, horrified but transfixed.

David gave her one of his measuring stares. He got up and placed Daniel's computer gently on the desk, then sat again and leaned forward with his elbows on his knees, knotting his hands together.

"Please, David," Eve pressed. "I have to know what happened to him—what was so bad that he would do what he did."

David nodded gravely. "I will tell you everything you want to know, Eve. In fact, I must. If you both are thinking of returning, you must know the full truth of what you are returning to."

CHAPTER FIFTEEN

DAVID LOOKED DOWN AT HIS HANDS PENSIVELY, as if deciding where to begin. He touched the tips of his fingers together, making half an orb, then flattened it, bringing his palms together.

Asa glanced at Eve, trying to catch her eye, but she was rapt, watching David as if his every movement meant something vital. Asa swung his arm up on the couch's back behind Eve, circling her protectively without touching her. Eve did not seem to notice, but David's eyes flickered past the gesture, taking it in as he had taken in everything they had done and said since they'd arrived.

David sat back in his chair and scrutinized them both in what Asa was beginning to see was his habitual fashion; then he stared off behind them with the same intensity.

"I do not know precisely what you have already been told," he said at last. "I will ask you to be patient. What you were taught contains absolute truth as well as blatant lies, and the two are so tangled, so bound up with each other, that at first you may think I am telling you things you already know."

"Okay," Asa said.

"I was a relatively young man when the world as we knew it began to end. I was a computer engineer. I was on the brink of great achievement. I was married with a newborn child."

"James," Eve said. "Daniel's father?"

David blinked. "No," he said curtly and cleared his throat. "My personal life is not important to the story of what happened."

Asa started to protest, but David kept speaking as if the interruption had not happened.

"The world as we knew it then was ending," he went on. "It had been since before I was born." He smiled suddenly. "We are all dying from the moment we are born," he said, and he sounded as if he was quoting something. "No one likes to think of their own demise. We are horrified of ending. Our minds have mechanisms to prevent us from dwelling too much on the inevitable fact of our own deaths. Otherwise, we would accomplish nothing or go about our lives haunted by our own terror."

"Some people do live like that," Eve said quietly, and David gave her a sad smile.

"Unfortunately, some do. So, imagine a species and a civilization facing the same prospect: they will die, their children will not be born, and the few that will be born will survive only to find their legacy is suffering and extinction. Of course, people deny it is happening. 'Don't worry,' they insist. 'Everything will be fine. The children are the future. They will devise some new technology to clean up any mess that we create today for the sake of profits.'

"But eventually, denial became impossible. The end began.

Everything started to happen at once. The oceans rose, and storms raged across the earth, bringing devastation."

"We do know this," Asa said quietly, and David nodded.

"I know. Let me continue. Communications were knocked back a century. We lost nearly all forms of contact. Storms and floods ruined crops, bringing famine. Famine forced people to flee their homes. Soon, people were crowded together in the only livable parts of the world, fighting for scarce food. Attempts to distribute scant resources turned into outright war, total anarchy." David raised a hand as if anticipating interruption. "I know. You know this too. But what you cannot possibly understand is how fast it all happened: not in generations, but in the space of only a few years. To know it will happen eventually is one thing, but to see it happen almost overnight . . ." He trailed off, shaking his head.

David stood and went to the window, gazing out at the ocean. The sun was still high in the sky, and it glittered off the water. Asa watched it, then looked away, his eyes burning with the afterimage of the light. David stayed where he was, speaking to the glass.

"We saw this coming. We tried to prevent it, and I do not mean a small group. Most of the world knew what would happen, because it was as plain as day. Year after year, the direst predictions were proven out. But no one wants to believe they are dying. There was another reason too, a more sinister one, and this I believe you know too."

He stopped and turned, his eyebrows arched, waiting for an answer.

"Greed," Asa said, slightly irritated at being questioned on history that every child knew by the time they could read. David simply nodded and turned back to the window.

"Greed. There was a saying: 'Knowledge is power.' But back

then, it was nothing of the kind. Information was everywhere. You could learn any subject known to man at the push of a button. But very few did. *Money* was the real power. Money created its own alternative truth. It was an age of appalling excess among the rich—they took more and more and more, stuffing it away for themselves while the masses struggled to survive. And when the end came, well, those were the people with the power to save the world. The billionaires, the politicians, the puppet masters of the human race. They were also the people who decided to do nothing and let the previous civilization burn to the ground. Who knows where we might all be if they had chosen to try to fix the broken system rather than hit the reset button?" He fell silent and didn't move a muscle.

"David?" Eve prompted after a moment.

He turned back to them and sighed, then returned to his chair and sat down. "I spend too much time alone," he said. "It makes me dwell on things."

"Some things are worth dwelling on," Eve said quietly, and he smiled faintly.

"No wonder Daniel liked you," he murmured. "Where was I? I tell this story in my head so often I get lost in it."

"You said something about a reset button?" Asa said, and David nodded.

"Thank you. When it became clear that we had failed, that we could no longer stop what had been set in motion, some gathered—the great minds of the time: scientists, of course, but more than that. Great thinkers, leaders, and several of the very wealthy who were also humanitarians, those of the rich who were seeking a solution to end the suffering like the rest of us." His voice took on a hard edge of irony. "Because, of course, nothing could be accomplished back then without a great deal of money."

"The Founders. You were among them?" Eve asked hesitantly, and he shook his head.

"No. I was not a great philosopher, just a computer geek. They needed technological infrastructure, and I was called in to do it. But that was later, when their intention had already been set in motion, when the plan was already in place. I'm a Founder in name only."

"The plan for us?" Asa asked.

David made a sound halfway between a snort and a laugh, then shook his head and continued. "In a way," he said dryly. "The Founders—they named themselves that, by the way—their debate began with finding a solution that would bring the world back to normal and ensure humanity's survival. How to gather surviving populations and provide enough infrastructure to help everyone survive. This was very early on. Hundreds of millions had died already, but the earth's population was still over seven billion. Many people who could still be saved.

"The Founders argued and ran computer simulations. They debated infrastructure and hypothesized over a thousand possible iterations of what might happen next, and then rather quickly, they came to their ultimate decision: they would do nothing at all."

Asa and Eve glanced at each other, then looked back at David, who was watching them expectantly.

"But they're the Founders," Asa said. "Without them we wouldn't be here."

"That's true. They planned this society: everything from the size of the ideal community to the age of childbearing. Everything modeled to its purest ideal and pragmatic in every way. But before they could do that, they had to wait out the storms and wars and famines. And once the earth had stabilized, once the population had dropped to a manageable level, they put their plans into action. At that time, they became the Founders, and the saviors of those who were left."

"Right." Asa nodded. "We know that too. But they didn't do . . . nothing." Puzzled, he turned to Eve, and she met his eyes with a stricken look. "I don't understand, do I?" he asked slowly, and she shook her head.

"Asa," she said, her voice thin, as if it might fade away. "Did you hear what he said? 'The saviors of those who were left.' He means that they let everyone else die. They just sat back and . . . *watched* while billions of people starved and drowned and murdered each other."

"What?" Asa stared at her. "No, that's not what he means, Eve. The world was in chaos—there was nothing they could do."

"Ask him," she said tightly, nodding toward David.

Asa turned to the old man, who was watching them with grave eyes.

"The world was in chaos," David said heavily. "Some say the seeds of this anarchy were planted many years before, when the powerful let weapons inundate our society. But aside from the violence, there were many things that could have been done. Flood zones could have been evacuated. The world's population could have been organized to migrate safely to higher ground. Farming and transport of food could have been arranged to feed the shifting populations. Alternate communication systems could have been put into place to maintain contact with other parts of the world. Most obviously, clean energy could have been put to use, both to mitigate the damage already done to our environment and to ensure that people would still have electricity, clean water, hospitals. There were many more things that could have been done that were not, and they had the ability to do all of them. So, Eve is correct.

"But they wanted to build a perfect society from scratch, one free of the problems and religious ideologies that had led to the destruction of the old civilization. They believed the perfect society could only be achieved with a small fraction of the population. A scattered people so brutalized by catastrophes, disease, and violence that they would gladly renounce the shackles of the past and embrace the new order wholeheartedly. So, the Founders allowed the destruction to continue unchecked until they had what they needed."

"And where did you come in?" Eve asked.

"I began building the computer system, the Network, once they settled on a plan. It changed as time went on, of course, but the basic framework was there from the beginning."

"Why did you agree to do it, if you thought what they were doing was wrong?" Asa asked, distressed.

"I didn't think they were wrong," David said. "I was not among them at the beginning, and if I had been, I doubt I would have approved of their decision. But once it had been decided, once it was the path we were taking, I didn't oppose it. You see, just like them, I had watched as the powerful allowed catastrophe and ruin to ravage the planet for their own selfish ends. I witnessed the carnage of the old civilization.

"I did not *want* the loss of life to continue, but if it was going to, then it made sense that whatever came next should be thoughtfully planned. Planned by people not motivated by greed. Planned so that no one could amass obscene wealth or benefit from holding others down in poverty for generations, so that everyone would have what they needed, so that we would truly all be on equal footing from birth. Totally pragmatic and completely unapologetic.

"If you are a good person, you have everything you need.

If you're a bad person, you are removed from normal society, as well as the future gene pool. Give the good people universal income so they can enjoy life and raise a proper family. Send the bad people to Work. A true meritocracy bound together by an unbreakable sense of community. We're all in this together. It was a stunning vision, and I became as true a believer as any of them.

"The individual citizens of our new society would use technology only sparingly, as the social ramifications were proven too dangerous by the old way of life. However, our new world would be run using a sophisticated set of programs. So, as the other Founders drafted philosophies of governance and population control, environmental conservation, resource distribution, and justice, I created the technological infrastructure to implement it—the Network, a system that could steward our society perfectly, and peacefully, for a thousand generations. That was the key, you see. Human history shows failure after failure when it comes to living together in harmony. The intent is often good—whole civilizations were built in the past using the most noble of principles. Yet always, the original intent crumbles beneath the inexorable weight of human fallibility. Greed, lust for power, the desire to subjugate—they always return, eventually. So, I was given the task of removing that possibility. I did so.

"When life began anew, I chose to live in the world we built. I wanted to see it from the inside—to be part of it. Most Founders felt otherwise, and over time I diverged from them in my vision for the world. I maintained access to the Network, which was necessary for any repairs or unexpected glitches, but I soon saw there was other work to be done. Several years into our great experiment, I broke with the rest of the Founders for good. We argued bitterly over the direction my work was taking, and an unspeakable transgression was made.

"But they could not take away my access to the Network—they didn't dare—and when my grandson showed an aptitude for the work I have devoted my life to, I shared my knowledge with him eagerly. We continued to work together even after I was sent here—at least until . . ." He broke off. He was knotting his hands together, gripping them so hard it looked painful, and now he closed his eyes and sighed deeply.

"I'm so sorry for your loss," Asa said awkwardly, the words falling flat even as he spoke them.

David shook his head and stood, going back to the window, where the sun was sinking lower in the sky, tinting the sparkling water orange.

"How . . ." Eve hesitated, and David turned around.

"Go on," he said. He strode over to the desk and opened Daniel's computer. "I'm listening," he assured her as he quickly typed something, then went to the workbench along the wall and rummaged through a small box labeled "Odds & Ends."

"You said you eliminated the possibility of human fallibility entering into . . . the State," Eve said, clearly choosing her words carefully. "Is that right? You mean greed and revenge? Things like that?"

"Yes," David said. He snatched an object from the box and nodded, satisfied, then returned to the computer. The thing was another, smaller strip of metal, and he slid it into a slot on the side of the machine, then looked up at Eve. "I'm sorry, my dear. You were asking me something important."

"I don't know if it's important or not," she said quickly.

"You want to know how I eliminated human weaknesses as

variables." He pressed a series of buttons on the computer key-pad, and it spat the strip of metal back out with a low-pitched hum. David closed the computer carefully and came back to sit facing them. "Well, I've been debating whether to tell you," he said.

"We want to know," Eve said with a quiet intensity, and he smiled at her, his eyes crinkling at the edges.

Then he sobered, and turned his attention to Asa. "What about you?"

"Yes, I want to know too," Asa said with a glance at Eve.

David nodded. "It's not a flawless innovation, but I do think it's quite brilliant. He is effortlessly authoritative yet perfectly empathetic—he makes those who follow him see the best in themselves. A leader who inspires his people not to fight but to lift one another up for the greater good. Because of him, we truly are all in this together," he finished pensively.

"The Chancellor?" Asa blurted out. "Are you talking about the Chancellor?"

David nodded. "No human being could inspire as he does—keep the peace as he does. Human leaders grow bored, fall in love, have children who usurp their power.

"There was a saying, long ago: 'Only the one who does not desire power is fit to wield it.' It was a witticism, an impossibil-ity. Yet that is precisely what we created with the Chancellor. Everything about him was meticulously designed, from his face to his voice to his speeches to every minute facet of his person-ality—every gesture, no matter how small. It was all compiled using the best traits from many of the great leaders through-out history—some you would admire, if you learned of them, and others who would strike terror in your heart even from the grave. Yet he cannot be vengeful or proud or greedy. He cannot desire anything except the well-being of the people. He does not desire power, and thus he is fit to wield it."

Asa looked at Eve. *What?* he mouthed, and she shook her head, wide-eyed.

"Are you saying the Chancellor isn't . . . a person?" Eve said at last.

David smiled. "No. He is so much more than a person."

"Then . . . what *is* he?" Asa asked, incredulous.

This man is insane, he thought, but David's calm countenance and reasonable tone made his wild claims seem believable.

As if Asa had spoken aloud, David chuckled. "I know I must sound insane, and I am sorry. Perhaps I shouldn't have told you the truth about the Chancellor."

"Well, you have, so answer Asa's question," Eve said, but she sounded more curious than irritated.

"He is a highly specialized computer program," David said.

"But I've seen him," Asa said. He was beginning to suspect the man was enjoying dragging this out, and it gave him the urge to force it to a conclusion.

"What you have seen is a holographic projection."

"That's impossible," Asa retorted. "I've seen him! I've seen him with people, real people. My father's brother was on one of his broadcasts, where he introduces people to all of us. Loads of people have been on those broadcasts. You can't tell me they were all holographic too."

"I'm sure your uncle is not a holograph," David said with a tone of mild amusement.

"If what you're saying is true, someone would have noticed," Eve said.

"He's a very *good* holographic projection," David said

reasonably. "Unless you tried to touch him, you would never know the difference, even from a few feet away."

Asa looked at Eve, but she appeared just as perplexed. She sighed.

"Fine," she said. "If what you're saying is true—*if*—then who controls him? You? The other Founders? Are they all alive here in Sanctuary too?" David laughed aloud, and she stood, glaring down at him. "You know you've told us something that's extremely hard to believe, right?"

"Of course," he said, shaking his head. "It's just nice to talk to you two. No, the other Founders are not here in Sanctuary—I don't know where they are. And as for the Chancellor, I don't control him, at least, not in the present. His programming is self-contained. It responds to atmospheric cues, artificial intelligence. But there are certain parameters that cannot be altered."

"Right." Eve was still looking down at him skeptically, and he stood smoothly and took the computer from the desk. He held it out to her, but she did not reach to take it. "Don't you want to keep that?" she asked.

"I can," he said. "But Daniel always said you have a curious mind, and all the answers you will ever want are in this machine."

"I don't know how to use it. He never showed me." David pushed the computer at her again, and she took it reluctantly as he held up the metal strip he had been fiddling with. "This contains basic instructions. Turn the computer on, insert this like you saw me do, and it will teach you how to use it."

"Thanks," Eve said doubtfully as she returned the computer to her backpack and zipped the strip of metal into one of its side pockets.

Asa stood to go, but Eve stayed where she was, hugging the backpack to her chest.

"I'm sorry, David. I appreciate your telling us all this, but you didn't answer my question. I wanted to know about *Daniel*. What *happened* to him? Was it something in his childhood? I just don't understand what could have been so bad that he would ..." She broke off, covering her eyes with one hand, and Asa could see tears on her cheeks.

David sighed and sat back down. "My dear, I was trying to explain. When Daniel was twelve, his father, my son James, passed away—a heart attack. It happened too fast for treatment. He was dead instantly. Afterward, the other Founders decided it was time for me to move on from the world we created and come to Sanctuary. It was an excuse, the death of my son—they claimed it was for my own good, to allow me to rest. In truth, they had been growing suspicious of me, and I believe they feared that such a great loss would drive me to some dangerous rebellion. They were right, though not in the way they imagined.

"James had known the story. I told him just as I told you. He was not disturbed by it in the way I was—to him it was just history. 'Done is done, and right or wrong, we must look to the future,' he told me, and we never spoke of it again.

"So, when I knew I was going to be sent away, I decided I had to tell Daniel as well—with James gone, there was no one else to tell him the truth, and I was out of time."

"You could have told his mother," Eve murmured, and David gave a choked laugh.

"His mother did not approve of me," he said dryly. "She wouldn't have listened. No, I had to tell Daniel so that he would not grow up in ignorance. I could not leave him there without telling him the truth—*someone* must always know the truth.

"But Daniel was not like James. After I told him, I could see at once that it would consume him. He dwelled on my history as if it were his own. I began to fear I had made a mistake in telling him—now I know it was the greatest mistake of my life. From the day I told him, he dedicated himself to learning every facet, every intricacy of the Network I had built. I don't know what he had in mind, and, Eve, I don't know what it was that he was working on. But I know he was consumed by the knowledge of our history—of the blood our State was built on. He saw the legacy of that history everywhere: a culture shaped by cold calculation and merciless indifference, a society ruthless in its quest for the greater good." David looked searchingly at Eve. "Do you understand?"

She shook her head. "I don't. What does history have to do with the present?"

David smiled faintly. "Everything."

"What could be wrong with a quest for the greater good?" Asa interrupted impatiently. David blinked, turning as if he had forgotten Asa was there.

"What indeed?" he said gently.

Eve sighed. "There's nothing else you can tell me?" she pressed, and David shook his head.

"I wish there were," he said.

Eve looked down at the bag in her lap, fiddling for a moment with a zipper, then she stood and swung it onto her back.

"Well, I guess this is goodbye," she said, wavering. "Will we ever . . . I mean, if I have this computer, will I be able to communicate with you?"

"Yes, you will." He smiled knowingly. "With me or anyone else you might know with similar technology."

"Okay, good . . ." Eve shifted her feet uneasily.

"So, our records are really clean?" Asa asked. "We can go back?"

"I promise both of your records are clean. You can walk into any municipal building in Horizon and be greeted with a smile and no restraints."

Asa cleared his throat. "Thank you, David Micah—I mean David Pasternak. You've given us something we can never repay."

"It was for Daniel," David replied,

As he said his grandson's name, all trace of mirth vanished from his face. His eyes looked suddenly hollow, as if he had aged a decade in moments.

Asa touched Eve's arm. "We should leave you alone," he said firmly. "Thank you again." He steered Eve out the door, and they walked out into the fading sunlight, heading back to the river.

CHAPTER SIXTEEN

THE FLOOR CREAKED OVER GABRIEL'S HEAD, and he backed down the wooden ladder as slits of light appeared, filtering down through the cracks outlining the trapdoor.

"So"—David Pasternak's voice came from above—"you have come here at last."

Gabriel glanced back at the high basement window where he had come in; a large trunk beneath it would make it easy to escape. *Five seconds, maybe three.* He hesitated for a moment, then climbed back up the ladder until he could reach the trapdoor, made a fist, and knocked three times. The door lifted open, and Gabriel climbed out of the basement to face the man he had been listening to for hours.

"Hello, Gabriel," David said quietly. Gabriel stopped himself from asking, *How do you know my name?* as he took note of the stunning collection of contraband technology that covered a whole wall of the small cottage.

"A hologram?" he asked instead. "Why? Why not . . . an autom? I've read of them being made to look human." David gave a small smile and walked to the middle of the room to sit beside what looked like a modified Bureaucracy desk. He gestured at the couch opposite him, and Gabriel went to take the place where Asa and Eve had been moments before.

"Automs that appeared fully human were mostly the stuff of fiction, even back in the old civ," David said as Gabriel sat down. "It was a problem we never quite solved—the closer to human they became, the more obvious, and unsettling, their deviations from humanity were. In theory, it would be possible, but I did not—and do not—have the technology to create an autom who would be truly believable. Besides which, a material Chancellor would require material repairs. Parts wear out over time. A single malfunction would blow the lid off the whole thing, as we used to say."

"Isn't that still the case? If you are telling the truth, which seems . . . unlikely," Gabriel said dryly. "I've been a Contract Enforcer for fifteen years. I'm not a scared kid. I need more than a story to be convinced the State was founded on a premeditated atrocity and is currently governed by a computer program."

David spread his hands out in front of him. "I'm not attempting to convince you of anything. You asked about the hologram. And the answer is, it can be repaired instantly and automatically. If a glitch does happen, if the deception is discovered, it is easy enough for the public to convince themselves that the Chancellor is a real man who sometimes has his image projected when he cannot be present physically. It would be harder to explain a robotic duplicate."

"All right," Gabriel said. "Then—assuming you're not lying or insane—why do you want me to know this? You knew I was listening from the basement the whole time. Why did you tell my runners this nonsense, knowing I could hear every word?"

"Your runners?" David asked.

"There is stronger evidence against them than what they claimed." Gabriel met David's measuring gaze with stone.

"Then why are you here with me instead of arresting them right now?" David asked mildly. Gabriel smiled, and David raised an eyebrow, an expression of distaste appearing on his face, then vanishing almost instantly.

"I will get to them," Gabriel said, but the conversation he had overheard nagged at him.

Daniel's own grandfather was unsurprised to hear he had committed suicide. Most people look for someone to blame, but instead he believed a woman he had never met.

Gabriel closed his eyes. He did not need to imagine Naomi's voice to know his duty here. "Why did you clear their records?" he asked. "*Did* you clear their records? Why did you take the word of a woman you didn't know and the man accused of your grandson's murder?"

David sighed and sat back in his chair. "You heard me tell them," he said. "Daniel and I communicated frequently. Often late at night, often when he was clearly drunk." He smiled thinly. "I would have to decipher misspelled words and half-finished sentences. He wrote to me about Eve. He sent me her picture. I knew who she was as soon as I saw her face."

"That doesn't mean she didn't have a hand in his death."

"No," David said thoughtfully. "Back in my day, when murder was . . . all too familiar, it was commonplace that the person closest to you was the one likeliest to kill you. The husband or wife, the ex-boyfriend . . ." He paused, his eyes flickering to Gabriel's face for an instant, and Gabriel swallowed, tightening his jaw.

Don't you dare mention her name, Gabriel thought.

David calmly continued as if nothing had passed between them. "Gabriel, more than once, I talked Daniel down from the ledge. I spent whole nights messaging back and forth with him, begging him not to kill himself, until he finally passed out." He looked at the blank wall of the cottage for a moment, as if seeing something beyond it, then met Gabriel's eyes. "I believed Eve and the young man she brought because I have been expecting this for years. I am just grateful to know exactly what happened. Do you understand?"

Gabriel hesitated, then nodded. "I do," he said.

To his surprise, with the words, he felt suddenly unmoored, as if he was giving up the only thing that tethered him to the world. David stood and dragged his chair to the wall of monitors and arcane tech. He sat and started pressing buttons, and one of the monitors lit up, white letters and numbers on the black screen. David typed a string of what looked like nonsense, then turned back to Gabriel.

"You asked why I told Eve and Asa about the Founding and the Chancellor, knowing that you could hear every word." He smiled. "My dear young man, surely you can deduce by now that you were really the one I was talking to?"

Gabriel rubbed his temple. "I don't like guessing games."

David shrugged. "I don't particularly like living in exile. But we all do our part."

"I'm sure the State is grateful for your service," Gabriel said tightly. He stood to go. "I'll see you in about twenty-five years, David. I'm sure you'll still be alive when it's my time to travel to Sanctuary."

"Where do you think you're going?" David asked before he

could move toward the door. "You've gone out into the Waste—do you really think you can waltz back inside those walls?"

"I was chasing runners," Gabriel snapped, but he stayed where he was. "I'll be granted an exception when I return with them," he added, hearing the defensiveness in his own voice.

"Will you?" David arched an eyebrow, looking up at him expectantly.

Gabriel glared back for a long moment, then relented. "I don't know," he said wearily. "Maybe. I'm the best they've ever had."

"So was I," David said with a faint smile.

Gabriel sat heavily. "Fine. Tell me what you want me to know."

"Thank you," David said, sounding utterly sincere. "If you will—for the moment—take everything I said as true, I will continue."

"For the moment."

"Do you recall what I said about Daniel? About his obsession with the history of the State's founding?"

"A society ruthless in its quest for the greater good, I think," Gabriel said, and David nodded, looking pleased.

"You have excellent recall," he said, as if he were complimenting a student.

"I know. Continue."

Gabriel gave David a hard stare, but the old man didn't seem to notice. There was something odd about his demeanor—something had changed since Asa and Eve had gone. *He wants to talk. He's comfortable with me.* Gabriel eyed him suspiciously. *When's the last time I inspired comfort?*

"What do you think of that description?" David asked. "Ruthless in a quest for the greater good?"

"I told you I don't like guessing games."

"Gabriel, it's important that I know your answer." David folded his hands in his lap and sat back, waiting.

"I think it misses the point," Gabriel said. "The greater good *is* the purpose of society."

"Even if it costs individuals their freedoms? Their lives?"

"If it is for the good of all people, then yes, of course. What is the purpose of this self-indulgent line of questioning?"

"What do you think of being a stalker, Gabriel?"

Gabriel stared for a moment; it was as if David had asked, *What do you think of being a human being?* "It's what I was created to be," he said at last. "There has never been anything else."

"But have you ever thought of having children?" David asked.

"Of course not." Gabriel straightened in his chair, affronted. "That's not possible for me, or any Ward."

"But have you ever thought of it? Imagined having a family? Or—"

"No," Gabriel interrupted. He looked to the blank wall, staring fixedly at it for a long moment. "I had a family," he said quietly.

"You remember your parents?" David asked, surprised.

Gabriel kept his eyes on the wall. "No."

"Then you must mean Naomi," David said in a tone of dawning comprehension.

Gabriel gave a short jerk of a nod.

David was silent a moment, and when he spoke, he chose his words delicately. "You never wanted a child with her?"

"What's *wrong* with you?" Gabriel leapt to his feet, knocking the couch back with his movement.

David was watching him intently, apparently unalarmed by his outburst. Instead he looked interested. "I asked if you wanted a child with Naomi," David repeated, implacable.

Gabriel shook his head and sat down again. "The role we serve as Authority Figures—as Contract Enforcers—is of far greater importance to the State than anything else we could do. Since Wards aren't raised in nuclear family units, we could not replicate healthy dynamics, because we didn't experience them ourselves. We were raised for a specific purpose. We would squander our years of training if we did not fulfill that purpose."

"But did you ever *want* a child?" David's tone was warm, as if he cared.

Gabriel forced himself not to snarl, biting off his words tensely. "Stop asking me that, old man. It was never an option."

"Because you and Naomi were sterilized as children, like all Wards of the State," David said.

"Yes." Gabriel felt suddenly exhausted, as if they had been fighting a physical battle. "And because our duty lay elsewhere." *Don't make me talk about her anymore,* he thought.

"Would you prefer to have had a choice?" David prodded.

Gabriel closed his eyes. "I didn't."

He stood and walked toward the blank wall, wanting to get away from David's kind eyes and inexorable march of questions. Children weren't something he had ever pined for; like all the rest of the Wards, he had known since early childhood what path his life would take. He had welcomed his role, never doubting for a moment that he was meant to be a stalker.

But Naomi, that day in the park . . .

They had paused on their route to have lunch, and a little distance away in the park were a young mother and father, playing in the grass with their two toddler children. Gabriel asked a question, and Naomi didn't answer; then he realized she hadn't heard him, her eyes set, just for a moment, on the family just a few yards away.

It was only for a moment, a shadow cast over her face, but

Gabriel's heart twinged as he suddenly witnessed a pain he had not known she had. He put a hand on her shoulder, and the shadow vanished; she turned to him and smiled and said, "What did you say?"

That night she came home with him, not for the first time, but on that night, something was different: that was the time she stayed for good. As she fell asleep, she whispered that she loved him, and for the first and only time he let himself imagine what it might be like if they could have their own children.

But he knew it was a futile daydream, and only four months later she was dead.

Gabriel sighed and turned back to David, who had turned around to face the monitors and was typing more of the incomprehensible white characters across the screen. As if he could feel Gabriel's eyes on him, he turned in his chair, waiting expectantly.

"I don't know that I believe you're telling me the truth," Gabriel said. "But I will listen to what you have to say."

David nodded soberly. "Good." He stood and put his hands behind his back. "I have told you all this history, Gabriel, not only because I believe you deserve to know the truth but also because I need your help." He paused, looking at Gabriel with a question in his eyes.

"Don't get ahead of yourself," Gabriel said. "Go on."

"I did not ask you what I asked in order to be cruel. I asked because Daniel's belief—that the merciless pursuit of the ideal society is not, in fact, for the greater good—has, over many years, become my own.

"I take responsibility for that, in large part. It was I who built the Network and I who programmed your leader, and no matter what we wish to think, societies reflect their leaders—a leader who is, in this case, inhuman. Now it is my intent, and not mine alone, to attempt to introduce a human element back into the State. To introduce mercies and liberties that have been stamped out in the so-called Social Contracts."

"The Social Contracts exist for the safety of us all," Gabriel said automatically.

"Yes," David said. "But they were devised in a different time. A dangerous, chaotic time. Many years have passed since then."

"So, what is it you want to do? Tear down the State and build from the ashes again?" Gabriel shook his head. "I'm not a revolutionary, David, and if you are, I'll arrest you right now. Sanctuary may be far away, but it's not beyond the law."

David raised his hands in a gesture of protest. "No, no. Not revolution. Only change—openness to change, even. That was among the sins that toppled the old civ, you know: resistance to change. Refusal to look with open eyes at the world we had made and ask, is this the only path? Or can we choose another one, a better one?"

"And what is the other, better path?"

"I don't know."

Gabriel inhaled deeply, trying to tamp down his growing frustration. "You're saying some fascinating things," he said. He couldn't keep the irritation from his voice. "But I still have no idea what you are planning to *do* and why you're trying to include me. Tell me something concrete, or I'm leaving."

David smiled. "We want to introduce the human element back into the government of the State."

"Who is 'we'?"

"A small but growing faction. Not only here in Sanctuary but in Work, in the heart of the State itself, and in the highest echelons of . . ." He trailed off, leaving the sentence unfinished, and Gabriel marked the omission but did not speak. "There are a growing number of people I am in contact with who support this effort," David went on. "The parameters of my computer program cannot feel. It cannot empathize as people do. It cannot make decisions with both reason and compassion. For that, we also need a human mind at the helm. Your mind, to be specific."

Gabriel stared at him, astonished. "*My* mind," he said at last. "Why mine?"

"Because," David said simply, "you are the best we have."

Gabriel sat on the couch and rubbed his temples. "I am *not* agreeing to anything. In fact, I still might arrest you. But fine, I'll keep listening. What do you expect me to do?"

David made a satisfied noise and went to his workbench, where he retrieved a stack of small notebooks from a drawer. He sat beside Gabriel and handed him one. "Are you familiar with cyphers?" he asked.

Gabriel shook his head and opened the notebook.

David began to explain the codes and their purpose as Gabriel paged through the books, half in a daze. He was beginning to feel as if all this were happening to someone else, or in a dream, as David continued his instructions. David's voice alone indicated his advanced age; it was hoarse and sometimes soft. He paused from time to time as he spoke with a pained expression, and Gabriel could not tell if it were the subject or the act of speaking for so long that hurt the old man. At last they came to the final book, identical to the others, and David held it out but did not let go when Gabriel put his hand on it.

"This is a distillation of what you have just learned," David said. He flipped the back cover open, and Gabriel saw a thin strip of metal affixed to the inside. "This is everything, but I don't know when or how you will be able to access it."

Gabriel nodded and took the book. He pried out the metal

strip and thought for a moment, then slid it into a hidden compartment in his shoe.

David looked on, amused. "Resourceful," he remarked. "A few more things before you go: I can't remove your act of insubordination the way I cleared Asa's and Eve's records, since not even I can erase human memory." He smirked. "At least not from this far away," he said, and Gabriel bit back a response, not really wanting to know if he was joking. "However," David continued, "I could not find an official State record of your desertion into the Waste. Whatever your fellow Authority Figures may decide to do with you, they have not yet made it official. Which, in my experience, means there is still hope." He stood, and Gabriel followed suit.

"How do I get out of here?" Gabriel asked. "By now, the boat has left without me, I assume."

"There's a tunnel that runs under the riverbed. You access it through the water treatment plant."

David went to his workbench again and turned on a monitor. The image was an aerial view of the cottage, and Gabriel came closer to watch as, slowly, the drone's camera panned to show a water treatment plant not far away.

"You just have to follow the sea wall," David said.

"I can see that."

"If anyone stops you, tell them you're from the State, but not—"

"Not a Contract Enforcer," Gabriel finished. "I can figure a few things out for myself."

David had turned away and was rummaging in another drawer. The drone turned slowly, and the image changed, showing what could have been a block of Horizon if it were not set right next to what could have been a farm in Rosewood.

"Lean toward me," David said, and Gabriel turned.

"What?"

David reached out, and before Gabriel could move, he felt a sharp pain in his neck, and a rush of cold swept through him. He gasped for breath, suddenly light-headed, and felt David easing him down to sit.

"What have you done to me?" he managed to ask, the dizziness beginning to recede.

"I gave you a vaccine," David said calmly. "You're having a mild reaction. It should ease within a few minutes."

Gabriel nodded, still half-certain he had just been poisoned, but the sudden chill was fading. The warmth of the room began to touch him again, and as he took deep breaths, he grew steady. "What did you vaccinate me for?" he asked when the room had stopped spinning and didn't seem likely to start again.

"*Naegleria algernoni,*" David said, bending down to peer into his eyes one at a time. "Better known as the Bug."

"What?" Gabriel started. "The Bug is incurable—everyone knows that."

David shook his head and straightened. "Oh, the things 'everyone knows,'" he murmured as if to himself, turning back to the monitors.

"Are you telling me you've come up with a cure for the Bug, and you haven't distributed it? Every man, woman, and child lives in fear of it. We are all at the mercy of the tainted water surrounding us and the danger of a treatment plant failure—it happened twenty years ago in Fairfield, and thirteen people died, raving and in agony. You're telling me you could prevent that? And you *haven't?*"

Gabriel was on his feet without realizing he had stood,

trembling with rage. His fists were clenched, and he carefully relaxed them, breathing slowly in and out. David had not moved an inch; he had turned on a different drone feed on a second monitor. It was fixed on an expansive cornfield.

When Gabriel spoke again, his voice was so cold he scarcely recognized it. "You tell me you want to introduce humanity into the State. I don't know how you would even recognize such a thing."

David turned around slowly. He had a strange expression on his face. *He almost looks pleased,* Gabriel thought and took an involuntary step backward.

"You're right," David said softly. "To have a cure for a deadly illness—to have the ability, even, to eradicate a scourge that holds all our people hostage—and not use it is monstrous. To allow, as you say, every man, woman, and child to live in fear so they avoid straying too far from home—too far from purified water—so they are dependent on the regulation of the treatment plants. So they are at the mercy of the tainted water everywhere. That is inhuman, indeed."

Gabriel scanned his face and understood. "You didn't create the vaccine," he said, and David bowed his head for a moment.

"I did not."

"The vaccine is not new," Gabriel said.

"No, it is not."

Gabriel nodded, the fury draining from him. His head ached, and it dawned on him that the dull throb had been going on a long time. "I have to go back now," he said tightly.

"There is far more than I have given you today," David said. "If you stay a few days—a week—I can teach you to work deep within the Network and leave no trace."

Gabriel took a long look at the wall of monitors, then met

David's eyes with a wry smile. "No. I'll figure it out myself," he said. "I always do."

"Then get to the tunnel as soon as you can." David's face was grim, and he glanced at the drone feeds on the monitors. "When the sky is full of eyes, the only safe place is underground."

Gabriel nodded, giving him a look of appreciation, then turned without another word and walked out of the cottage. It was almost dark, but he could see the water treatment plant not far away. He set off toward it.

Would you prefer to have had a choice? David's question nagged at him. *Yes, damn it. I'd prefer having one now too.*

✦

David leaned back in his chair. He sighed, feeling more tired than he thought he should. He felt like a man at the end of a very long race. His eyes found the monitor presenting the drone footage. One screen followed Gabriel until he reached the water treatment building.

The Contract Enforcer entered without being stopped. David smiled; that didn't surprise him. Gabriel always acted as if he had the right to be exactly wherever he found himself. It was a useful talent.

Using remote commands, David manipulated drone flight patterns to ensure no observational platforms would be near his residence for the next hour. Secure in the knowledge he'd avoided unwelcome attention, he stood and went downstairs to the basement. There, he flipped a hidden switch. A section of wall slid back to reveal a secret video booth.

Once inside the dark little room, he typed a string of numbers that he knew by heart. For a moment nothing happened, then a bright light flashed across the screen. Her face was revealed. If he was happy to see her, it didn't show in his expression.

"He's on his way," David said without preamble. "I've given him everything he needs. The rest is up to him now."

She seemed poised to reply, but he cut the link and sat for a time, alone in the dark. He thought of Gabriel, of all that lay before him. For the first time that he could remember, he felt old.

CHAPTER SEVENTEEN

EVE WAS QUIET AS ASA STEERED THE BOAT back across the river.

He glanced at her from time to time, but she was just sitting half-turned around in the seat beside him, looking at the way they had come. She had the strip that David had given her in her hand, and she was rubbing the metal with her thumb as if it were some kind of good luck charm. Asa wanted to say something, to reach out to her somehow, but the current had picked up; the boat was drifting downstream more rapidly than before. He locked his eyes on the boathouse and accelerated, trying to offset the rapid sweep of the water.

He managed to bring them alongside the riverbank and spent another few minutes battling ten feet upstream before he managed to get the boat to the opening of the boathouse. "Eve!"

She looked up with a startled expression.

"Help me—get the ropes," he urged her, and she put the strip in her bag and hurried out into the back of the boat to help him maneuver the rest of the way.

When they were inside the little building, Asa cut the engine and went to the back of the boat. Eve was leaning over the side to reach the lift lever, and she yanked it into position. With a loud grind, the boat began to rise, water dripping from the hull as they rose out of the river.

When the boat stopped moving, Eve went back in the cabin, grabbed her bags, and rushed out onto the deck almost as if she were being chased. Asa followed a pace behind, pausing to make sure he had not left any of the switches on. When he emerged from the boat, Eve was leaning against a shelf full of storage bins, clutching her bag to her chest and breathing shakily.

"Are you okay?" Asa asked, putting a hand on her shoulder.

She nodded, then shook her head, looking at him with an expression he could not read. Gently, he took the bag from her hands and set it down, then hugged her, letting his cheek rest against her hair as she wrapped her arms around his waist.

"We're okay now," Asa whispered. "It's all over. We can go back."

She tightened her grip. "Can we?" she asked, so quietly he scarcely made out the words.

"Yes," Asa said firmly. "Everything will be okay."

Eve sighed, then straightened, pushing away from him. She gave him a weary smile. "If you say so."

"I do. Come on, we can get back to your brother's . . . community before it's dark, then leave out from there in the morning."

Eve nodded. She slung her bag over her shoulder again, and Asa did the same. He took a last look at the boat, still glossy with river water. They made their way to the door and stepped out of the boathouse onto solid ground.

"Asa Isaac Rosewood! Eve Layla Ashland!"

They froze and turned to face the voice. It was the stalker who had tracked them to Saul's compound. He was standing on the bank of the river, ten feet away. He was holding something out, stiffly, in front of him, and his face was red with fury. Asa noticed that his ear was crusted with dried blood where the earlier shot had grazed him.

"Put down what you're carrying and raise your hands where I can see them," the stalker said evenly.

Asa eyed the car, only a few yards away, then saw that Eve had already dropped her bags and had her hands raised in a gesture of surrender.

"Asa, he has one of those weapons," she hissed, and Asa looked; the stalker was aiming a gun at them. Asa suddenly recalled him seizing the weapon from Saul's guard as he fled. Now he held the thing with steady hands.

Asa dropped his bag and matched Eve's pose. "What do you want?"

The stalker's face twisted into a ghastly smile. "By authority of the State—"

A shot sounded, a loud crack splitting the air, and before Asa could think, the stalker rocked backward. For an instant he kept his footing, his eyes wide with shock as a bright red spot of blood bloomed on his left shoulder. He fell backward without even a cry of pain. There was a splash as he hit the river below, then only silence.

"Eve! Evie!" someone called as people ran to them.

Their feet pounded in the dirt as the sound of their breathing and their voices filled the air, blending together as Asa turned to see Saul surrounded by a dozen of his people. Eve turned too, looking dazed as if in a dream, and Saul embraced her, lifting her off the ground and whispering something to her Asa could not hear.

"Are you all right?" asked the woman Asa recognized as Lilith.

He nodded, then turned his eyes back to the river. The stalker's body was still visible, growing rapidly smaller as it bobbed downstream with the current.

"I don't think he'll bother you again," Saul said, setting Eve down. He touched the gun at his hip reflexively and nodded. "Everything is going to be okay," he said and smoothed down her hair.

Eve cast her eyes back to Asa and smiled. "I know it is," she said.

"We've got two more cars," Cyrus said abruptly, giving Asa a sidelong glance as he approached the group. "We had to cram in tight on the way here, so we'll split up four and five apiece. I'll drive this one." He gestured at the car Asa and Eve had come in.

They sorted themselves into the cars; Asa sat beside Cyrus in the passenger's seat, while Eve, Saul, and a small, thin young man took the back. As they drove, Cyrus kept his eyes on the path ahead, and Asa gazed out the window. He heard Saul and Eve speaking quietly, but he could not make out much of what they said and gave up trying.

The sun was setting as the long, flat-topped compound appeared ahead of them. Asa followed Eve and Saul inside with impatience.

Why can't we just leave now? I can drive in the dark, he thought, knowing it was unrealistic.

"Get cleaned up, then we'll gather for dinner," Saul said cheerfully as they reached the habitation area where Asa and Eve had spent the night before. "There's a bathing room down that hallway—conserve water, obviously. It's pretty scarce out here."

"Of course," Eve said quickly.

"I'll send one of the kids to get you for dinner. So you don't get lost." Saul grinned, then left them alone.

"You can go first," Asa said quickly, and Eve nodded.

"I'll be fast," she said.

True to her word, she returned a few minutes later wrapped in nothing but a thin white towel, her amber skin scrubbed clean and her black hair wet and shining.

"I'll . . . I'll go get cleaned up," Asa stammered, and she smiled.

"Don't take too long."

"Okay." Asa tore himself away, the image of her gleaming skin, so slightly covered, returning to his mind each time he blinked.

When he returned to the room, however, she was wearing a new dress, bright blue and knee length, with thin straps across her shoulders. It was clean but wrinkled from the days in her backpack. She flashed him a brilliant smile.

"A girl came by to take us to dinner," she said. "You should hurry."

She had a book in her lap, an old one that must have been in the room. She picked it up and turned her attention to it. Asa hesitated, then took his bag to the opposite side of the room and put on his only change of clothes, glancing nervously at Eve every few seconds. She kept her eyes on her book, never glancing up. He finished buttoning his shirt, which was more worn and crumpled than he would have liked, and cleared his throat. Eve set the book down and turned to him.

"Ready?" she asked, and he nodded. As if on cue, someone knocked on the door, and Eve opened it to let a teenage girl in.

"Are you ready to come to dinner?" the girl asked.

"Lead the way!" Eve said merrily, beckoning Asa to follow her.

He watched her still-damp hair swinging against her back as they followed the girl through the maze of corridors. She seemed happy—almost giddy—now that they had returned; maybe it was just the relief of making it safely across the river, the adrenaline rush of evading the stalker's clutches.

Or maybe she's just happy to be back with her brother.

The dining room was already crowded and noisy when they arrived; it took Asa a moment to orient himself among the chattering voices and unfamiliar faces. There were dozens of people there.

Saul waved to them from the far corner of the room, where he was seated with what Asa recognized by now as his core group of . . . *advisors? Enforcers?*

Asa followed Eve as she wove her way through the tables. No one turned to look at them as they passed, but a path of silence opened before them, each table falling quiet as they came to it, the backs of the diners going still with the awareness of their presence.

Saul had left two places open beside him; Eve sat next to him, and Asa on the other side, at the corner of the table.

Simon was at his right hand, halfway through a plate of stew. He smiled at Asa and pointed at his full mouth, then swallowed. "Welcome back," he said in a confidential whisper.

"Thanks," Asa said with genuine appreciation.

The first time they had stopped at the compound, he had been eclipsed entirely by Eve's presence, and this time seemed no different. He did not particularly care what the people out here thought about him—it was not as if they were ever going to see them again—but it was nice to be acknowledged.

Saul thumped his fist twice on the table, and the dining room quieted, all eyes turning to him as he stood.

"I'd like to welcome my sister Eve back to our home," he said, "along with her companion, Asa."

He gave Asa a nod, and there was an incoherent cheer from the assembly; then Saul sat, and the room swelled with conversation again. Asa glanced around the table. Cyrus had not looked up from his plate when Saul made his brief toast, and he did not acknowledge Asa or Eve now. Lilith and Aquila were at the far end of the table, talking quietly together.

Now or never, Asa thought and cleared his throat. "Saul, I want to thank you for all that you've done for us," he said.

Saul gave him a sidelong look. "I'm just glad you've both returned safely," he replied coolly. "Despite the odds."

"We did what we had to do," Asa said, trying to keep his irritation in check.

Like Eve sometimes did, Saul seemed as if the world could not touch him, his face a blank. In Eve, it was to Asa an exquisite vulnerability. In Saul, it was just annoying.

"You did what you had to do?" Saul repeated.

"Yes," Eve said quickly. "We talked about this, Saul. There was no other way. We had to do it, and now it's done."

"It was a fool's errand, and what's your reward?" Saul demanded, turning his chair to face her, the metal scraping loudly on the concrete floor.

"I don't know what you mean," Eve said icily.

"I mean, you risked your life so you could return to that . . . fantasy land, where all the real sacrifices are made by people you never even have to see."

"That 'fantasy land' is my home," Eve said. "It was yours too."

Saul sighed. "I'm sorry, Eve." He reached for her hand, and

she let him take it. "It's just that I'm happy here. I'm happier now than I ever was back home—than I've ever been. It's a harsh life out here, I know that, but we are free to create, to think . . . and to believe."

"I've seen that," Eve said quietly.

"I'm happy here," Saul said again. "The only thing missing is my family—my sister. If you would stay . . ." He broke off and looked away, and Asa saw his hand tighten on Eve's. "If you would stay," Saul went on, "we could be a family again. I want that more than anything in the world. I miss you so much, Evie."

"I miss you too," Eve echoed.

Asa watched with rising despair. "Wait," he said, breaking the spell between them, and Eve and Saul turned to him as if surprised he was still there. "Wait," he repeated. "Eve, we were going to go back home. Our *lives* are there."

Eve turned to him, her eyes pinched with emotion. "Asa, I don't know if my life is there. Daniel was all I had, and now . . ."

"Now you have me," Asa said firmly, and her eyes widened. "Didn't you know that?" he said, surprised.

She smiled, her eyes shining, then ducked her head, covering her face with her hand. Asa waited nervously as she recovered her composure, casting his eyes around the table. Everyone seated there was watching them unabashedly; only Saul seemed distant, staring across the room at something no one else could see.

Eve took a deep breath. "What does that mean, Asa? If I have you, what would that mean? Where would we go? What would we do?"

"We would go back inside, then go anywhere you want," he said, realizing only as he spoke how clearly he had envisioned their lives together. "We could live in Horizon, but I think you should come with me to Rosewood to see what it's like there."

"I've been to Rosewood," she said, her lips curved in a hint of a smile.

"Only for a few hours," Asa pressed.

"I liked the trees," Eve said. She had a faraway look in her eyes.

Asa gazed at her, pleading silently. *See what I see. See how wonderful our lives could be if we could be together.*

"Eve, you can't be serious!" Saul exclaimed, smacking the table with his palm so hard it shook. They both jumped, and Eve shoved back her chair.

"What if I am?" she demanded, turning on her brother. "What if I do want to go back inside? To the only home I've ever known?"

"I . . . I wouldn't stop you," Saul stammered.

"Oh, thanks for that," Eve said bitterly. "I'm so glad to know you wouldn't *stop me* from leaving your impenetrable fortress in the middle of the damn desert."

"We can go straight back tomorrow," Asa said soothingly. "We can go see every tree in Rosewood."

"Oh, *every* tree?" Eve stood, turning her scathing gaze on Asa. "How nice. What if I don't *want* to go with you? What if I *want* to take this chance—this *one* chance to start over? I thought Saul was *dead* for *five years*, and you expect me to leave him again to go look at *trees* with you?"

"Uh . . . no?" Asa guessed, bewildered. "Eve, I'm sorry, I didn't mean . . ."

"Neither did I," Saul put in quickly. Eve shook her head in frustration.

"I know," she snapped. "You both want me to be happy." She wavered for a moment. "I need to think," she whispered, then lifted her head, turned, and stormed out of the dining room without looking back.

Saul's face had gone blank again, and when he saw Asa looking at him, he cleared his throat. "I don't know what she's thinking," he muttered, then bit his lip, his eyes anxious.

Asa smiled in spite of himself. "I think that's her point."

Saul laughed abruptly and clapped Asa's shoulder with startling force. "I don't dislike you," he said, then shook his head.
"Sorry, that's not quite what I mean."

"I know what you mean." Asa stood. "I don't dislike you
either."

Saul raised his glass and nodded, and Asa left the dining
room, pretending not to notice the people turning from their
plates to watch him go.

✦

Asa wandered the near-identical corridors aimlessly, allowing
himself to get lost, then finding his way back to the main stairs
several times. He passed a few open common spaces, where people were reading in corners or talking animatedly in groups; on a
raised platform, a group of musicians were playing a discordant
song unlike anything he had heard before. As he passed room
after room, some of the doors ajar, he heard bursts of laughter,
arguments, children playing, and music, some of it odd and some
surprisingly familiar.

The compound really was like a small community in many
ways, he was forced to admit, and no one he passed looked hungry or frightened—only curious at the sight of a stranger.

Maybe it wouldn't be such a terrible place to live.

It was the first time the thought had struck him, and he
was ashamed; he had not taken Eve's indecision seriously. She
was distressed at the thought of leaving her brother, but surely,

Asa had assumed, she realized that remaining in the Waste was impossible. He had not really believed she would choose to stay among these people.

If she did, could he remain with her?

No.

The reaction was instantaneous and weighty, like a punch to the chest.

My mother and father—Hannah. There was no future in which he did not live among them again. *Yet that is what I'm asking her to give up.* Asa opened the door to a stairwell, sat on the steps, and leaned against the cool concrete wall.

I can't ask that of her.

He sighed and closed his eyes, picturing her as she had been that first night, when he walked into the Horizon nightbar and his life was forever altered. At first, he had not even seen her face, only the white dress against her dark skin, her hair shimmering down her back like an obsidian waterfall. Then he had seen her face and had been undone.

She had stunned him then—she stunned him now. Each time she touched him, he was stirred with a longing beyond anything he'd felt before. He felt something desperate, something deeper than mere sexual attraction.

Asa took a long, shaky breath and let himself imagine what he had been afraid to dream of.

Eve—yes, Eve—her skin smooth and electric, her hair falling silkily over his face, all the unfathomable things he so urgently desired, and then . . . life. Eve, the weight of her past lifted from her shoulders by the constancy of his love; their home, some warm, safe place that belonged only to them, as they belonged always to each other. Eve, smiling without fear or sadness, her belly swollen with the first of their babies as they argued cheerfully over what to name it. Eve,

272

always beside him, raising their children to be happy and safe, to have all the things that had been taken from Eve at such a young age. Eve, an old woman, and he an old man, making the journey to Sanctuary, sharing their secret, that they were actually going there for the second time. Life—all of it, from now to the end—always with Eve.

Asa opened his eyes, looking around the stark, bright stairwell. *How can she not want our life?* His chest hurt, as if something had been ripped out of him, and he put a hand over the hollow-feeling place. *What else could she want but our life together?*

Then he knew.

Asa leapt to his feet and ran down the stairs.

✦

Asa came to the end of the stairs and halted outside the room, listening, but he could hear nothing. He hesitated a moment, then opened the door and went inside.

Eve was kneeling, her face upturned and her eyes closed beside the giant tree at the center of the vast domed room. The underground sun filtered down through the slope of the branches, setting her face aglow. Asa let the door fall shut, and her eyes snapped open. She looked at him for a moment as if she did not recognize him; then her expression cleared.

"I'm sorry," Asa said, abashed. "I didn't mean to interrupt you. I just—"

"It's okay," Eve said. She got to her feet. "I've never seen anything like this, you know. Except in pictures. We were taught . . . our mother and father taught us the rituals—the history—at home. Sometimes there were other children, but usually it was just me and Saul. It's the strangest thing, because I know it isn't true, but I always remember it as if we were taught in the dark.

273

I remember the lessons as if we sat together in darkness, with nothing but a little candle to light the room. It's not what happened, of course. We just went in the basement. There was plenty of light. But it felt like dark. Do you understand what I mean?"

"I don't," Asa said. "But I want to. Eve, I want to understand everything about you, and I think in time I will, if you'll let me."

"I still need to think, Asa."

"I know," he said. "I just wanted to tell you—I don't understand all of this." He gestured at the room around them, the glowing golden branches that adorned the sloping walls. Eve looked as if she was about to speak, but he hurried on. "I don't have to understand it, not yet. I know it matters to you. And I want you to know that if you come back with me, I don't expect you to give it up."

"What about our children?" Eve asked softly, and his heart stopped for a second when she said "our children." He looked into her wide, dark eyes, unable for a moment to speak.

"I want our children—" His voice broke, and he took a breath, steadying himself. "This is a part of you, Eve, and I want our children to have *you* in them. If you want to raise them with your beliefs, we can. I'll even try to help."

Eve reached out for his hand and raised it to her lips, then met his eyes again. "Saul and I were taught to worship in secret," she whispered. "I think in a way the darkness made it precious, kept us bound together. But in truth, being forced to hide like that . . . it shrouded all the beauty in something very sad."

"Does that mean you won't come with me?" Asa's voice was hoarse; he felt as if he had forgotten how to speak.

Eve shook her head. "It just means I'm still thinking."

Asa forced a smile. "I'll be in our . . . in the room when you're done thinking," he said as despair hollowed out his chest again.

He left the sacred chamber and started back through the maze, getting lost a few times before he made it back to the room.

◆

Back in their room, he closed the door and lay down on the bunk they had shared. Someone had changed the sheets; they smelled clean, like soap. Eve's scent, and his, had been erased. He closed his eyes.

How can she not want our life?

The future he had imagined in such detail rose unbidden, and he forced it away, wishing he had not allowed himself the fantasy.

What can I say to her? How can I convince her to come with me? How can she choose superstition and make-believe over a real, true life with me? He put his hands over his eyes, pressing until spots of color appeared in the blackness. *How can I make her choose me?*

Greed.

He sat bolt upright, the accusation shocking him with adrenaline.

This is greed. I want her greedily. I want her more than I want her to choose freely. My love of Eve is not pure; it is tainted by greed.

His face went hot; he was flooded with the shame of it. He stood abruptly, itching to shed the realization, and began to pace the length of the room, back and forth across it, five steps each way.

I want her to be with me, but we will only be happy if she is happy. I will only be happy if she is happy. Asa grunted in frustration and kicked the metal bed frame. It rattled noisily in the empty room, and he hurried to steady it.

"I will only be happy if she is happy," he said quietly. "I want her to be happy, even if it makes me sad. I can't be happy with her if she isn't content with me."

Asa sighed, the rush of adrenaline draining all at once. He lay back on the bunk again and closed his eyes. *I will only be happy if Eve is happy.* The words were like tin, but he repeated them over and over in variation, until at last he drifted into sleep.

✦

"Asa."

Asa slowly roused to the sound of his name and opened his eyes to see Eve beside him on the bunk. It was dark in the room except for a thin bar of light shining in under the door from the hallway.

"Asa," Eve touched his shoulder. "Are you awake?"

He smiled. "I am now."

"Good."

She brushed her fingers back through his hair, sending a shiver down his spine. Before he could speak, she pulled him to her, pressing the length of her body against him as she touched her lips gently to his.

Half in disbelief, Asa slid his hand to her waist, marveling at the curve of her hip and the give of her stomach beneath the thin fabric of her dress. He kissed her back eagerly, his pulse quickening; then, without warning, she pulled away and stood. Asa sat up.

"Is something wrong?" he whispered, and she smiled.

"No."

Asa stood and put his arms around her, burying his face for a moment in her hair, and she wrapped her arms around his waist with a contented sound. Asa swallowed; he had held her before, but not like this and not for so long—her full breasts were soft against his chest, and her hips brushed against him enticingly, her long legs already half-bared by her dress.

Eve looked up at him with uncertainty. Gently, as if he were touching something terribly fragile, Asa bent to kiss her. She slid her hands up under his shirt, stroking his bare back, and he shivered. She tugged at his hem with a smile and started to unbutton his shirt. Asa hurried to help, fumbling at his collar, then cast aside the shirt as Eve traced her fingers across his abdomen. She kissed his shoulder, then bent to brush her lips against his chest. Asa gasped; he stiffened as she licked his nipples delicately, sending little thrills through him with each movement of her tongue. She looked up at him again, and he cupped her face in his hands, kissing her thirstily, desperate to hold her against him.

"Sit," she whispered, nodding toward the bed, and he sat. She climbed onto his lap, straddling him.

Asa's eyes widened. For a moment he wasn't sure where to put his hands; then, with a nervous glance at her face, he set them on her bare thighs. Her skin was warm and smooth, and he ran his hands up and down her legs. Then, hesitantly, he slid one hand under her skirt, caressing the firm, supple curve of her ass. She made a small sound, and he stopped, lifting his hands off her as if he had touched something hot.

"No, don't stop," she whispered. She kissed him again, then took his hand and brought it to the nape of her neck. "Help me."

She placed his fingers on the zipper of her dress, and Asa felt for the tab and slowly pulled it down, his hand brushing the length of her spine as he undid her dress. He carefully took hold of the cloth and pulled it over her head, dropping it on the bed beside them as he gazed at her. She was wearing nothing but a

small pair of undershorts, cut just below her flat stomach. He
touched her slim waist, then met her eyes, silently asking permission. She smiled, took his hands, and guided them to her breasts.

He held them lightly, surprised by their weight in his hands.
Eve gasped, and he bent to touch his lips to her nipple. He took
it carefully in his mouth, and she moaned aloud, clutching at his
shoulders. The sound sent a jolt of desire through him, and he
sucked gently, growing harder as she mewed with pleasure.

Eve tugged at his waistband, and he let her undo his pants.
She got up off his lap and pulled down her underwear, and he
hurriedly stripped off the rest of his clothes. She came to his
arms again, and the feeling of her bare skin naked against his
almost brought him to his knees. Eve's breath was shallow and
hot against his neck.

She took his hand and went back to the bed, pulling him on
top of her. She pulled his face down to hers and kissed him, then
reached down to guide him. He gasped for breath as he finally
slipped inside her; she was wet and warm. As he thrust inside, he
felt her tighten around him.

Eve cried out with pleasure as he moved back and forth
inside of her, over and over, and finally Asa reached his breaking
point. He shuddered as it took him, clinging to Eve with all his
strength until he was breathless in her arms.

Neither of them spoke. Asa closed his eyes, not wanting the
moment to end. She stroked his hair, and he kissed her breast as
his fast-beating heart began to slow down. For a long time, they
did not move.

"Eve," Asa whispered at last, half hoping she was already
asleep and would not hear him.

"Hmm?" She pulled back so she could look at him, her eyes
alert.

He took in a deep breath, filling his lungs with her scent as if it would strengthen his memory of the night. "I wanted to say, I understand if you want to stay here," he said. "I can't ask you to leave your only family. I just want you to be happy—"

She cut him off. "I'm going with you." Eve kissed his cheek, then his lips. "I want to be with you."

Asa was taken aback for a moment; he had steeled himself for the opposite but had not prepared for what he wanted most. Eve's smile faded.

"Is that not what you want?" she asked, and he nodded urgently.

"Yes, yes, of course that's what I want. I want to be with you, Eve. Always."

He hugged her fiercely, kissing her hair. He felt as if his chest might burst with joy and with the sheer overpowering reality of it all. Eve made a contented sound, settling sleepily into his embrace.

"We'll live in a little house," she said. "I'm tired of those giant buildings. We'll have a house with no one above us or below."

"That sounds nice," Asa said cautiously. "And children?"

She nodded against his chest. "Yes. A boy and a girl, sister and brother, like you and Hannah, or me and Saul."

Asa smiled. "So, the boy first."

"Yes." She laughed. "We've all gotten into some trouble, though. Maybe the girl should come first."

"It's decided, then." Asa couldn't stop smiling; his face felt as if it were about to split open. *Life, all of it, with Eve.* He kissed her forehead, and she sighed dreamily.

"Goodnight, Asa," she whispered.

"Goodnight," he answered, though he doubted he would ever sleep again.

✦

"Good morning!" There was a sharp knock at the door. "Good morning!" called a young man. He sounded irritated, as if he had been trying for a while.

Asa blinked, disoriented. The room was dark, and the soft glow of the night-light provided just enough illumination for him to make out his surroundings. The knock came again.

"Uh, good morning!" Asa called. "Thank you!"

"Saul wants to see his sister," the young man shouted through the door. Asa glanced at Eve, who pulled the sheet up over her head without opening her eyes.

"Can it wait?" Asa asked.

"Soon as possible." No footsteps followed; the young man was clearly not going away until they came out.

"Okay," Asa called. "Give us a few minutes, okay?" The boy outside the door didn't reply. Asa nudged Eve. "Hey, I think we have to wake up," he whispered, loath to disturb her.

"I heard," she said, her voice muffled by the sheets.

She pulled them off her head and sat up. Asa stifled a laugh; her long hair was sticking out in every direction, still clinging with static to the sheets.

"What?" Eve asked, and he reached out to smooth her hair down.

"I just can't believe you're here," he said. "That I'm here—that you're coming home with me." He was suddenly seized with the panicked notion that it had all been a dream. "Wait, you're still coming with me, right?" he asked.

Eve laughed. "Yes, I'm coming with you." She kissed him and hopped out of bed, dragging the sheets with her like a long, messy dress.

Asa grabbed a pillow and put it on his lap, suddenly self-conscious. Eve grinned.

"Get dressed," she said. "Then we'll go home."

✦

Saul was sitting at his desk when they entered. The boy who had escorted them downstairs closed the door, leaving the three of them alone. Saul turned, and his eyes flicked from Eve to Asa and back again.

"I instructed that you come alone," he said curtly, but his face did not show anger.

"Saul," Eve began, and he shook his head, cutting her off.

"No. I don't understand, Eve. I can't see why you would return to that . . . police state to be watched and controlled the rest of your life. To hide our beliefs, when you could openly worship if you stayed here with me. If you stayed you could be free, Eve, and you could be with me."

He looked at her pleadingly, and she went to him and wrapped her arms around his waist, leaning her head against his chest.

"I never believed I would see you again," she said softly. "I never imagined. You've come back to life, Saul, my own miracle."

"Then why won't you stay?" he whispered. She stepped back from him, looking up at his face.

"Here I could be free," she said. "Here I could worship openly, honor our history and our family and our beliefs. But, Saul, I want children."

"You could have children *here*. He could stay here with you if he wanted to—he's as free to choose as you are."

Saul shot Asa a dark look, and he leaned back involuntary, then steadied himself. He pushed forward, knowing Saul wouldn't like what he had to say.

"It's me who doesn't want to stay, Saul," Eve said. "Me. If we had children here, how would they live? Underground all their lives? Or worse, snatched away? And if they survived, what kind of life would they have? Their only goal would be survival itself: all their days spent making food, creating shelter, seeking water, and purifying it. If we go back inside, they can do anything they wish."

"But at what cost?" Saul looked appalled.

"I know the cost, maybe better than you do," Eve snapped, then her face softened. "I am sorry. I love you. I don't want to leave you, but I am going back."

"How?" Saul demanded. "How will you go back? Do you think you can walk through walls or sneak by the drones unseen?"

Asa glanced at Eve, but she appeared unruffled.

"I hoped you would help us," she said calmly.

"What makes you think I can help you?"

"You and I both know there's nowhere on earth you couldn't get in and out of if you really wanted to," she said, and Saul shook his head, smiling in spite of himself.

"Are you trying to flatter me, little sister?" he asked.

"I know you have a way in," Eve said with perfect confidence. He shot her a worried look.

"Did Daniel tell you something?"

"Daniel never told me anything. But I have eyes and a brain, and I know you can get in. Help us."

Saul threw up his hands in mock surrender. "Okay. You're right, I do have a way in." His face turned stony, and Asa straightened his shoulders. "No one knows about it, though," he said, lowering his voice. "No one *can* know about it. The safety of this community and everyone who lives here depends on that."

"We won't tell anyone," Eve said, and Asa nodded. Saul looked at him expectantly.

"We won't," Asa added, and Saul went on.

"There's a tunnel. You'll have to walk. It's a long walk, but it will get you back inside, under the wall."

They waited, but Saul said nothing more.

Eve cleared her throat. "I came here this morning to show you something."

"You came because I told you to," Saul muttered, barely audible. Eve ignored him. "What is it?" he asked in a normal tone, and Eve held out her backpack.

"Show me how to use this. Show me how to talk to you with it."

"Eve, I told you, I don't know. Daniel kept a lot of secrets, even from me."

Eve smiled and held up the strip; Asa wondered briefly where she had been concealing it. "David said this would show me everything I needed to know," she said. "All I want to know how to do is communicate with you, and with him if I need to. You can keep the computer. Just give me something that will let us talk to each other."

Saul nodded and took the bag from her hand almost reverently. "I've got something that should work," he said.

He looked from her to Asa and sighed, then went to his desk and opened a drawer that was jammed with wires and electronic parts.

If I organized things like that, the harvest would rot in the field while I was still untangling the plough, Asa thought, half-amused and half-annoyed.

Saul rummaged through the jumble of parts. "So, what's it

going to be like, this beautiful new life of yours?" he asked with a deliberate casualness, not looking up from the drawer.

"I thought we'd start by going back to my parents'," Asa said carefully. "We've got to let them know that everything is all right now—that we're safe. Rosewood's a beautiful place. We might just stay there." He glanced at Eve quickly. Her face was impassive, and he felt a pang of apprehension. *Did I say the wrong thing?*

"You're going to live a simple life on the farm? Eve's always been a city girl." Saul pulled a long cord out of the tangle with concentration.

"*Eve* has always been unhappy," Eve said. Saul looked up, dropping the cord. Eve shrugged uncomfortably under his sudden, attentive stare. "I just . . . I haven't been happy in Horizon for a long time. Maybe Rosewood will be a nice place to start over."

"What if it's not?" Saul asked.

"Then we'll go somewhere else," Asa said firmly. "Right?" He smiled at Eve, and the tension left her face.

"Right," she said.

"Got it," Saul announced, pulling a smaller version of Daniel's computer from a different drawer. "Eve, come here. I'll show you how to talk to me once you're back on the inside. You can even send pictures so Uncle Saul will feel like part of the family." His voice was brittle, but he smiled at Eve, and she went over to him as the screen lit up.

Asa hesitated. "I'll go make sure all our things are packed," he said loudly, and Eve turned.

"Thank you, Asa." She smiled brilliantly, and he grinned.

"Just come find me when you're finished." He left the room

and bounded up the stairs, taking them two at a time. *A lifetime of that smile.*

◆

An hour later, Asa was gazing at the ceiling, tracing every moment of the night before so that none of it would be lost. Eve hurried into the room.

"Are you ready?" she asked breathlessly, and he sat up, swinging his legs over the side of the bed.

"Yes."

"Saul is going to drive us to the tunnel. It will take us to Horizon."

"Horizon?" Asa frowned. "I guess I thought we'd go right back home. To Rosewood, I mean."

Eve bit her lip. "I know. But we left our phones back in Daniel's apartment. We should get them if we can—it might draw suspicion if we apply for new ones. There's something else I need to get too, and . . . well, we have to test out what David said, don't we?"

"He said he fixed our records," Asa said with alarm.

"I know. But, well, we can't know for sure until we test it—until we try to buy something or go somewhere with facial recognition, we won't know for certain that whatever he did worked."

Asa nodded grimly. "So, we have to go back to Horizon."

"If we don't test it, we'll spend the rest of our lives looking over our shoulders, wondering if there's a stalker lurking behind us," Eve said softly.

Asa stood and touched her hair. She moved in to embrace him, and he closed his eyes, breathing in her scent.

"We're not going to live like that," Asa said. "Come on. Let's go."

Saul drove the car in silence, but he did not seem angry—whatever had passed between him and Eve after Asa left them alone appeared to have resigned him to her departure. Asa sat in the back, looking out the window as the desert gave way to low, flat-leafed plant life again.

If we don't test it, we'll spend our lives looking over our shoulders. He had not considered that David might have failed in his attempt to clear their records, but now he could think of nothing else. *If we risked all that for nothing . . .*

He shoved the thought away. Eve was right; they had to check, but only to be certain. David had done all he could, and David could be trusted.

The sun was high when Saul stopped the car. Asa twisted in his seat, looking out the windows. They had been driving for the past hour on the bumpy remains of what appeared to be an old road, lined on either side by sheer rock. It stretched behind them and before them as far as Asa could see, with nothing to indicate that this place was different from any other. Saul got out, and Eve and Asa did the same, grabbing their bags to follow as he headed toward a jagged outcropping in the rock.

As they approached, Asa saw there was a pile of large rocks at the corner where the outcropping began. When they were beside the rockfall, Saul turned and studied their faces.

"Once you're in the tunnel, it will be a day's walk. You'll be safe. No one knows about this except me and a few of my people, but if by some wild chance you see someone, tell them you're my sister, Eve."

Eve nodded, her face serious.

"Asa," Saul said, "help me move these."

Asa followed Saul's lead as they carefully moved aside several of the large rocks in the pile, exposing a low passageway just high enough to crawl through.

"Saul," Eve said, alarmed.

"It's okay," he interrupted. "It's only that way for a few feet. Once you're inside the main tunnel, you'll be able to stand up and walk. Just turn left when you reach the end of this passage."

Eve looked dismayed. "Are you sure this is the only way back inside?" she asked, and Saul nodded gravely.

"When the sky is full of eyes, the only safe place is underground," he said.

"We'll be okay," Asa said quietly. "I'll go first."

Without waiting for an answer, he dropped to his knees and swung his pack around to the front so it would not scrub against the top of the rocky passage. He glanced back to see Eve embracing her brother. When she let go at last, Asa smiled at her, beckoned her to follow, and crawled farther into the darkness.

CHAPTER EIGHTEEN

THE CRAMPED TUNNEL SOON WIDENED INTO A
cavern high enough for them to stand, and Asa crawled out into
it with relief, then turned to Eve, offering her a hand as she got
to her feet. She brushed her hands off on her skirt as Asa pulled
off his backpack.

"Next time we do that, I'm wearing pants," Eve remarked. She
flicked on a small flashlight, and Asa saw that her knees were
bleeding, her legs scraped and bruised from crawling exposed
across the rock.

"I'm sorry," Asa said, instantly contrite, and rummaged in his
bag until he found a clean undershirt, which he handed to her.
"Eve, I didn't think—I'm so sorry."

She took the shirt and dabbed at the cuts, wiping away
the trickles of blood. "What were you going to do, give me
your pants?" she asked lightly. She handed the shirt back, now

covered in fresh red blood and streaks of dirt. "I didn't think of it until we were already in the tunnel," she added. "Come on. We turn left, right?"

"Right," Asa said. "I mean left—you're right, we go left." He swung on his backpack, uncertain why he had suddenly become as tongue-tied as if he had just met her.

She took his arm and kissed his cheek. "Asa," she said. "We're going home."

He smiled, and his momentary disquiet melted away. "Do you have another flashlight?" he asked.

"No," she said, sweeping it up and down the long, empty passage. "You're just going to have to trust me."

"Easy enough," Asa said, and they started walking.

The passage was as deserted as Saul had promised, but as they went, they saw evidence of others who had come this way before. There were markings on the walls here and there, mostly symbols they could not read, but some people had etched their names into the rock, and some had left messages:

JUDAH CAME THIS WAY.

CONDEMN THE ABUSES OF THE STATE—REJECT AUTHORITARIAN RULE!

TARA LOVES CESAR

SIC SEMPER TYRANNIS!

Here and there, they saw nooks in the rock walls large enough for someone to sleep in, and when Eve swept her flashlight over them, they saw that some had small black boxes stashed inside. Opening one, Asa found preserved food rations, a first aid kit, and most preciously, a bottle of water. They left the water but paused long enough to disinfect the scrapes on Eve's knees and bandage them.

"I feel like we should leave something," Eve said.

Asa shrugged. "We're not going much farther, right?" He took his own travel rations from his bag and tucked them inside the box before sealing it shut.

"Are you sure?" Eve asked.

"We're going home. And if we somehow get stuck here, we know where I left it." He picked up a small stone and put an X on the wall above the sleeping nook, then looked up at Eve with a mischievous grin. He scrawled a message with the rock:

ASA + EVE

"Asa! What if someone sees that?" she chided him.

"Who's going to see it but other people on the run?"

Eve shook her head, but as they continued along the passage, he saw her look back and smile.

They walked for hours, until Asa began to feel dazed from their plodding pace and the dark monotony of the cavern. After a while, they stopped talking, the novelty of the intermittent graffiti and other signs of travelers wearing thin as they wound around corners, climbing up steep slopes, then back down again as the tunnel plunged into the earth. It was impossible to tell how far they had gone—they could be halfway to Horizon or half a mile from where they started, looping endlessly back through the terrain. They went grimly onward, trusting Saul's promise that they would make it through.

Then, abruptly, the passage stopped. What Asa had assumed was a bend in the tunnel was a dead end.

"Now what?" he asked.

"This must be it," Eve whispered, sweeping her light along the walls. "We must be at the end of the tunnel. We have to find the way out. There has to be a way out," she added uncertainly.

"Of course there does," Asa said.

He went to a pile of stones along one wall and began clearing them away, but when he reached the end, there was only sheer rock. He sighed and looked around for another, but Eve stopped him.

"Wait, there's no reason it will be the same. It comes out in Horizon. It has to be less conspicuous—anyone digging their way into a hill like that would be seen by drones."

"What, then?"

"I don't know." Eve paced along the perimeter of the dead end, shining her light at the walls and ceiling. Suddenly she stopped, lowered her flashlight, and stared straight ahead.

"Eve?" Asa came up beside her.

"It's okay," she said, and a small blue grid appeared on her face for a moment—a scanner, mapping her features. It vanished after a second, then a door slid open in the wall of the cave, and Eve nodded and took Asa's hand.

They stepped through, into a small, dark room. The door slid shut again behind them, and a dim bluish light flickered on.

The room was empty and no larger than a closet. Directly in front of them was a door with a crash bar across the middle. Eve turned off her flashlight, they exchanged a glance, and Asa went to the door. He pushed it open cautiously, then blinked in the sunlight. He stepped out onto the pavement and found himself facing a brick wall.

The door swung shut with a soft click, and he turned to see Eve beside him. The door they had come through was gone; a black concrete wall stood behind them, with no indication of a way through, and there was noise coming from all around them— shouting and chattering, footsteps on pavement, and the general clamor of a crowd of people going about their day. Asa looked up. They were between two buildings that stood three or four stories high; on either side of them was a round water tank. He peered past the tanks and saw that they were between two streets, one wide and bustling, the other narrower, with fewer people passing.

"Are we . . .?" Asa looked confusedly at Eve, and she nodded.

"We're in the middle of Horizon." She glanced to either side, then took his hand and pulled him out of the alley and into the wide, crowded street.

"Shouldn't we go the other way?" Asa asked hoarsely, trying to whisper and be heard at the same time.

"The more people there are, the harder it is to be seen," Eve said in a normal tone of voice. Asa glanced around worriedly. "We've got to go back to Daniel's," she said, lowering her voice, and Asa nodded.

"I remember."

Eve led the way briskly through the streets, and soon they were in front of the gleaming building where she had once lived. The front door scanned her face and opened, and Asa felt a little part of himself relax. One test was passed, at least. They crossed the lobby, and Asa couldn't stop himself from looking at the place where Daniel's body had fallen. Daniel was gone, of course, but Asa still found himself surprised—it seemed like such a thing should be impossible to erase. Eve kept her eyes forward as they walked to the elevators, and as far as Asa could see, she never cast her eyes toward the place where Daniel had been.

They rode to the top floor in silence, and Eve's face was scanned again before the door opened to let them in. Inside the apartment, they both stopped dead. The place had been torn apart. The furniture was pulled out of place, couch cushions overturned, drawers opened, and their contents spilled out onto the floor. Eve surveyed the living room without expression.

"They searched it," Asa said in shock, though some rational part of him realized, *Of course they did.*

"They used his death as an excuse. They've been desperate to get inside here for years, but it doesn't matter," Eve said. "Even the State's sniffers won't have found anything Daniel didn't want found. Come on."

She led him into the bedroom and dropped her bag on the floor, then crawled into the closet as she had done the last time they were here, before they ran. Asa waited, nervous. The mattress had been tossed off the bed, and it had been ripped open; foam fragments littered the carpet and clung to every surface.

Eve emerged after a moment and held out Asa's phone. As he took it, he felt a pang of homesickness so strong it half choked him.

"Thanks," he said quietly, turning it over in his hands to see the inscription: *Asa Isaac Rosewood.*

Eve put hers into her bag, then turned away from him. "Can you fasten this?" she asked, and he saw that she was holding up a necklace.

He took the clasps from her hand and fastened them, careful not to ensnare the wisps of hair at the nape of her neck.

"All done," he said, and she turned to face him.

The necklace looked like the one Saul had given her and she had given back to him, the same arcane symbol at the center of a circle.

"It's religious?" Asa asked, and she nodded.

"When Saul went away, I gave him mine. This one was my mother's."

"It's beautiful." Asa swallowed, not sure what else to say, and Eve took his hand.

"Let's go."

"There's nothing else you want here?" he asked.

The apartment had been ransacked, but he knew from his last visit that it was filled with rare and beautiful things. But Eve shook her head and tucked the necklace under her dress.

"There's nothing else for me here," she said. Asa nodded, and they left the apartment together in silence.

Asa followed Eve from street to street, not tracking their movements because everything was still unfamiliar. After a while, they emerged into the plaza, where the rail station was, and Asa looked at Eve, questioning.

"Do you think we can just get on a train? The apartment building let you in."

Eve shook her head. "Daniel tampered with everything in that place," she said. "I would have gotten in even if I'd been declared dead. We have to try something else—the bank is easiest. We can have the autom check our accounts."

"No."

"Asa, we have to."

"I mean, I'll go. You wait for me. Go to the bridge over the park. You'll be able to see me. I'll go in, and you watch what happens. If everything is okay, I'll meet you on the bridge. If not, you'll see me get arrested."

Eve let out a nervous laugh. "Oh, good. Then what?" she said, her voice tight with worry. Asa put his arms around her, and she hugged him back fiercely.

"If anything happens to me, you'll go somewhere safe, send a message to Saul, and go back through that tunnel," Asa whispered.

Eve jerked back, her eyes wide. "You want me to leave you here? You'll be sent to Work, or worse!"

"Yes, I want you to leave me, if it comes to that. Eve, listen to me."

Asa stopped and glanced around, suddenly aware of their exposure, but no one passing even seemed to see them. Eve smiled faintly.

"That's the nice thing about the city," she said. "No one notices you—no one *wants* to notice you. Just talk to me quietly. It will be all right." She took his arms, pulling him closer to her. "Talk to me."

"I was just trying to say, if my record hasn't been cleared, neither has yours, and there will be nothing either of us can do about it now. You have a family out in the Waste. You could make a life. One of us has to."

He smiled and swept her hair back behind her ear. Eve nodded.

"I'm prepared," she said.

She kissed him lightly and turned to go. Asa watched her walk away, waiting until she was visible at the top of the bridge to make his way across the plaza. The bank was the first place he had come when he arrived from Rosewood, and then too, he realized, it had been a way of checking his own legitimacy: *Am I really supposed to be here?*

He went to the farthest door at the end of the building and let himself into the small private booth. The door closed behind him, and he jumped, thinking briefly of the cell where he'd been detained, back when all this started.

"Good morning, Asa Isaac Rosewood," said an automated voice.

"Good morning," Asa said nervously, glancing around. He wasn't sure what he had expected to happen—an accusation by the autom itself or a pair of Contract Enforcers appearing out of thin air. He cleared his throat. "Can I . . . Can I check my account, please?"

"You have 199,980 credits available. They are valid for all transactions, except those that violate your Social Contract."

Asa's phone lit up. On the screen he saw the number, and the two transactions he had made: twelve cred for the train to Horizon and eight for the moonshine on the night he met Eve.

"And there's nothing else?" he asked hesitantly, unsure how to phrase the question he really wanted to ask. *Am I a fugitive?*

"Is there anything else I can do for you? I can offer personalized financial advice based on your individual needs. My records show that you are twenty-one years old and unmarried, with a clean record; no outstanding debts; and a permanent address in Rosewood with your parents, Isaac Thomas Rosewood and Sarah Anna Rosewood."

Asa's heart leapt. *A clean record.*

"I'm . . ." He grinned, overcome with sudden, intense joy. "I'm getting married," he said, realizing it was the first time he had told someone outright.

"Congratulations, Asa Isaac Rosewood. I can offer personalized financial advice for your future, based on your family's needs."

"Thanks," he said. "Maybe later."

Asa stepped out of the bank booth and into the fresh air, feeling light-headed with relief. He looked up at the bridge, where Eve was standing high above the park, her hand cupped over her eyes to block the sun. He stood where he was for a moment, then waved and started running to her.

He was flushed and out of breath when he reached the top of the bridge, and he lifted Eve off her feet and spun her around.

She was laughing as he set her down. She grabbed his hand to steady herself.

"You made me dizzy," she said. "What happened? Is it okay?"

"The autom said my record was clean," he said.

"You asked?" Eve said, looking suddenly dismayed, and he laughed.

"No! It offered me personal financial advice and said my records showed I'm twenty-one, unmarried, with a clean record and no outstanding debts."

Eve heaved a sigh of relief. "So, it's all right, then. We're all right?" Asa nodded, then made his face serious. Eve mirrored his expression. "What is it?"

"I think we need to change the unmarried part as soon as possible."

Eve smiled radiantly, and Asa's heart skipped. "We should tell your parents we're still alive first," she said. "Come on, let's catch the train to Rosewood."

✦

They bought their rail passes easily, just like the dozens of other people in the station, and when they took their seats at last, Asa felt, for the first time, that it was real—that they were free, that they were going home. The train pulled out of the station, and as it gathered speed, Eve yawned and laid her head on his shoulder. He put his arm around her.

"Sweet dreams," he whispered, and she murmured something incoherent, already on her way to sleep.

Asa stroked her hair. *I can't believe you're here with me,* he thought as he watched her eyelashes flutter; she was dreaming. *I can't believe we're going home.*

As they neared Rosewood, Eve woke up, stirring Asa from his dozing as she sat up straight. He grinned at her sleepily.

"Morning," he said, and she blinked, looking confusedly out the window.

"Is it?" she asked.

"No, it's evening. It just started getting dark a little while ago. We're almost there," he added.

Eve nodded. "I'll be right back."

She took her bag with her to the compartment's restroom and did not return for several long minutes. When she returned, she was wearing another green dress, this one long, falling nearly to her ankles. Asa realized she must have packed at least a few other things while getting their phones from the hidden compartment in Daniel's closet. She sat next to him and shrugged her shoulders.

"I thought I should cover my knees," she said.

"My parents won't care if your knees are covered," Asa said bemusedly, and she hiked up her skirt to show the bandages. "Oh, right." He blushed. "I forgot."

She rearranged her skirt, plucking nervously at the folds.

"What's wrong?" he asked.

Eve hesitated.

"Eve, what is it?" He nudged her, smiling.

"I know your parents are good people," she said at last.

"Of course," Asa said.

"And they love you." She rubbed the fabric between her thumb and fingers, not looking up at him.

"I know that. Eve, just tell me what's wrong," Asa insisted.

"What if they don't want me around you? What if they don't like me? I'm the one who got you into all this trouble in the first place." She looked up at him, her eyes troubled.

298

Asa put a hand on her cheek and kissed her gently. "Eve," he said, "if there's one thing my family knows, it's that I can get into trouble just fine all by myself."

She smiled, but there was still worry in her eyes. As they pulled into the rail station, Asa felt worry of his own begin to creep in. *What if I got them in trouble? Did the stalkers come? What if something terrible happened? What if they don't want me around?*

They walked through the woods to Asa's parents' house, coming up behind it as they had before. Asa stopped walking when they reached the tree line. The lights were on in the little house, and he could see shadows in the kitchen. They were home, probably just starting dinner.

"Asa?" Eve asked nervously, and he took her hand. *We can't both be worried,* he resolved, and they crossed the backyard.

Asa gave Eve an encouraging smile and knocked on the kitchen door. After a moment the door opened, and Asa found himself face-to-face with his father. Isaac started, astonished, and Asa could not tell whether he was happy or upset to see him.

"Sarah!" Isaac shouted abruptly. "Sarah, come here!"

"I'm so sorry," Asa said as his mother appeared, looking just as startled. "I'm sorry I—"

"You're here now, you're safe," Isaac said roughly. "You're home. That's all that matters."

Isaac gripped Asa in a hug, pulling Sarah in too, and Asa let his parents embrace him, relieved. After a second, he thought of Eve and pulled away gently.

"You remember Eve," he said nervously.

"Hello," Eve said with an edge of trepidation.

Isaac smiled widely and placed his hand on her shoulder. "How could we forget such a beautiful girl?"

He opened his mouth to say something else, but Hannah

clattered down the stairs, pushing past her parents and almost knocking Asa to the ground. Asa lifted her off her feet, laughing with relief, and when he set her down, she turned to Eve and hugged her just as excitedly. When she had released them both, she took a step back, scrutinizing their faces.

"Are you going away again?" Hannah asked, and before Asa could speak, Eve cut in.

"No," she said firmly. "We're staying here in Rosewood."

Asa's heart leapt to hear her say it, and he caught a glimpse of his parents, their arms around each other. When Eve spoke, they both closed their eyes, clasping together for a moment as if to make sure the moment would not escape. Then Sarah pushed her husband away and clapped her hands together.

"You are both late for dinner," she announced. "Wash your hands and go take a seat."

Asa winked at Eve. "Come on, the sink's over here," he said.

As they cleaned up, Hannah dragged a kitchen chair to the dining room. They followed her in, and she sat down and beckoned.

"Eve, you can sit by me," she said, and Eve sat, looking pleased, if slightly bewildered. Asa took the seat at Eve's other side.

"Now, Asa," Isaac said as he set plates in front of them, "I don't want to get ahead of myself."

"Oh, don't you?" Sarah said with an amused smile. Isaac laughed.

"Perhaps I'm getting ahead of myself," he admitted. "But I don't think you two are going to want to stay here with us for too long, and there's a nice property up the road that's itching to have a house built on it. Not too much land, but I think that's probably best for starting out."

"Dad, they're not even married yet." Hannah rolled her eyes, but Sarah looked suddenly alarmed.

"Oh, you're not, are you? You wouldn't get married without us?"

Asa laughed. "No, we're not. I would have told you, Mom!"

"And I'd certainly hope you'd have told *me*!" Eve put in, and Isaac threw back his head and laughed.

"I'd certainly hope so! You brought back a good one, Asa— you're a lucky man."

Asa grinned and took Eve's hand under the table.

"You have no idea how lucky," he said.

She smiled at him and squeezed his hand; she was beginning to look more relaxed already, and his heart lifted.

"Are you going to have a baby right away?" Hannah asked eagerly, and Sarah shot her a warning look.

"That's their own business, Hannah," she said, but Eve laughed.

"It's okay. We will if we're lucky," she said.

"And if you're luckier still, the baby will take after its mother!" Isaac joked. "Who's hungry?"

Later, after dinner was finished and Isaac and Sarah had gone off to bed, Hannah gave Asa a fierce hug, then seized Eve just as eagerly. "I always wanted a sister," Asa heard her whisper to Eve, then Hannah slipped off to her bedroom, finally leaving them alone.

Asa closed the door to his childhood bedroom. Eve sat on his bed and abruptly began to cry. Asa hurried to her.

"What's wrong? I'm sorry, I know they can be a little much, especially Dad, but . . . we won't have to live with them for long. There's a small inn near the square. We can stay there until the house is built . . ."

He trailed off; Eve was shaking her head. She sighed and wiped her eyes.

"Your family is wonderful, Asa. We can stay with them as long as you want. I just . . . I never thought I could have all of this." He hugged her, and she buried her face in his shirt for a moment, then straightened.

"This is everything I ever wanted," she whispered.

"You're everything I ever wanted," he whispered back.

He kissed her, and with a contented sigh, she lay back and pulled him down beside her. She ran her fingers lightly down his chest, and he gasped with a sudden swell of desire. He brushed back her hair and traced his thumb down her cheek; she still stunned him with her beauty.

A lifetime of her smile, a lifetime of her touch. A lifetime with Eve, always.

CHAPTER NINETEEN

GABRIEL BLINKED IN THE BRIGHT SUNLIGHT as he stepped out of the darkness and into the alley. The noise of Horizon swelled around him: shouts and movement and laughter, all jostling against one another. It had been days since he climbed out of the river and started the long journey back to the city.

His shoulder ached where the shot had gone through it, but, in a distant way, pain had become a manageable constant. He had cleaned and sealed the wound, along with more than a dozen other cuts and scratches he'd gotten as he was dragged, unconscious, down the river. *The river.*

The Bug had not begun to devour his mind. *Would I know if it had?* he wondered from time to time as he made his way back home, but it was only an idle thought. He believed David had told him the truth about the vaccine. Gabriel no longer feared the untreated water.

Gabriel touched the codebook in his breast pocket reflexively. During his long journey back from Sanctuary, he'd gone over the things David had shown him incessantly. At times, they seemed preposterous, but at other times, they seemed like the only way to make sense of the world.

I have to know for myself. See it for myself. The thought ran through his head in a loop.

He stepped out into the street, half-conscious of the unnerving hush as the crowd parted before him. He oriented himself quickly, then set off. He walked steadily, not looking from side to side as he took the familiar turns, then stopped at the edge of a small clear plaza. Gabriel tapped his finger against the book in his pocket again, then strode toward the shining edifice of Municipal 1.

As he crossed the open space, he was vaguely aware that people were coming toward him. They were all Authority Figures, dressed in crisp black suits and speaking calmly to him as he walked on, ignoring them.

"Excuse me!"

"Are you all right?"

"You're bleeding. Are you okay?"

"Gabriel? Gabriel, is that you?"

Gabriel did not turn to see who had spoken his name but pushed open the wide, heavy front doors of the building and walked straight to the elevators.

"Authorization Gabriel Ward," he said hoarsely, the first words he'd spoken aloud in days.

The glass elevator door slid open and closed behind him. He saw two Security Enforcers hurrying to catch up.

"Lock door," Gabriel said and took the codebook from his pocket. "Open manual override panel, authorization—" He hesitated.

Behind him, someone knocked on the door from the outside, shouting something too muffled to understand. Gabriel cleared his throat.

"Authorization David Pasternak, open manual override." He held his breath for a moment.

You can't falsify a voice print, he thought, almost at the point of panic. Then a small rectangular panel sprung open in the sidewall of the elevator.

"Confirm, David Pasternak," said the smooth voice of the elevator autom.

Gabriel started breathing again and opened the codebook. It had been mostly undamaged by the fall into the water; what looked like old-fashioned paper must have been an insoluble polymer, and the ink had only smudged a little here and there.

Quickly, Gabriel keyed in the long series of numbers and symbols. As soon as he had finished, the elevator began to rise. It passed the normally accessible levels and kept going straight to the top floor, gaining speed along the way.

When it stopped, the door remained closed.

"Open door," Gabriel said nervously, and the back of the elevator slid open.

Gabriel whirled around, bracing instinctively for an attack, but there was only an empty hallway. He gripped the codebook tightly in his hand and cautiously touched the weapon he'd taken from the Waste.

I should have left it out in the desert, he thought. He had intended to, but every time he thought to bury it in the dirt or leave it among the barren rocks, something stopped him. *I can always get rid of it later,* he had told himself. He squared his shoulders, then stepped cautiously out into the hallway.

It stretched out wide in both directions; the walls on either side were floor-to-ceiling murals of pastoral life, intricately painted to represent the outlying communities. One scene faded into another seamlessly, so as Gabriel walked, he watched as the snowy forest of Rosewood in winter faded into the lush green of Fairfield in summer, which soon became a festival in the central park of Horizon.

The painted people looked joyful, and as Gabriel peered at them, he thought he recognized a few of the faces, though no one he could name. Under his feet was a thick, bright-blue carpet that looked untouched, and at the end of the hallway was the only door in sight—a heavy wooden door that looked somehow both stately and humble. As Gabriel approached it, he saw a sign; the words were carved into the wood itself, blackened with ash and lacquered over.

Official Office
Chancellor of the State

Beside the door was a small panel with letters and numbers, and again Gabriel consulted the book and entered the appropriate code, glancing back toward the elevator every few seconds.

Someone must know I'm here, he thought. *Someone must be coming.* But no one came.

The blue light of a scanner flickered over his face, then a lock clicked open. Gabriel put the book back in his pocket, pushed the door open, and slowly stepped into the dark room.

His hip banged against something hard, and Gabriel ground his teeth as he felt a cut begin to seep blood again. Abruptly, the room lit up, and he drew back in surprise, shoving the door closed behind him.

The room was the size of a large closet, crammed with racks of computer equipment—some resembling the things David had in his home, others wholly alien. Only a few square feet in the middle were open, and at the center of that small space stood the Chancellor himself.

The Chancellor smiled and spread his arms wide in a gesture of welcome; Gabriel watched dazedly as his hand seemed to pass straight through a large, blocky piece of equipment.

It is true. Everything David told me is true.

"Hello Gabriel," the Chancellor said warmly. "I've been expecting you."

For a moment, he could only stare in disbelief. Then he composed himself and met the Chancellor's familiar blue eyes with his own. The Chancellor calmly motioned him forward, and Gabriel began to smile.

END

ACKNOWLEDGMENTS

A special thanks to:

My parents, Reynolds and Gloria, for all the love and support they've always given me. Thanks for staying that extra night at the lake house all those years ago. Without that night together and a few bottles wine, I probably wouldn't have been here to write this book. Dad, I hope Amazon has figured out a way to sell books in heaven. If not, I'm sure it will soon.

My uncle Jeff and my uncle Jim. They both spent a lot of time reading this book in its infancy and giving me much-needed feedback and the confidence to keep writing.

All my friends and loved ones, especially Christina. She was sitting beside me when the crazy idea for this book entered my brain. She listened graciously for hours on end while I talked through every character and plot twist. Thanks for letting me ramble.

All my animals, whom I love dearly, the ones who are here

and the ones who have passed. Every day, they give me unconditional love, the most powerful thing in the world.

The people everywhere who are working hard to make this world a better place. To those people who are providing a helping hand to the less fortunate and fighting to protect our planet from environmental disaster, please keep it up. This world will never be perfect, but it can always be better.

ABOUT THE AUTHOR

 **J. R. HARBER** is a writer, humanitarian, philanthropist, and environmental advocate. He believes it is vital for society to take a more common-sense approach to how we live and consume resources to ensure a world worth living in for future generations. When he's not exploring ideas for new writing projects, J. R. dedicates much of his time advocating for stronger environmental and watershed protections and directing his nonprofit animal rescue and rehabilitation center in Georgia.

Made in the USA
Columbia, SC
30 April 2020